DIVINE CHALLENGES

Rise of the Stria Book Two

TESSA MCFIONN

To those who look up to the skies and know we're not alone. And to those who believe that, even in the darkest hour, love can conquer all.

Acknowledgments

A long time ago, I sat in a darkened theater with a bunch of like-minded fans and marveled over the greatest space opera to hit the big screen, *Star Wars*. The classic tale of good versus evil set in "a galaxy far far away" truly transported me into a world where even in the middle of a massive rebellion, two hearts found love.

When I began my own science fiction story, I drew on that sensation from all those years ago. I wanted to create a world that was immersive and new, yet familiar. To that end, I needed a whole team of readers, rereaders, and re-rereaders. Mary-Anne, Ri, Elma, Michelle, Mona and Emma-Louise: couldn't have asked for better betas.

To my amazing Romance Writers of America San Diego Chapter buddies, especially Tami, CJ, Cindy, Pam, Margaret, HelenKay, and Christy, thank you for letting me vent when the world seemed against me. You all inspire me to be my best every day.

Dani, my cover artist and dear friend, thank you for bringing Kahlym and Evainne into the world for all to see.

Finally, to my loving friends and family, thank you for your patience when I spend hours working. To my husband, for accepting my craziness.

And to Mom, thank you for fueling my love of reading. I owe the magic to you.

Chapter 1

Home.

The word had a different meaning to Evainne Wagner now. Up until a week ago, home was a closet of an apartment, with enough money in her pocket to cover rent for one more month before she was out on her ass. Home was a city she had never truly lived in, only survived in, without the luxury of family or friends, thanks to the notoriety of her parents. The idea of packing up everything and starting all over elsewhere had been percolating in her mind, even before she'd headed out for a run on that fateful morning.

Today, as she stared out through the massive convex window into the vast stars surrounding her, her definition of home had turned upside down. The whirring hum of an alien engine droned in the background as she shuffled her rambling thoughts into organized piles. The silence was sobering, giving her much-needed time to sort through her heart as well as her head. A bright shooting star streaked across the twinkling dark, sparking her mind, and the events of a few short days ago jumped to the forefront.

Kahlym and Brel run toward the open loading dock and to her wildly beck-

oning arms. The brothers keep pace, closing the distance as the engines roar to life. A glimmer of muted silver catches her eye as the traitorous navigator, Qaen, raises his weapon and fires one blast. Time slows to a crawl as Brel knocks his younger brother and her lover, Kahlym, out of the path and falls hard to the floor. Her screams echo in her ears as she watches in horror, her ill-timed and poorly aimed dagger doing only minor damage to the fleeing culprit. She recalls being shoved out of the way as Dhaerin barrels past her to help carry Brel back on board.

"Are you certain you should be out of bed?"

Lost in her thoughts, Evainne had missed the approaching, shuffling steps of the ship's doctor. She shifted her gaze to the reflection of the rotund, blue-skinned alien, his head bowed respectfully while his stubby fingers twisted around each other. Four green eyes searched for answers on the well-worn tiles beneath her feet.

She reminded herself that, to all of the people living on this ship, she was a reverent-worthy saint. A Divine.

Boy, I wonder what Daddy would have to say about this little nugget.

Might explain a bit about her current wardrobe. Whisper soft, the long and flowy burgundy layers made her feel more like an escapee from some college toga party. Granted, the pale blue, leather-like jumpsuit she'd been wearing had been pretty ripe. Not to mention slashed, torn, blast-damaged, and bloodstained, but she was getting used to the skintight fit.

The dress looked no worse for wear, considering all it had been through. She recalled the honorific presentation by Falka, while Kahlym had played tour guide on the outer space version of the swap meet. The extremely alien alien had used two arms to hand her the simple box, while the third limb had rested across her heart. As soon as Evainne had revealed the stylish attire, she'd used it as a disguise, tossing it over Kahlym's head to cover his face as they hid from the white-clad enemy forces. After that, it had been crammed into a small backpack, along with a minor arsenal of weapons, while they broke out of jail the crew of his ship, *Tiamat's Revenge.*

Now, she slid her hand along the resilient material. Not a

wrinkle or a tear in it, even after all of the abuse it had endured. She wished the same could be said for herself. So much had been rattling around in her mind after she'd awoken naked and alone, the soft fabric laid out on the bed for her. No answers would be found in solitude, and she was never one to sit in silence, so the dress would have to do.

Once her birthday suit had been hidden from sight, she'd headed toward the room's main door. Since she was only going for a short walk, she'd opted to go barefoot, hoping the cool metal floor would help to ground her in reality, even if the reality was still unreal to her.

She smiled weakly as she turned from the giant picture window and faced the man. "Probably not, but I just needed to…"

Her pause was enough reason for him to lift his gaze to hers. Four pupil-less eyes stared back, serving as another undeniable factor that she was in outer space.

"Were your legs in need of stretching again, *Dym Char'ann?*" Without the black dots in the middle of that quartet of milky white, it was really tough to figure out what he was thinking. But the quiet concern in his voice told her all she needed to know. Her shoulders drooped as she pulled apart the meaning of the title he'd tacked on to the end of his question. She knew he was a cleric, trained in healing skills, very serious in his beliefs.

Still, she had a name and would rather be called by it than that honorific.

Well, at least he'd gotten out the habit of dropping to his knees when she walked by. Guess that would have to be enough.

"Yeah," she said. "Figured a little walk would help get the blood pumping."

The face before her paled, and he waddled closer. "Did your heart cease to function? Is that normal for your people?"

Evainne screwed up her face, a light smile warming her lips. Damn, she really needed to learn how to speak right if this stupid translator program was going to keep taking her so friggin' literally.

With a slow shake of her head, she reached out and patted him on the shoulder.

"One of these days, I'm gonna have to sit you down and tell you about the wonders of colloquial language, Yhan'tu. No, my heart is…well, the actual organ is still beating away."

She replayed her words, pondering over why she'd halted herself when she did. Is her heart fine? Another memory flashed.

She's standing over Brel's paling body, his insides more on the outside. Without hesitating, she rests her left hand on his forehead while the right flattens on his chest. The voice of her old sensei, Whetutoa, rings through her ears, and she begins the centering exercises she hopes will save his life.

She'd held a man's life in her hands. Not just any man, either. The brother of the man who was the reason her heart was a mess: Kahlym cal Jhuen, rebel leader. The very captain of this ship. The man who'd rescued her, and with whom she'd fallen in love.

"*Dym Char'ann?* Your skin is showing signs of a rising temperature. Perhaps you should return to your rest."

She pinched her bottom lip between her teeth to choke back a vulnerable sigh. Her blush had little to do with her weakened state, though he did have a point. As her energy waned, the promise of bed looked more and more tempting. The cleric waited patiently until she nodded with a tired smile. He bobbed his head and, moving his hand to her elbow, guided her back down the corridor.

At first, she thought he would take her back to the med bay and she tensed, mid-stride, feet skidding against the slick surface. He must have misread her stumble, though, using the moment to tighten his grip on her arm, offering more of his bulk to lean on. After a few more steps, the med bay doors were at their backs, and a relieved sigh escaped her lips as they continued toward the crew's quarters.

If she had her way, she would never set foot in that room ever again, not quite ready to tackle the memories that lined those walls. The farther they traveled, the clearer the voices grew. She picked out Dhaerin and R'uan, the two giant leonine brothers, in a heated discussion about something that had R'uan on the defensive and Dhaer laughing.

The pair were as opposite in their mannerisms as they were in their coloring; R'uan's dark and shadowed grays and blacks were contrasted by the bright and sunny oranges and tawny beige of Dhaer. She remembered the man who called the leonine brothers "his sons" and the huge part he paid in her current situation. She remembered the flight, the hiding, the pool.

Evainne sighed as the journey took them past the open door to her final destination: the captain's room.

She was sleeping in the captain's room. More than that, she was sleeping in the captain's bed. With the captain, himself.

Her sexy space vampire pirate captain.

This time, her sigh turned into an introspective chuckle as Yhan'tu opened the door.

"Is anything amiss?" he asked.

She shook her head, opting to keep her silly mental ramblings to herself, and stepped into the luxurious room. Being the head honcho did have its perks, namely the biggest room in the crew's quarters. A large bed took up residence along the far wall. A pair of round chairs were suspended from above by thin, solid cables, and a rectangular desk decorated the facing walls. Faint light shone down from the muted ceiling. The sheets were jumbled and cool, the sleek, brick-red fabric unlike anything she'd ever slept in before.

Well, before she dropped onto the scene, like Dorothy in Oz.

She had no desire to click her heels three times, though. She was home.

"Dym Char'ann?"

Evainne turned back to find the medic just beyond the door's threshold. She hit rewind and remembered his question. Another formal request. Back on Earth, she had never heard anyone use the word "amiss." Hell, she'd only seen it in crossword puzzles or in Jeopardy clues. But here, it was the word of the day. Every day. Especially when anyone had something to ask her.

Which seemed like every five minutes. Granted, she'd used some serious unknown magic to pull more than just a rabbit out a hat and had blacked out moments later. Still…

A forced smile tugged her lips up, and she shook her head. "Nah, I think I'm gonna get some more rest. Thanks for the escort back."

She gnashed her teeth as the medic offered her a low, reverent bow before backing away. Sheesh, before she showed up here, she was lucky to get someone to hold a door open when she had her hands full. Being seen as a semi-deity had an upside, she supposed.

The door slid shut, and she was alone once again. Alone to wrestle with her thoughts. She had a vague memory of Kahlym slipping out of the room, but for the life of her, she couldn't remember how long ago that had been. Not that she missed him or anything sappy like that.

Yeah, right. Keep telling yourself that, sweetheart.

She crossed to the bed and flopped onto her back, sinking into the thick, spongy mattress. "Gawd, what am I doing here?" she muttered as she draped an arm over her eyes. But the shielded dark only provided a pristine canopy to roll out another memory in full Technicolor.

Red splatters the ground at her feet. She hears the stream slow to a trickle and she knows time is running out. She stacks the little torn and damaged Legos she finds in her mind's eye, hoping she's doing some real good. This is the same thing she did last time, but that was on her. One final block adds to the pile, and a blast of golden light surrounds her. She returns to her own body, almost unaware of having left it in the first place. The flesh beneath her hands is whole, the heart beating against her palms is strong and steady. All the while, during the ordeal, she hears Kahlym's voice over her shoulder, his mournful and blame-ridden words spilling around her.

If I pull this off, I'm gonna have a long talk with that boy.

"Evainne? Is something amiss?"

As if on cue, Kahlym's voice echoed through the room, a sound too all-encompassing to have been delivered in person. Evainne kept her face covered and barked out a sharp laugh. How much of that question she was ready to answer?

"Sweetie," she finally replied, "I don't think anything isn't amiss. Never mind. I guess I need my head examined, or more sleep, or something. Maybe I just need to get friggin' blitzed."

Silence filled the room, with only the distant humming drone of the engines encroaching upon the quiet. She frowned, eyebrows drawing together, and she lifted her arm for better access to the surrounding emptiness.

"Kahlym?"

The door whooshed open, and she popped up onto her elbows, managing to make it to a reclined position before the object of her inquiry was sitting next to her on the bed. Panic oozed off of him as he stroked her cheek, while his intoxicating bi-colored eyes scanned her head for any blood.

"What has happened? Are you injured, *ziat'xahn*? Did you fall?"

Evainne laughed, shaking her head, and she captured his frantic hands.

"Relax, sweetie, I'm fine. Okay, so maybe 'fine' is a stretch. But physically, I'm all right. I promise I'm not hurt." Scooting into a more comfortable position and trying not to slip out of her dress at the same time, she tucked her legs beneath her and faced him.

Her personal hero.

Her lover.

She couldn't seem to use the juvenile term "boyfriend" when she looked at him. There was nothing boyish about his appearance: standing at six-and-a-half-feet easily, with polished copper skin and thick waves of dark charcoal hair that twisted into tight bands. And those eyes—swirls of deep green and bright fuchsia that bored straight into her soul.

No, he was pure man—strong and battle-honed—though his demeanor around her could at times fall into the boyish category. For someone as drop-dead gorgeous as he was, he had a refreshing and sometimes innocent charm. And he fretted over her, which made her feel cherished and special.

His face lost some of its tension as he exhaled in relief, and he dropped his shoulders, slipping his hands free from her hold. His rough fingers tickled her skin as he cradled her face and pressed a soft kiss against her forehead.

"I am sorry if I startled you, *ziat'xahn,* but your response took me off-guard."

Her laugh was easy and light. His ability to state the obvious with such flair always brought a smile to her lips. She rested her fingers on his wrists, eyes drifting close as she took solace in his tender touch. Inhaling deeply, she dragged his wild scent into her, the mouth-watering fragrance soothing her soul, centering her mind.

Since her arrival, he had been her anchor, never doubting her, even though her appearance had created a massive shitstorm of troubles that had cost him the life of one of his crew and almost the life of his brother. His unwavering belief in her boosted her spirit and gave her the strength she needed to accept her new fate.

Now, she would return the favor.

She opened her eyes and lifted her chin to meet his gaze.

"Kahlym. We need to talk."

Chapter 2

Kahlym tensed, his heart rate ratcheting back up, having calmed after his sprint from the pilot's deck. The voice of his angel had been so muffled, her words so troubling, his instincts had kicked his legs into gear.

After she had collapsed in his arms following the miraculous healing of his brother, Kahlym had refused to release her from his embrace. He almost pitied Yhan'tu. Almost. Not enough to give her over for more than a visual exam, though.

Blood raced through his veins as Kahlym gulped in air, gaze glued to her face. Her breaths fell soft and steady against his arm, so he knew she wasn't dead. But his ship's healer had mumbled something about psychic damage, and that halted his impending retreat. With delicate care, he lowered her onto the other available table.

He knew his hovering irked Yhan'tu, but leaving the med bay was simply not an option. Kahlym's gaze swung between the two most important people in his life as they lay on separate exam gurneys. The longer he stared at their rhythmic breathing, the more shallow and rapid his own became.

"Kahl? You might as well sit down." Kahlym looked away from

the sleeping figures to Dhaerin on his right, his left eye swollen and shut. "I know you well enough, brother. Yhan'tu's gonna take good care of them both." His friend motioned to the nearest chair, close enough to be in the room, yet far enough so he wasn't a hindrance. Sighing in reluctant agreement, Kahlym shuffled backwards until his knees bumped the edge of the seat.

Seconds turned to minutes, which turned to hours, while he waited for the cleric to finish his assessment. The moment he'd gotten a nod from Yhan'tu, Kahlym scooped Evainne up into his arms and hastened back to his chamber, his long strides eating up the hallway. He forced his body to move at something just below hyperspeed as he easily navigated the empty corridor. A sniff of her tangled hair urged his feet to quicken their pace, the stench of blood and grief souring her flowery fragrance.

After jabbing his elbow against the keypad, Kahlym stepped through the door, sliding between the wall and the receding barrier and, without missing a stride, carried Evainne straight to the bed. He laid her down, making short work of her tattered battlesuit. Small slashes and angry bruises marred her ivory skin; lingering hints of her healing powers had paled the deep blues to sickly greens.

As soon as he had assured himself she was in one piece, Kahlym once again scooped her into his arms and entered the shower stall, where the warm water made short work of the dried blood and grime. As he gently lathered her hair and her skin, his mind spun in circles, each thought turning back upon itself to reach the same conclusion.

He was in love with a Divine. Even if she hadn't saved his brother's life before his very eyes, she still held his heart. From the instant she'd placed her trusting hand into his, he was lost. Her radiant smile and refreshing perspective gave him hope; she spoke from the heart, even if, at times, those words made little sense to him.

She gave him a reason to smile. She gave him a reason to believe.

He took the gravity chair so he could watch over her while she slept. His body wasn't happy with the decision, but one night of discomfort would be a small price to pay for the promise of a future with his Divine. His heart and mind warred with the prospect of loving one of the sacred; both knew the Emperor would rather see Kahlym's entrails wrapped around the High Counsel House before he'd allow him peace with his love.

But for her, he had to try. For her, he would do anything.

Even now, as he sat across from her, as his breath caught in his chest and his throat locked in fear.

His expression must have relayed his trepidation. In the blink of an eye, a warm smile lit up her angelic face, and her light laugh, so like the tinkling of the wind bells that hung on the eaves of his house, calmed him down a hair.

"Don't look so scared, hon. I'm not breaking up with you."

Kahlym nodded slowly, his mind picking apart this "breaking up." *Did people on her homeworld cause physical damage to others?*

Her smile deepened, and she caressed his cheek. "Means I'm not leaving you, Kahl. I said you were stuck with me and I meant it."

He nuzzled into the palm of her hand, turning his face to kiss her soft skin. Her affections for him were dangerous, possibly even deadly, but his heart would not let her go. She had shattered the barrier that protected his soul, and he could not go back to how he was before she had come into his life. Did she feel obligated to him?

"But I cannot burden you to—"

She yanked away her hand and met his stunned gaze. "This is what we need to talk about." Her porcelain skin had lost a touch of its luster, her deep brown eyes clear and intent. She scooted farther away to sit stiff and regally rigid before him. In the room's dim glow, she appeared the reverent Divine he knew her to be.

Habit forced him to lower his eyes and drop his shoulders, his heart threatening to crumble into the woven pattern of the bedding. She deserved more, and she now knew this to be true.

"See? This is what I mean!" she declared. Perplexed, Kahlym raised his chin as she slid back to her original place directly in front of him. "Look, we can't have any kind of serious relationship if you keep acting like I'm some sort of goddess, or some shit like that. I'm not. I'm just me. Just a terrified girl who landed in your lap. I'm some freak from another planet who got lucky and can do some pretty cool stuff here. And I wish to Christ that I could kick the crap out of whatever bitch screwed with your head and your heart so much that you feel that you're not worthy. If anything, I feel like I'm the one not worth the attention you are giving to me."

His mind reeled, frantically pulling meaning from her unexpected tirade. Her regular use of profanity still surprised him, but the word that hit him harder than a physical blow was *relationship*. She had even said a *serious relationship*. He blinked slowly as he continued to process her words.

"You…you wish to…?" Although his voice failed him, the curling of her lips told him she understood what he could not say. She reached for his hands and laced their fingers together, and her jaw started to open more than once without her speaking. Her eyelids drifted down, and she swallowed before she spoke.

"Kahlym, I've never been good with people, much less good with any kind of strong emotions. But here, in this place…?" She paused, and he looked down at their conjoined hands, her delicate ivory intertwined with his dark bronze, and he trailed his thumb along her finger, turned his wrist to examine her small, pink fingertips. He traced the edge of one with the tip of his own sharpened nail.

"What about this place, *ziat'xahn*?" His throat tightened, letting only a whisper of air escape.

"Here, I…Well, I feel like I belong here, you know? Like I matter." She lifted her gaze, dark brown eyes shimmering in the faint starlight. "You. Your brother. Even Falka and Yhan'tu, with all of their bowing shit. I just feel like I was meant to be living here. All my life I just wanted someplace where I'd feel welcomed. I got so used to being by myself, I was convinced that was the way it would always be. I've never had anyone to really care about what I thought or what I felt. But, here? I'm not looked at like something you just stepped in."

She sighed, slipping her gaze from his. He released her hands and scooped her into his arms. The instant her body rested against his, all of his tension vanished. If he'd had any doubts of his feelings, these evaporated as soon as he brushed his lips across her hair.

"You have no need to be afraid, Evainne. I will do all I can to keep you safe, for you do matter in this world."

Evainne laced her fingers in the open neckline of his gearsuit and clung on tightly. Tremors crawled up her arms, and he tightened his embrace. To his surprise, she shook her head, pushing away from his offered comfort.

"No. I don't mean 'matter' like that," she amended. "Safe has little to do with this. Shit happens whether you're playing it safe or living on the edge. Gah!—I have to finish this. My brain is about to turn to mush, and I want to say this before I lose my nerve." She pulled back enough to meet his eyes. Silvery tracks of spilled tears sparkled on her upturned cheeks. The sadness he'd seen earlier had been replaced by something deeper, something that spoke of tender passions and unbelieved joy.

But the moment was fleeting; her lids shuttered down as she drew in a stuttering breath. Unable to resist a moment longer, Kahlym pressed a soft kiss against her hair, the clean fragrance swathing his soul, centering him.

"I do feel safe here, Kahlym," she whispered. "I feel safe with you. I want nothing more than to stay. But I need something from you."

Her mumbled words gave him pause, though he'd offer up his own liver on a jade platter just to see her smile.

"What is it you need from me, *ziat'xahn?*" he asked, choking past the lump in his throat. She'd already said she wished to remain, so he had to believe she wouldn't ask him to take her back to her homeworld. He only hoped he could deliver on her request.

She wrapped her arms around his waist, hugging him close. "I need to know I'm your strength, not your weakness. I need you to stop pushing me away."

Kahlym leaned back and held her at arm's length, while a frown chiseled furrows across his forehead. "How have I pushed you away?" He froze, terror streaking through his veins like ice. He had done exactly what she'd asked him not to do, and his jaw dropped in mute anguish.

Evainne shook her head, stroked her fingers across his cheek. "No, by acting like you're not worthy of me, telling me I shouldn't care about you. Kahlym, I've never met anyone as caring or as amazing as you. You always think of others before yourself, and you give so much to your crew. I've never heard you say anything negative about anyone, even that douchebag, Qaen. Hell, I think I've thought meaner things when some rotten Beamer driver would speed through the gutters after a downpour."

More of those bizarre references. But as long as her hand touched his skin, he didn't care. Kahlym smiled, brushing his fingertips along her smooth brow. "I have no idea what most of that denotes, but I'm certain you're overestimating my goodwill."

Sighing, she captured his hand. "I mean it, hon. Kahlym, I...I need to know you're doing this because of who I am, not what I am. I don't know if that makes any sense. All I can think about is how you were when we first talked. Well, when I first understood what you were saying. I was just a girl, and you were my big, bad knight in leather armor, sweeping in to save the day. Can we just go back to being those people? Could you please try? For me?"

One blink of those soft brown eyes and he could resist no longer. He closed the distance between them, lips pressing tenderly against hers, and the ice that had stilted his movements melted in a flash as heat zinged though his veins once her mouth opened to him. His possessive growl mingled with her heady sigh, and his tongue twisted and danced with hers as he plundered her mouth, savoring the pure innocence and love in her kiss, fingers threading through her hair.

He slid his other hand around her waist and lowered her back to the bed, nestling his hips at the apex of her thighs. She dug her fingers into her shoulders, holding him tight. He deepened the kiss as her legs wound around him, her body undulating and teasing him to distraction.

"Captain?"

Kahlym dropped his head onto the mattress, a frustrated groan resonating through his chest. Talk about shit for timing. His body rebelled, arguing with his logical brain, and he forced his jaw to work as he answered Falka's interruption.

"What?" His grumbled reply had drawn a tempting chuckle from the beauty pinned beneath him. Rising up onto his locked arms, Kahlym gazed down and drank in the impassioned blush on her cheeks, the impish, tilted grin on her kiss-swollen lips. "Be careful, *ziat'xahn*," he whispered, voice ragged and breathy, "or I will ravish you with my crew listening in."

Her laugh shifted to a wickedly dark rumble that snapped his cock to painful attention. She laced her fingers through his hair, dragged him back down, and he lowered onto an elbow as she nipped along his chin. "Oh, baby, that's no threat as far as I'm concerned." She rocked her hips against his rigid shaft, and his eyes rolled back into his head, a hungry groan slipping from his clenched teeth.

"We're getting a message from Raedyn Primus."

He stilled, his playfulness disappearing in a flash. Kahlym lifted his head, dread quenching the fire in his blood, and Evainne's smile faltered as she stopped her sensual teasings. Her eyebrow knitted together in confusion as he asked the question that tied his gut into knots: "From whom?"

"It's encrypted, so that should give you a good idea."

Fuck.

They knew. Somehow, word of his passenger's identity had reached the Thrall, and his allies were verifying the intel. That also meant his family would know his ship transported a living Divine. She'd be sought after as both a guiding light and a bargaining tool.

Looking down into Evainne's questioning gaze, Kahlym searched for the strength to lie to her. He wished he could assure her that all would be well, but things were moving faster than he'd anticipated. The longer he fell into her entrancing chocolate brown eyes, the more he knew she deserved nothing less than the truth. He brushed his fingertips along her forehead, trying to wipe away the worry lines creasing her pale skin as he offered her a weak smile.

"I have to go." His heart ached at the hateful words that tripped off of his tongue. He wanted nothing more than to remain in her calming presence, to take comfort in the tender embrace that set fire to his soul and burned away vengeful memories. But he was captain and a leader in the Chandaran Stria, and duty would always take precedence to his wants.

She met his gaze without hesitation, offering a soft smile to carry with him. "I understand."

As he climbed off of the bed, Evainne followed his movements, sitting up and tucking her legs beneath her. The deep maroon robes that cascaded off of her shoulders brought out the rich beauty of her bloodwine hair, streaks of black and red tangled in the exotic blend. With her creamy complexion and chestnut brown eyes, she stole his breath as well as his heart and his reason. He lingered another moment, trailing his fingers through her tempting locks before turning toward the door.

"Kahlym?"

He peered over his shoulder just as the wall slid open. In the shadowed light, she looked like the sacred Divine he knew her to be, but her womanly pleas rattled through his mind. She paused, her lips moving, yet she made no sound, and his heart ached as he sensed she warred with herself in some fashion. After a short stall, she wet her lips and smiled.

"Be safe."

Her honest concern lit up his spirit, and the corners of his lips curved upward. He placed his hand over his rapidly beating heart and inclined his head. When he again raised his eyes, her cheeks wore a most tempting shade of pink, and if not for the urgency of his summons, he'd be sampling the warmth of her inviting lips.

Instead, Kahlym turned and stepped through the opened door.

Chapter 3

Kahlym's trip to the comm bay was a frustrating blend of a pained limp and a one-way argument. How could he be torn in so many different directions and still continue moving forward? Part of him wanted nothing more than to tell Brel to handle the message so he could return to finish his interrupted discussion with his angel.

Discussion? Perhaps an over-simplification of the situation. But talking had been involved.

Another part, however—the part controlling his legs—wished to retrieve the cryptic request, to tell his allies they now had the Thrall by the balls. He wanted to gloat that a Divine Healer was sympathetic to their cause and now fought for them.

Could he? Did he dare speak for her?

His rational voice told him it'd be safer to return her to her own time and to her own planet. Move her away from his enemy's clutches … and far away from him.

He stopped at the threshold, hand hovering over the door release. That last thought was the most dangerous. His greatest enemy was his own fear of her rejection. He replayed her words in his mind. She wanted to stay, and his desire to respect her wishes caused his heart to sing and his gut to knot.

How could he keep her safe and happy, knowing the part she'd eventually play in achieving their ultimate freedom? Could he force her to join a fight that had nothing to do with her or her people?

The flat surface before him fell away, and he stood toe-to-toe with Falka, her expression dark and guarded.

"You forget how to use the door?" she asked, wiping off two hands on the rag held in the third.

Scowling half to himself and growling half at her, Kahlym pushed past her and crossed to the console, where he leaned over the vid screen, placing his hand on the red pulsating light.

"Jhuen cal thra'Ahx Kah'lym."

The flashing ceased, and the image solidified into a face he was truly not expecting. He locked his knees to stay upright as he stared at an older reflection of himself, yet with eyes of pure red. A pair of thin lips were framed by a perfectly trimmed beard and moustache, the firm line slashed across the harsh planes of his chiseled face. Long gone were the warrior locks, his ebony-and-silver hair now close-cropped. The severe crew cut drew more focus to his piercing crimson eyes. Time had done little to mar Anaxar du Jhuen's stern appearance; it only added to the man's innate cruelty.

In a blink, Kahlym hid his surprise, burying any emotions behind the protective mask that had allowed him to survive living under his father's oppressive thumb. He squared his shoulders and stood his ground, careful to lock his arms behind his back lest he slam his fist through the video monitor.

"Father. To what do I owe this honor?"

A sharp gasp behind him was followed by a hasty shuffling of feet and the closing of an internal door. *Gee, thanks, Falka. Way to have my back.*

"You look well, Kahlym. It appears your time playing space captain is finally starting to turn you into a respectable man."

Last week, that off-handed comment would have churned

Kahlym's insides and hammered his ego. Now, he had given his heart to a Divine, and the mere knowledge of her presence on board his ship steeled his nerves. He unclenched his hands, releasing the pre-attack tension from his fingers, and folded his arms across his chest.

"I no longer live or die by your approval, Father. Why have you contacted me?"

The stern gaze widened, eyebrows raising in piqued curiosity. "Never one for pleasantries, were you?"

Kahlym resisted his father's baiting him, responding with tense silence, hoping the man would get to the point. Brel still rested in the med bay, but as soon as Kahlym finished with this lovely family visit, he'd need to let his brother know what had been said. That is, as soon as something *was* said. Kahlym maintained his stoic façade until the emptiness crept closer to an uncomfortable realm.

"Word has reached us that you are in possession of a female wanted by the Emperor. We have also heard rumors that she is a Divine."

Kahlym paused, eyes locked on to the condescending crimson in the vid screen. "Is that a question?"

Hands smacking against a distant tabletop cracked through the terminal, and his father bolted up from his chair, the image shifting and blurring to keep focus on a now-moving target.

"Don't get smart with me, boy. If you have her, this could be the chance for our family to regain our seat in the Rimmarian Thrall. Perhaps the Emperor would reconsider the marriage arrangement since your brother never consummated the betrothal with the royal heiress."

A tic started in Kahlym's jaw, brought on by the bone-breaking clench of his teeth, and the air swirled around him in hot, angry waves.

"I will not hand her over to you as a bargaining piece, Father." Kahlym had spat out that last word, and his arms shook in contained rage while icy terror ran through his veins. "It is time for the Emperor to relinquish his stranglehold on this system. Far too many lives have been destroyed, and the Divines he controls are dying out. It is time for—"

His father rolled his eyes and waved off Kahl's words. "You always were such an idealistic fool. Good intentions and peace have no place in leadership. You fight for what you want and kill to keep it. This is the way in all things. Now, bring the brood bitch to me, and you will earn your place once again as a true son of the Ruling Hand."

The monitor blinked, then went silent. Kahlym stood frozen, his blood pounding in his head and his breathing the only sounds in dark room. How the hell did his father find out about her so quickly? The Emperor would never publicly announce the missing Divine. Unless he meant to paint the Stria as kidnappers of the faithful, which would seriously reduce the number of safe places to regroup.

Snarling in cornered frustration, Kahlym slumped heavily into the chair beside the now blank video monitor.

"Great. Perfect. Just fucking perfect," he grumbled as he dragged his fingers through his hair. With a heavy sigh, he dropped his head back and stared at the muted chrome above, praying for some guidance. It offered no answers, though, only a glowing sliver of light that crept across the ceiling as a sliding door opened behind him. Knowing he was no longer alone didn't help much. If anything, he feared the accusatory looks he'd receive once he made public the nature of the message as well as the messenger.

"I figured you wanted to take that call in private."

Falka's timid intrusion and friendly attempt to break his glum mood only added to his irritation. Snarling at the unhelpful ceiling, he hid behind the safety of his eyelids, mustering the courage to ask his crew yet again to place themselves in deadly peril. For him.

For her.

"News was that good, huh?"

He barked out a mirthless laugh and opened his eyes. "Yeah,

you could say that." He paused. How best to phrase his request? "Falka? I need—"

"Does this have to do with Lady Evainne?"

Recalling Falka's great reverence to his beautiful angel, Kahlym nodded in the dark before rising from his chair. "I wish to hell it didn't, but I fear news of her existence is traveling fast." His tech expert slowly approached, head bowed in respect, and she placed two of her hands on his shoulders as the third pressed flat against her heart.

"Then whatever it is you ask to see to her safety, I will do."

Confusion puckered his brow, and he regarded his crew member. Falka had come to them after her homeworld had been ravaged by Thrall forces. She had managed to survive by sheer will alone. He knew little of her people on Shee'Van, but he assumed they were not a warring race; it was said the battle that had decimated their planet had lasted less than three solar cycles. She was at home with the computers and the ship's engines, but she was also handy in the kitchen and able to convince even the most stubborn plant to bear fruit.

Her smoky, greenish eyes were focused and intent, and he reached up and gripped her shoulder as he nodded sharply. She responded with a dip of her long neck and moved away. Curiosity spurred him to keep hold on her arm.

"Not that I don't appreciate your support," he said, "but why? Why would you possibly risk your own life for someone you barely know?"

For a moment, he thought she'd leave the question unanswered and, believing he had overstepped his bounds, he released her and headed toward the door.

"She is not like the Divines who had visited my home before… before ordering the cleansing of my tribe." Kahlym snapped his head around as sympathy coursed through his veins. Her gaze was vacant, searching back through what he suspected were horrific memories.

"Since our race had not gifted the Emperor with a Divine to replenish the sum, we were deemed 'useless,' and those white-robed sycophants sat by while my father, our tribe's elder, as well as my sisters, were butchered. Had I not concealed myself under piles of the dead, I would have joined the rest of my people."

With a blink, she returned to the present, pinning him with a staunch stare. "She is special, and I would lay down my life to protect her."

Kahlym swallowed hard against thick emotions clogging his throat. "Thank you," he croaked out before stepping through the open door.

As he contemplated his newly discovered information, he meandered back toward the pilot's deck, his mind churning with each deliberate step. He was going to need his crew, as well as his allies, to back him. This was not about just him.

This was about saving the whole of the Seventh Quadrant.

And his biggest fear lay sleeping in his bedchamber. How was he to keep her safe, yet ask her to fight by his side?

Chapter 4

Evainne cracked open her eyes, yawning as she stretched her arms above her head. She hadn't realized she'd crashed out. After a couple of minutes and when Kahlym hadn't returned, fatigue had slammed her hard and the bed had been just too comfortable. Now, she felt around in the sheets, her questing fingers unsuccessful in their search for another physical body.

"Damn."

With a resigned sigh, she sat up and rubbed the sleep out of her eyes while continuing to coax movement from her heavy limbs. Saving someone's life sure did take a lot out a person.

I'd really done that, hadn't I?

Blinking in the soft darkness, Evainne climbed off the bed and crossed to the desk where, in perfect descending size ratio, lay her phone, her iPod, her wallet, and her keys. She chuckled, imaging Kahlym staring at the bizarre items that had been her lifeline back home. Timidly, she reached for her music player, the other things tits-on-a-mouse useless at this end of the universe. She paused, hand hovering over her faded black-and-red plaid billfold, knowing that behind the worn-out fabric sat the only pictures she'd ever have of her familiar places.

A frown drew her eyebrows together. Did she even have pictures in her wallet? Did she have anything in it? Driving curiosity soon had her fingers sifting through the lonely scraps of her tattered life. One photo of her and the closest thing she'd to a pet growing up, a German Shepard/black Lab mix she'd called Max, brought a sad smile to her face. A lapsed insurance card, an expired library card, and a student ID for Bunker Hill Community College rounded up the contents.

Tucking away the faded photo, she picked up her iPod and tested the battery.

Yes.

With a happy chuckle, she thumbed the device off. Might as well keep as much charge as possible.

She scanned the Spartan room, thoughts trailing to its owner. The walls were bare, with no windows or pictures breaking up the shimmering blue-and-gold surfaces, and two of those weird hanging chairs were the only other furnishings.

Even with her screwed up life, at least her own place had plants and art, and her fish. Her heart went out to someone with a sadder existence than hers. Kahlym was kind and compassionate, and she would do all she could to make things better for him.

How? You gonna buy him a puppy and hang a velvet Elvis on his wall?

Yeah, there was that. At times, she felt about as useful as her keys in this world. They called her a "healer" and believed she was something special. She prayed she wouldn't let them down.

What did healers do anyway? Well, the only time she'd seen a nurse during school was when the hand-shaped bruise on her cheek had been a bit too defined to explain away as a mere fall. With a wistful smile, she remembered the kindly older lady checking in with her over the next couple of days. And the doctors on those TV shows would do that, too: visit their patients.

She suppressed a shudder, realizing she'd be, once again,

walking into that confined medical room. But, she should see how her patient was doing. Maybe she'd totally screwed things up and he'd grown a second head. Or worse still, perhaps he had inadvertently picked up one of her personality quirks.

As she headed for the door, Evainne caught the sway of her flowing robes from the corner of her eye. She had never been one to wear a dress, and her gaze drifted over to the floor-to-ceiling mirror next to the exit door. Her hair looked like a rat's nest—tousled waves in desperate need of taming fell about her overly pale face. Evainne narrowed her eyes, peering deeper into the reflection. Wait—was she really that pasty?

She stepped closer and realized her skin only appeared lighter because of the surrounding dark contrast of colors. The rich brick-red of the gown gave her fair complexion a healthy glow, and her normally dark-ringed eyes popped and sparkled. With a flourish, she twisted from side to side, the layered fabric masking her less-than-favorite body parts—namely everything below the waist. The surprisingly soft gossamer dress flowed off of her curves to pool around her bare toes.

"Huh," she remarked. "Not bad." She gave one final spin before opening the door.

The earlier bounce in her step faltered as she glanced down the blank corridor. A slight frown touched her lips while she swiveled her head to look behind her. The path trailed off to the right, a few feet before it led to a narrow-rung ladder.

That wasn't the right way. She had no recollection of going up any kind of steps. Taking a steadying breath, Evainne turned back to her left and headed down the silent hall.

Mechanical whirs and distant voices filtered through the overhead vents, and as she walked on, she pondered the reasons for a small crew on such a decent-sized vessel. Was it a big ship? She searched her memory for images of other ships when they'd stopped at the space station, yet all she could access were visions of the Enterprise and Darth Vader's TIE fighter.

Captain Kirk probably wouldn't stop by for a drink with the Sith lord.

As Evainne walked toward a door on her right, one with an eye-level white sign embossed with a strange Red Cross-like symbol, her pace slowed. She shrugged and, taking an educated guess, pressed her hand against the glowing black square on the wall. The door slid open to reveal the familiar white-and-chrome room in which she'd first awoken; the room in which she realized she was in a whole new chapter in the book of her life.

Peeking into the room, Evainne spied only one occupant. Long black dreads draped across an ivory pillow, and the chest beneath the silvery sheet rose and fell in a relaxed rhythm. Evainne rested her shoulder against the door jamb, entranced by the sleeper's simple action, not wanting to disrupt the peaceful scene.

"Don't worry about waking me, *learom-xahn*." The glow of the room brightened as the bed levered upwards, and Brel turned to her, a sleepy smile on his burly face. "Come in, little sister. Please. Besides, I could use some company, aside from Yhan'tu and his mothering attentions."

She returned his grin and entered, absentmindedly lacing her fingers in front of her. "Hey," she stammered. "I just, um…wanted to see how you were doing."

"I am alive, thanks to you. A bit tired and sore, but that is to be expected."

She lingered near the door, shifting her weight from foot to foot before shuffling farther into the chamber. "I guess so. I mean, you did lose a lot of blood, and I don't know anything about how much it hurts to get healed. I'm sorta new to all this."

"Please," he said, "sit down. You're making me nervous watching you hover by the door." He motioned to the chair beside his bed, and she scooted it closer. The long skirt snagged underneath the bent metal base, and it took her a couple of tries to escape from the entanglement. Once free, she huffed in petulant frustration, dropping heavily onto the seat.

Her awkward actions deepened Brel's grin, and his chuckle filled the mechanized silence with warmth.

"Not used to the regal robes, I take it?"

She looked up from her current task of rearranging the scads of material under her ass so it didn't bunch uncomfortably. His sympathetic smile helped to ease her panic, and she slumped forward dejectedly, leaning her forearms against the narrow railings along the edge of the hospital bed.

"That obvious, huh? Oh, who am I kidding? I'm not all this." She punctuated her brief tirade by plucking at one of the loose split sleeves. "I'm just a girl, Brel. I never asked for any of this."

His citrine gaze softened, and he rested his hand on top of hers. "Sometimes Fate doesn't ask what we want. She only puts us where we are needed."

"Yeah, well, the bitch needs to have some serious etiquette lessons," she groused. "'Cuz this shit sucks."

Brel smirked and patted her on the shoulder. "Couldn't have said it better myself." He wriggled his back, attempting to sit up higher, and Evainne jumped out of her seat to offer a hand. Granted, it was like trying to move a Mack truck with a feather, but between the two of them, Brel found a more comfortable position.

"Should you be moving around this much?" she asked, then halted. Meeting his eyes, she realized the medic's words had slipped from her own mouth. They shared a laugh as she returned to the chair.

"Are you certain you are not a healer? I almost pictured Yhan'tu with that last statement."

She shook her head. "Yeah, no. Trust me on this one. I kill fake flowers. I just stopped by to make sure you were still breathing and hadn't grown a third arm or something."

Brel covered her hands with one meaty mitt, a quizzically sad smile on his face. "You underestimate yourself, Evainne. You have traveled far from your home and all things familiar, and you still wear a smile. You saved my life, and you have done more than that for my brother."

Butterflies in combat boots tromped around in her gut as the conversation drifted to the nitty-gritty, touchy-feely part. She sighed, her gaze slipping away from his golden eyes. "Are you sure?" she said. "I just feel like every time he looks at me, he's…aw hell, I don't know. It's like he's terrified I'm going to decide I'm too good for him, or some crap like that. I'm no prize catch, honest; I'm crass, I swear like a sailor, and I totally suck in social functions."

Brel's smile warmed as he shook his head. "*Learom-xahn*, all the traits you berate yourself for having are the exact reasons you are a perfect match for Kahlym. You challenge him, bringing out qualities in him I have never seen. You must understand that the females in his past believed him to be disfigured and therefore undeserving of compassion. Even his birth was put to question. Had there not been myself and our other brother, Xandar, present at the event, he would have been cast out. Only the words of prophecy cemented his right to live, in the eyes of our mother."

Evainne recalled hearing much of these details from the kindly lion-man, Bhaan, when she and Kahlym were hiding from the Thrall soldiers on the space station. Hearing it now from Kahl's brother gave the tale added weight.

"Why?" she asked. "I mean, I did get some of this from Dhaerin's dad, so I know the whole 'pure eyes,' superficial song and dance. But how could a mother who carried a child until finally bringing it into the world, how could she just throw that child away because of some archaic rules?"

Her words must have struck a chord. Brel's features hardened, and his gaze grew distant. "Love has little place in our family." He paused, and Evainne forced herself to stay still. "The men of the house of Jhuen," he went on, "have held the title of Ruling Hand for millennia, and that honor was to fall on Kahlym. His betrothal before his birth, to the daughter of the Rimmarian Emperor, would have forged an unbreakable foundation which would have meant another millennium of unyielding power."

Brel blinked and turned those bright gold eyes back to her. "Kahlym was born to be a pawn in a game, nothing more. But the Goddess Ishtanti had other plans for him." He tightened his fingers around Evainne's, his gaze boring straight into her soul. "She set his feet on an arduous path because She knew you would be there to save him."

The once-sharp images blurred as Evainne's emotions threatened to stream down her face. She bit the inside of her cheek to hold back the impending flood, shaking her head sadly.

"I don't believe in any higher power, Brel." She felt like shit for saying these words aloud, but during her hellish solitary upbringing, no god had ever listened to her pleas. Why should she put her faith in one now?

Brel lifted her hands and placed a gentlemanly kiss upon her knuckles. "You may not believe in them, Evainne, but you do not need to feel the sun to know it shines beyond the clouds."

She squeaked out a strangled laugh. "Why does great wisdom always sound like a riddle from a fortune cookie? How come the universe doesn't just say: 'Here's the map to happiness. Don't be a douche.'"

He joined her in the mood-lightening levity. "I know not what this 'fortune cookie' nor this 'douche' is, but I do agree with your desire for straightforward answers."

The needed tension release centered her thoughts and Evainne wiped at her eyes, telling herself the tears were from the bout of laughter and not something deeper.

"Kahlym's lucky to have you as a brother, Brel."

His eyes twinkled with a mischievous glint.

"And he is lucky to have you as a lover, *learom-xahn*."

Sudden modesty heated her cheeks, and her gaze slid to the floor. Did she honestly think things would be kept secret, especially with such a tight-knit crew? Not to mention, she was talking to Kahl's brother.

A dark and cold thought crept down her spine, chilling the air. She shuddered and wrapped her hands around herself, rubbing away the persistent dread.

"Brel," she confessed, "I'm afraid he's gonna do something really stupid over me."

Brel shrugged. "You are going to need to be more specific. My brother has a nasty habit of doing stupid things on a regular basis."

"I don't mean that," she said, chuckling. "I don't want him to risk his own life, or hand it over to someone else, because of me. I'm not weak or helpless."

"Yes, I did notice that." His brow furrowed as he pinned her with a serious stare. "I saw some of your battle. I don't think anyone bothered to tell you just who you were fighting against, did they?"

"That purple chick? She was good, I'll give her that. And since she helped that asshole, Qaen, escape, I'm guessing she was his girlfriend, or fuck buddy, or something."

Brel shook his head slowly. "That, Evainne, was one of the most dangerous and deadliest of all the Thrall's assassins: Kaxxahn tu'Ertta. She has never missed a mark. Except for you, little sister. You have made a powerful enemy, *learom-xahn*. Be certain to keep your wits about you should you be away from the security of this ship, and of us."

Evainne opened her mouth, poised for a sharp retort, when a voice spoke, the mechanized male coming from both everywhere and nowhere.

"Crew, prepare for descent. Planet fall in one hour."

Another impish grin warmed Brel's face, probably in response to her apparent confusion. "Evainne, would you like to watch the landing?"

Childlike excitement crackled along her arms like electricity, and the fine hairs all stood at attention. She practically bounced in her seat at the prospect of seeing an alien world. Not much of a traveler back on Earth, she did love the take-off and landing. The worst plane experience she remembered was a class trip to Washington, D.C. during her eighth-grade year. She'd only been allowed to attend since her father would have been lobbying for his firm and he would have been able to keep close tabs on her.

She'd ended up spending the entire trip holed up in the hotel, though, after one of the boys had snuck a small bottle of bleach into her luggage and the bottle had melted on the way, splattering her wardrobe with pale splotches and discolored smears. She begged her father to contact her mother to have some clothes sent, or at least to give her some money to buy something. But he sneered, telling her this should be a lesson in taking better care of her own baggage.

She never again begged for anything from either of her parents.

Shoving away the memory, Evainne nodded, a broad smile crossing her face. Brel pointed a small oval device with several buttons at the far wall, and the chrome-and-white barrier shimmered before it blinked away.

Evainne gasped in surprise as the star-filled skies surrounded her. Ahead and looming closer sat a cluster of planets, the nearest a swirling mass of oranges and blues.

Why didn't Yhan'tu just open the window while she was in here? *Oh yeah, you didn't tell him you just wanted to look outside. YOU blabbered on about needing a walk.*

A pair of voices murmured behind her, but she was too entranced by the approaching sphere to turn away.

"Is that where we're going?" Her voice sounded thin to her own ears, but she didn't care. Even in her science classes, she never would have dreamed of other worlds, much less one she would be walking on soon.

A pair of warm and comforting arms wrapped around her waist. "No, *ziat'xahn*. That is Raedyn Hectar. But if you like, I can take you."

Kahlym's breath wafted hot against her cheek, and she leaned back against his chest, her fingers gripping his forearms. His body acted as a nice backdrop, giving her the perfect amount of support while she gazed at the beautiful and bizarre planets as the ship easily navigated the obstacle course outside.

"Is it pretty?"

Pretty? Really! Ugh. What are you, five? She cringed at the juvenile comment that had slipped from her lips. Maybe she'd been lucky and the boys had been paying attention to something other than her dumb self.

Kahlym squeezed her lightly, and a tender kiss landed on the top of her head. "I will allow you to make that decision. However, if by 'beauty' you mean natural outcroppings and growing things, then perhaps you would find Raedyn Septicon more to your liking." His lips brushed against the shell of her ear. "It is also our destination."

Raedyn Septicon. The name had rung a bell, and she glanced over her shoulder at Kahlym. His face was so close, his stubbly chin tickled her forehead, and she craned her neck back to capture his gaze. Her mind had prepped a necessary question, but something in his eyes now stalled her words. That previous call hadn't brought good news. As she recalled a little of her earlier conversation with Brel, she opted to keep her inquiry to herself. Or at least until they were alone.

Instead, she decided on a safer question. "How did you know where to find me?"

Kahlym smiled, kissing the tip of her nose. "I could say it was my mental powers, but the truth is, Brel told me you were here."

"Traitor," she mumbled, glaring with a crooked grin at the beaming buffoon lying in the bed.

The door slid open, and Yhan'tu joined the group. His large head swiveled, taking in the trio as another enormous sphere, its surface blanketed by dark pink clouds, passed by the giant window.

"If I cannot have order in my med bay, Kahlym, I will be very cross."

Brel laughed as he cautiously swung his leg over the side of the bed. "Relax, Yhan'tu. We've got a healer right here in the room, and you've not allowed me to lift anything heavier than a fork. I've taken worse beatings."

"But you've never knocked so hard on death's door before," Kahlym chimed in.

Evainne tuned out the friendly banter, redirecting her gaze to the ever-changing starscape. What about air? What if she took one breath and her lungs collapsed, or exploded, or froze? What if the planet's sun fried her skin? Her knees knocked against the glass; so entranced by the unfolding scene, she hadn't noticed she'd stepped in for a closer look.

Her heart started to race in a feeble attempt to catch up with her panicked thoughts. What if the gravity was so horrible she couldn't move? But a tiny, more sensible, part of her mind tapped an impatient foot at her ridiculous fears. *Face it,* the mini-Spock whispered, *it would be illogical for an alien species to generate artificial gravity and an oxygen-rich environment if it was not necessary for their own survival.* The smug Vulcan even arched an imaginary eyebrow at her.

Evainne didn't realize she was telegraphing her worries until Kahlym nestled up behind her and ran his fingers through her hair.

"Shhh," he breathed against her skin. "You have no need for concern. I promised to keep you safe, and I will not fail you."

The dusty-rose poofs grew larger as they circled the massive globe. Soon, pinpricks of light from the ship cut through the atmospheric layer, and she spied the outlines of the planet's surface. Once the ship was clear of the thick cloud covering, Evainne gasped again. The skies above teemed with activity—Spaceships of every size and shape imaginable hovered or zoomed past the vast picture window, and their own craft maneuvered easily through the traffic to approach a shimmering silhouette on the horizon. Upon closer inspection, she noticed the skies were a pale orange, though she couldn't find any recognizable sun as the light source.

"Welcome to Raedyn Septicon, *ziat'xahn.*"

"Is this your home?" She'd squeaked out her question while

gawking at the new vistas. The ground presented rolling hills of yellows and deep reds, dotted by large golden bodies of water that trailed finger-like tendrils toward the distant horizon. Shining silver and black turrets reached toward the heavens as the monumental city sprawled beneath them. Lights twinkled from steepled peaks while the glint of something behind them sparkled and danced on the cramped columns.

"This?" said Kahlym. "No, this is only the landing terminal for the Achtilles, the ruling capital of the planet."

She nodded as the ship angled steeply, headed toward a large, open balcony. Kahlym chuckled lightly, patting her fingers as they locked around his wrist, knuckles white and trembling.

"Have no fear, Evainne. Dhaer has never misjudged a landing bay this open. Not even when he was less than sober."

Brel's voice had sounded over her head as he joined them at the picture window, and more details clarified before her. Each balcony held a craft, or space for one at least. Workers with strange hand-held tools moved to unload cargo and adjust things, while people of every imaginable size strolled to and fro in organized lines. It was like riding in one of those glass elevators, looking at everyone while none even realized they were being watched.

Evainne began to recognize some of the species, only because they looked like crew members. Lion-people hurried by, boxes piled high in their arms, and she even thought she saw a couple of those owl-guys in the mix. Her heart dropped. Someone would need to tell Lozzan's family that a friend had betrayed him and was responsible for his death.

The platform loomed closer and, after a light jostle, the whirring engine sounds vanished. *That was it?* She'd expected something more. Hell, she'd gotten more of a jolt parking her car.

"Safe and sound."

Kahlym stepped away and tapped the glowing box on the wall, transforming the clear surface back to shimmering steel and chrome. "Nicely done, Dhaer. Might as well lock her in. I think we're going to be here for a while."

"Thank the goddess. I could use some time away from you lot. No offense, but only one of you have parts I'm interested in and she's not on the menu."

Evainne barked out a sharp laugh, triggering the others to join in.

"Bloody hell, Kahl. You coulda warned me she was listening. I'm sorry. I didn't mean— No, I mean, what I meant was—"

"It's okay, Dhaer," she interjected, saving him from any unnecessary backpedaling. "It's actually kinda refreshing to hear I have interesting parts."

Continued mumbled apologies filtered through the whole ship, blending with growing raucous laughter. Buoyed by a renewed sense of purpose, Evainne turned to face Kahlym, a confident grin firmly in place.

"All right, if I'm gonna make my big debut, I can't be running around in my pj's. Or maybe it would be better if I said it this way: I'm not going out in public dressed in a shower curtain. I don't care if you didn't get all the references, I'd just feel a whole hell of a lot more comfortable if I were wearing pants."

KAHLYM BLINKED SLOWLY as the beautiful female before him transformed from a timid observer to a force to be reckoned with. She settled her fisted hands onto her full hips, and he immediately rethought his original view. Her words were now direct and she spoke from her heart; no guile ever colored her intentions. She'd asked to be his strength, not his weakness.

She was intelligent, compassionate, and at every turn, she met each obstacle with a graceful determination. And she held his heart in the palm of her hand.

Out of the corner of his eye, he caught Yhan'tu twitch, the cleric's deeply ingrained training warring with the blanket "no bowing" clause set up by their unique Divine. She was unlike any of the ancient fools under the Rimmarian Emperor's thumb; she rebelled against any and all preconceived notions of proper behavior of the gifted ones. Even as she stood before him, the robes currently clinging to her with loving care seemed…wrong.

She looked more at home in the gearsuit that accentuated her womanly curves.

"I believe another gearsuit could be arranged," he said.

"Out of the question!"

He snapped his head toward the uncharacteristically angered medic. Yhan'tu shook with indignity as he glared at the three pairs of eyes staring at him. He shuffled closer, huffing and jiggling during the short journey.

"I will not hear of it." He lifted his droopy chin and leveled all four eyes at Kahlym. "She is a Divine Healer. I will not see her paraded around in anything less than the appropriate garb. She must be recognized and treated with the reverence deserving of her title."

A flurry of voices exploded into the once-peaceful room; Yhan'-tu's flustered tone rose in righteous indignation above the low growls of himself and Brel. Gestures flew as wildly as did their words, arms outstretched and fingers all pointing toward the only silent person.

A high-pitched screech sliced through the chatter. Kahlym scowled, gaze sweeping in search of the hideous sound's source. Brel covered his ears, and Yhan'tu's mouth froze in mid-yell.

"Are we done here?"

Kahlym's frown deepened as he swiveled his head toward Evainne. She smirked, shaking her own head slowly, folding her arms across her chest.

"So, now that I have your attention, let's start this again, shall we?" She walked over to Yhan'tu and placed her hands onto his shoulders. Even though she was only slightly shorter than the cleric, his bulk made her look like a delicate angel, the flowing robes adding to her ethereal beauty. Kahlym's libido took a backseat to his driving curiosity, though.

<Just how did she make the horrid noise, kherdes-xahn?>

Kahlym could only shrug in response to Brel's question.

"Look, I get that you believe I'm some divine something" —she lifted her hand just as Yhan'tu's jaw began working— "but I need you to hear me out. I also get that some people out here aren't too happy that I'm not with them. So, while I appreciate the comfy, flowy stuff, I think it would be better if I remained as mundane as possible. I'm already gonna stick out like a sore thumb, unless you happen to know of a local planet of pale people."

Brel grinned, his movements stilted and heavy as he hobbled closer to lean on Kahlym's shoulder. "She does have a point. I'm sure the Overlord will be on high alert trying to find her."

Kahlym's gut knotted as he recalled his earlier conversation with his father and, swallowing past the rising bile, he broke the news. "He's not the only one we need to worry about," he said, then shifted his gaze, hoping strength would materialize out of the scenery.

Silence encouraged him to continue and a centering grip on his shoulder helped him to turn back to the crowd, but dread still froze his voice.

"Don't worry, *kherdes-xahn.* I had a feeling dear old Dad would be showing his ugly face around soon. Is he here?"

Kahlym shook his head. The relief that his brother was unsurprised by their father's machinations did little to dispel the snakes writhing inside him. "Not at the moment," he replied. "But who knows how long that reprieve will last? I just hope we can slip in with relative swiftness before he knows we've landed."

"Then we don't have a whole lot of time to waste arguing about fashion." Evainne turned her eyes back to their medic still uneasy in his stance. "I'll make you a deal," she said. "As soon as there isn't a price on my head, I'll wear the frilly crap all day long. But for now, I need to be able to move and fight, and I sure as shit can't do it in this. Just ask Brel. I nearly strangled myself with the damned thing trying to sit in a chair."

Kahlym couldn't stop the corners of his lips tilting upward at her logical argument. She'd already proven herself a Divine Healer. Perhaps she had a touch of a Divine Seer, as well, with her quick thinking and mental acuity cutting through to the heart of any matter. She also said "fight," and he'd witnessed her prowess at hand-to-hand combat.

Was it possible? Had those doddering fools stumbled upon a Divine Fury hidden in a faraway galaxy?

Evainne had managed to pull a begrudging nod from Yhan'tu, and she rewarded him with a dazzling smile. A faint twinge of jealousy tickled at the base of his skull, but it vaporized in a heartbeat when she turned to face him.

"All right," she said, "now that that's all cleared up, I suggest we get this party moving."

Chapter 5

Anaxar du'Jhuen paced the expanse of the black marble floor, his boot heels clacking out an angry tattoo. Ornate tapestries of gold and burgundy draped from the ceiling and clung to the walls in a lavish array. Chairs organized in a wide circle within the domed room were nothing more than obstacles to be avoided as he stalked from end to end.

"The ship is the *Tiamat's Revenge*. It shouldn't be that hard to locate. It escaped Thrall forces on Skirnahn Station two days ago."

"I'm sorry, sire, but we don't have any ships matching that description requesting a docking bay."

He spun around and slammed his hands down on the chiseled stone desk. "Dammit. Find that ship. I want the entire crew. And alive." He cut the link, halting the sputtering affirmative response from the useless drone.

That malformed bastard of his held the female Divine on board that pathetic vessel. He knew it in his bones. His bitch of a mother had spared him because of some spewed crap about a prophecy. First, she disgraces him by sleeping with Ishtanti-knew-what to birth the freak, and now that abomination held hostage the entire Thrall and the future of his own family.

His talons carved furrows into the aged granite beneath his palms. Since the untimely death of his son, Xandar, his position in the empire had slipped. The marriage to the emperor's out-of-wedlock daughter would have guaranteed his title, and the name of Jhuen would be once again favored as the Ruling Hand of Raedyn Prime. Had that misfit Kahlym not sabotaged the ship, causing it to lose control and explode upon landing, Xandar would have bedded the stupid, spoiled cow and his lineage would have prospered.

Instead, Anaxar spent his time scrounging for scraps of respect from those who'd once served him, forced to hear the lesser pleas from the wealthy merchant class, having been demoted to mere Sub-Confidant.

Enraged, Anaxar roared, dashing to the ground the neatly stacked briefing ledgers. The thin sheets fluttered in the air before decorating the dark floor with bright, geometric squares.

A timid knock stalled his tantrum. "Enter." He dragged in air as he rose to his full height, the veneer of control safely in place once again as he prepared to greet his guest.

The door swung open and, while his clerk remained out of sight, admitted an entourage of sharp, white-uniformed officials. Anaxar narrowed his eyes and the corner of his lip curled in disgust as the current Ruling Hand of Raedyn Prime sauntered in under heavy guard. The man was a weasel who shouldn't have gained such a position of power.

But until Anaxar could deliver to the Emperor his prize, he would swallow his pride and kowtow to this impudent pretender. Family loyalty would win out in the end. His son wanted his title and his honor restored, and that desire would be his undoing. Dangling in front of Kahlym the temptation of redemption would drag the little shit out of hiding, though it didn't mean he had to agree to any such reversal.

Anaxar locked his arms behind his back to keep at bay the drive to strangle the effete fraud. Rules dictated he must bow to a superior, though his ego would only grant the man a slight dip of his chin.

"Why, Grand Counsel Xhineer, what an honor you do me. May I ask the reason for this visit?"

His obsequious words were lost on the approaching man, whose pristine white uniform bore praise ribbons from battles Anaxar knew the fraud had never seen. Gold braid dripped from the Grand Counselor's shoulders, looped beneath his wiry arms. Anaxar could have broken the man in two like a twig. And the sniveling bastard knew this, too, which explained the military guard surrounding him at all times.

The four enforcers took up positions at the door and beside the room's main windows, leaving their conversation in relative privacy.

"Anaxar. You know why I am here." The man's nasally tone did little to add to his feigned authority. He plucked off his white gloves and settled into the chair directly across from the desk. "The Emperor demands the Divine."

"Divine?" Anaxar blinked, expression bland, emotionless. "But the Emperor already has all the Divines born of the Seventh Quadrant housed in his temple on Rimma."

The black diamond eyes across from Anaxar flared wide, flashing in shock, and his pale, brushed silver skin shimmered with a sheen of fear. He held his loose stance, though, delighting in discovering a new bargaining chip: Xhineer believed Anaxar knew nothing of this new Divine's existence.

Anaxar lowered himself into his high-backed seat, careful to keep his face neutral.

"Apparently, you have been kept out of the informational know, Ax," Xhineer said. "It seems a Divine was found on a distant world. A female, to boot, so naturally she was transported to Rimma. But somehow, she did not reach her destination, and it is rumored she has been taken to a Chandaran Stria outpost." Xhineer's eyes narrowed, and Anaxar sensed the glorified lackey's clumsy attempt at a memory scan.

"Is that why you have darkened my door?" Anaxar growled menacingly.

Xhineer blinked, then lowered his gaze, a hint of embarrassment painting his cheeks. "Apologies, sir, but I must inform you that your son, Kahlym, has been named as the possible perpetrator of the kidnapping."

Anaxar scoffed and leaned back into the thick padding. "That name has no meaning to me. The boy is not from my lineage, so what care have I if the bastard is a thief?"

The trap had been laid. Now to see if the bait was enough.

A slippery smile spread across the council member's face, and Anaxar knew he was successful.

"I know that his dishonor and the lost wedding to Gha'jahn's daughter struck a hard blow to your family. If you were to deliver this woman and her kidnapper to me, I would be able to put in a good word with the Emperor. Perhaps even a promotion could be arranged."

Anaxar took to his feet, chair legs scraping along the slick tiles. "I assure you, High Counselor, should I receive any news regarding this Divine, I will not hesitate to inform you."

Xhineer grinned like a fool as he rose. "I look forward to hearing updates on your progress."

Anaxar remained standing while the counselor and his men exited, and as the door clicked shut, he snorted out a derisive laugh. He'd sooner eat glass than hand over such a powerful weapon. His wayward son would seek out sanctuary within the ranks of the Stria, and that was how he'd destroy them both. By taking out the bastard and the thorn in the Emperor's side, his honor would be restored. Ishtanti, be damned. His son was no harbinger of prophecy, and it was time he erased that mistake.

After tapping rapidly against the touch pad on the desk, Anaxar hovered by the blank screen, waiting until he was certain the communique had been received. A moment passed, and his answer arrived. He grinned in cruel pleasure and sat back down.

Soon, the source of my troubles will be the engine of my success.

Chapter 6

"Are you ready for this?"

Evainne looked up. Kahlym stood by the open door, the hint of a grin on the edges of his luscious mouth. If she had half a brain, she'd say no and drag him back to bed; their earlier conversation had been rudely interrupted before they'd landed on the alien planet. Why couldn't their destination still be days away? She wanted to resume their kiss, feel his weight pressed on top of her.

Especially when he was looking at her the way he was right now, with the warm glow from the overhead lighting turning his eyes an even more exotic color. The combination of his coppery skin, silvery black hair, and those "to die for" eyes made him sexier than any Calvin Klein model. Tingles traipsed down her arms as she replayed their night in the pool; his single-minded attention to please her and his toe-curling skill to do just what he'd promised, warmed her even now. But what had captured her the most was his heart. His open honesty and fiercely protective streak were such new experiences for her, and it gave her hope in the existence of love.

"Evainne?"

She shook her head, clearing out the emotional distractions, and closed the lapel on her new jumpsuit. No, she told herself, they called them gearsuits. As the material cocooned her into its protective embrace, she pondered the name—gearsuit. Personally, she thought they should be called "Ziplocs," since she felt like a well-cared for sandwich in the thing.

"Yeah, sorry. I'd be better if I had some coffee." After a couple of necessary tugs in the crotch, she was ready to go. She jammed her fingers into her unruly hair, weaving the strands into a thick braid as she covered the short distance to the door, her gaze hitting the floor as her hands worked in rote routine. "This thing takes some getting used to," she muttered, "but it sure beats standing in front of the closet, deciding what to wear, right?"

A pair of boots appeared in her narrowed vision, and she halted before she bumped her bowed head into Kahlym's chest. He steadied her by the shoulders, and she lifted her gaze as she reached the ends of her hair. His piercing tourmaline eyes were clouded with apprehension and a deep furrow of concern had cut across his forehead.

"If you are not ready, we can—"

She touched his lips with her fingertips, stopping the sure-to-be-tempting proposition.

"It's not safe here, sweetie. You know it, and I know it. Hiding our heads in the sand is not going to make things go away." Kahlym's apprehension turned to confusion, and she smiled, shrugging sheepishly. "Yeah, I know it sounds weird. But trust me, it makes sense. Besides, enemies are around every corner, and wouldn't you feel better with a full crew and loads of needed supplies?"

She could see emotions warring on his handsome features, and the hardest thing to do was to remain still while he worked things out. If she hugged him, they'd both give in to the sexual tension. She'd never been this horny in her life. Then again, no man had ever fired her blood in quite the same way as Kahlym did.

Right now, though, she had to keep her mind on business: the business of staying alive and staying one step ahead of the bad guys. Kahlym must have picked up on her vibes because his demeanor shifted. He let out a heavy sigh and nodded in slow acquiescence.

"You are right. This place is not safe."

Unable to resist, Evainne smiled deviously. "Oh, baby, I'm always right," she said and gave him a wink. "The sooner you realize this, the better."

He quirked a suspicious eyebrow, unable to hide the trace of a smile on his kissable lips just beneath her fingertips. She shrugged innocently before dropping her hand.

"Okay, so maybe not all the time. But it helps my ego to think I am."

The familiar voice of the ship's captain, Dhaerin, cut through the air—*"Kahl? We've got transport clearance."*—and their playful mood shifted. Back to business.

"Thank you, Dhaer. Have you heard back from Khundyl yet?" Kahlym gestured toward the open door, and Evainne couldn't help smiling at his chivalrous action. Knowing they were on a time crunch, not a first date, she stepped through the door but hung back to give him the lead.

"Sorta. I heard from one of her lackeys that she is indisposed at the moment. However, she is aware of our need and will meet with you prior to moonrise." They moved in an almost unconscious synchronicity, though Evainne did need to take almost two steps to his one. Grateful for the exercise, she kept pace, listening as they discussed further details. She struggled to lock all of the mentioned places and names into memory; they were firing info at such a furious pace that, by the time they'd reached the ship's loading bay, she was completely confused.

The door was already open, and her steps faltered as she took in the scene. She was about to step foot on another planet—an alien-friggin-planet. *And me, without my camera.*

"Damn." The word had come out as a breathy chuckle as she

stood on the edge of the ramp, drinking in all of the sights and sounds just beyond the ship's safety. The vast, open space reminded her a little of the space station from her previous off-board venture. Boxes and pallets of cargo were stacked in neat towers along the walls, leaving clear the center of the landing platform. The air tasted different; heavier, with a slightly bitter aftertaste. It could have been the lingering traces of exhaust from their recent parking job, but it reminded her of the lowest level of the underground garage at Boston Common.

She peered farther, past the ship's tail and out at the strange, rosy sky.

After taking a few steps, Kahlym stopped, apparently aware he was going on alone. He turned toward her, his handsome face lined with concern. In the artificial light from an unknown source overhead, he looked completely in his element, body encased in deep blue leather that highlighted his exotic features, a sidearm strapped to his muscular thigh, publicly displayed as a warning to all.

The rest of the crew waited just beyond Kahlym—Brel was casually propped up between both Dhaerin and R'uan, as Yhan'tu and Falka fidgeted, probably fighting the urge to grovel.

Taking a deep breath, Evainne stepped off the ramp and onto another planet.

KAHLYM WATCHED as his beautiful female hesitantly joined him on the tarmac. Even back in his quarters, he'd sensed her trepidation. Still, she was strong-minded and brave, willing to face the impending danger. His heart skipped a beat as she strolled over to him, chin lifted proudly and confidently. Her voice rang in his head as he remembered her request: *I want to be your strength, not your weakness.*

Kahlym wanted nothing more than to prove himself worthy. Even now, as she walked with him and his crew toward the waiting transport, he suppressed the urge to wrap his arm around her shoulders and pull her in close. He had to stop himself from shielding her from the uninterested stares, their owners lost in their own thoughts and worries.

She was right. On more than one occasion, he'd sheltered her to the point of endangering the both of them. His head was in the right place, though. She had no idea what this world was like, and she was far too precious to fall into the wrong hands.

But neither was she helpless, as he'd learned during their escape. Even so, his heart jumped into his throat each time she looked away, debilitating fear nearly crippling him, and all rational judgment flew out the nearest airlock. No one had ever made him feel the myriad of emotions he did when she was near, and he dared not let her farther away than arm's length.

R'uan knocked into his shoulder, jarring him out of his mental wanderings, and Kahlym shifted his eyes over to match his surrogate older brother's fierce stare.

"You good, kid?" asked R'uan.

The strong vibes R'uan threw off had a much more direct message: *<Best watch yourself, Kahl. Anyone gets their hands on her because you're daydreaming and you're gonna wish Qaen had killed you.>*

Words failed Kahlym, so he nodded sharply and followed as they reached the small craft, where he turned to face his crew. The lot looked like they'd been through one hell of a meat grinder—healing cuts, black eyes, and bruised cheeks dotted every expression as they awaited his orders.

"Go on," he said. "Get out of here. You all deserve a rest. We can regroup in a couple of days."

Yhan'tu cleared his throat, concern reflecting back through his four pale eyes. "Do you think it wise to separate?" he inquired.

Kahlym shook his head as he processed all the possible "what if" scenarios. "I don't really know," he replied, "but I do believe our chances are better if we don't remain together."

"He's right," Brel chimed in, adding his support. "We all have people we can trust and places we call safe. I say we let the dust settle for a couple of days and see what happens."

Falka and Yhan'tu shifted their gazes between him and their precious cargo and, after an uncomfortable silence, Falka stepped away from the group. With reverent care, she placed a hand on Kahlym's shoulder.

"We will take word to Lozzan's family. He will be remembered with his due respect."

Kahlym nodded, gripping her own slender shoulder in response. "Thank you," he said, then slid his eyes toward his quiet angel. She'd remained silent during their short trek, eyes never still as she surveyed the sheltered dock. If she was amazed by the station and the small bit of Septicon she'd seen during their landing, she was about to experience the surprise of her life. His gaze rested on her as she swiveled her head, jaw slightly agape in wonder.

"Dhaer. You, Yhan'tu, and Falka, take the second transport. After your stop on Outer T'chan, you can head to wherever you desire. R'uan, Brel, and I will take Evainne to Khundyl's place. After two days, unless you hear something new, meet us back at the ship. Sound good?"

Evainne spun on her heels and shifted her wide, brown eyes to him. "I'm sorry," she said. "What?"

Brel chuckled. "Damn, *kherdes*. If it makes you feel any better, I was paying attention."

"Me, too." Dhaerin raised his hand, feigning a serious scowl. "I never know if there's going to be a test on things around here."

Kahlym arched an eyebrow, shaking his head. "Why me?"

Relaxed laughter filtered through the quiet dock. Dhaerin ducked his shoulder and left Brel in R'uan's care, heaving an overly dramatic sigh of relief. Rolling his shoulders, he crossed to Yhan'tu and thumped him on the back. Shock from the friendly gesture earned him a surprised squeak from the portly cleric.

"Well, sweet cheeks, guess you're stuck with me, eh?" He winked at Kahlym as Falka rolled her eyes. Another mirthful bout of good-hearted conversation broke out, tension releasing in a cacophonous array of highs and lows.

"All right, time to get moving." Kahlym said, and half of his crew climbed into the waiting transport pod. The door closed, and Dhaerin flashed a toothy grin, flipping them off as the small craft took off.

"Someone tell me again why I didn't drown him in his sleep when he was still a cub?" R'uan shook his head, grumbling good-naturedly as he helped Brel inside the other vehicle.

"Same reason I keep that one around, *kherdes*," Brel said with a slight hiss, tipping his chin toward Kahlym waiting outside. "It's always so amusing to see what kind of shit they're going to get into."

Kahlym sighed as he closed the chuckling pair into the back seat, then he triggered the front door release and reached out toward Evainne. "Maybe I should have sent these two off with Dhaer. At least that way, the ride would be filled with silence instead of snark."

Evainne smiled as she took his offered hand. "Yeah, but I think I'd prefer some conversation rather than all that worshipful, whis-pering crap." Once inside, she angled her shoulders, a panicked expression aimed at R'uan and Brel. "Please don't tell them I said that. It's just—"

Kahlym joined in on the laughter as the door slid shut. "I do not believe you have much to worry about. I'm sure your secret is safe. Not to mention, all of us have spoken to both of them about their overly reverent actions."

She let out a relieved breath and settled into the seat. Kahlym brushed his fingertips against her trembling hand with a reassuring smile as she clamped tightly on to him. He kept a hold on her as he programmed in the coordinates of their destination.

"Do not worry, *ziat'xahn*. We will reach the rendezvous location soon."

She glanced at him, wide, brown eyes sparkling. "Not too soon, I hope. This is my first alien planet, after all."

Chapter 7

Evainne wandered around the vast, round room, her movements slow and soothing as her brain shuffled through the images of the ride there. Their cab had started the trip by dropping straight down like an elevator from heaven. Buildings streaked past the window, and she finally glimpsed the sky—the clouds' pinkish shade did not do justice to the fiery fuchsia over her head. Twin suns glowed, one a pale sapphire blue while the other contrasted with a deep burnt orange, the pair perched off-kilter high above the horizon.

The beauty of this alien world stunned her, and she only half listened during the ride as the men discussed strategies and next steps. Rays of orange and blue bounced off of the gleaming towers of ebony and the lakes of golden fire. Other small ships similar to theirs zipped past them, as did large, cargo-laden transports and sleek, single-occupant racers. Traffic moved at breakneck speed, the rules clearly defined to the participants, though completely lost on her.

Evainne gaped as, through the window beside her, she saw a little boy with creamy lapis skin playing with a toy rocket, the vehicles keeping pace together toward their mutual destinations. He blinked his bright silver eyes at her and waved, an innocent grin splitting his happy face. Evainne struggled to return the same exuberant expression, but fell short; faltering a moment, she managed to send the signal to her hand to respond, her weak gesture earning a silent laugh from the child. Soon, the two transports parted ways, and she continued to stare out at the vacant space.

Her brain searched for something familiar, flipping through memories of every sci-fi movie she'd ever seen, but this was truly an alien landscape. No billboards lit up the skies or jumped from the mirrored walls, and Kahlym's hand remained on her knee throughout the journey, his touch grounding her in this new world.

During their journey, so many images blew by, many of them blurring as tears misted her eyes. All around, everything was pristine and shining; no hint of pollution darkened the distant horizon, nor did she spy any trash on the streets as they began to descend.

Once their pod came to a complete stop, Evainne vaguely remembered stepping out. *Thank you, and enjoy the rest of your day at the Magic Kingdom.* She had never been to Disneyland, yet somehow she knew none of the attractions there held a candle to the roller coaster she'd just experienced.

A mechanized beep caught her ear and halted her circuit. The door slid open to admit Kahlym, deep in thought. He paused mid-stride, surprise drawing him out of his reverie.

"I am sorry, *ziat'xahn*. Please excuse my intrusion." He tipped his head, and she quickly covered the distance between them before he could backpedal through the door. She grabbed his arm and pulled him toward her.

"Don't you dare. No bowing and groveling from you, remember?"

She shuffled in reverse, a firm grip still on his hand as she bumped into a table and then a desk before reaching the large bed that dominated the far wall. "We still have a conversation to finish, if I'm not mistaken."

"I have not forgotten," he said, eyebrows knitting together as he dragged his feet after her. "But you are still in need of rest."

That did it. With an impish grin, Evainne hooked her ankle around his and spun him, guiding his momentum backwards to land on the soft bed. She swung her leg around his waist, planted herself firmly onto his hips and, kneeling akimbo on his crotch, aimed her best glare at him.

"Look, how about if I decide what I need most, all right? Been doing that since long before I stepped into the Twilight Zone, and if you don't mind, I plan to continue right on doing it. So zip it, pal."

His expression melted from shock to sultry, and fire coursed through her veins, pooling at the juncture between her legs. And judging from the growing bulge currently nestled beneath her ass, his thoughts were taking the same lusty trip. He gripped her hip bones and rolled his thickening shaft against her sheathed core. A needy groan slipped from her lips, and her eyes drifted back.

She flattened her palms against his chest, her fingers moving of their own volition as they searched for the elusive release latch on his gearsuit's collar. His exotic tourmaline eyes darkened, but to her surprise, he touched her hands, stilling her frantic scratching.

"*Ziat'xahn*, if you continue in this, I fear we will not do much conversing."

Undaunted, she shook her head before bending low to brush her lips against his. At the light touch, she nearly purred, arching her back, grinding her heated core against the massive erection just two layers of material away.

"Actually," she said, "I'd rather pick up our conversation exactly where we left off."

Seemed neither wanted to fight the growing hunger, and Kahlym silenced any more rationality with a hot kiss, thrusting his tongue past her slack jaw. He threaded his fingers through her hair, allowing her freed hands to work at getting him out of the damned

Ziploc. Granted, he looked friggin' sexy as hell in skin-tight leathers, but right now, she wanted to see him out of them.

Their tongues twirled and danced, and the world spun until the soft mattress pressed against her back, and she squirmed under his weight. He broke the seal of their lips and nibbled along her jawline, giving her a chance to suck in some much-needed air.

"Please tell me we're not going to get interrupted again," she rasped as she arched her back, eager to feel more than his sheathed body against her aching breasts. He ground his swollen shaft into her weeping core, while his wicked tongue tantalized the shell of her ear.

With delicate and erotic care, he pinched the sensitive tip between his sharp teeth, and she bucked beneath him, her orgasm exploding in record time. She cried out, digging her fingers into his shoulders, hungry for more than this heavy petting, and she clawed once more at the thick layers separating them, growling in frustration and ecstasy.

"I've issued orders for us not to be disturbed, *ziat'xahn*, and our host will not arrive until much later this evening." His whispered words had blown hot against her and drove to greater heights her need for direct skin-on-skin contact. Without warning, he levered up on his arms, pulling away from her questing lips. Primal fire glowed behind his bi-colored eyes and he slapped at his neck.

The once-tight material gave way, and a tempting V of bare sweat sheened copper appeared before her. Frantically, she latched on to the ever-widening gap to yank the pliant leather farther down his body. So intent was she on her mission, Evainne nearly missed the sudden shock of cool air against her own sensitive nipples. The rosy nubs snapped to diamond peaks, and she dragged her gaze down.

"No fair," she groaned. Kahlym had made easy work of her Ziploc, having peeled her arms free in a blink while she still fumbled with his sleeves. For a moment longer, his face remained curtained by the thick fall of twisted obsidian waves before he raised his heated gaze. Their eyes locked, and a wicked smile teased at the corners of his firm lips.

Kahlym shrugged out of his offending garment with practiced ease. Evainne forced her gaze to remain lost in those swirling seas of pinks and greens, without much success; her salacious id wanted nothing more than to drag her tongue across every inch of flesh revealed by his slow striptease. As soon as his leathers vanished from her periphery, hunger overrode honor and Evainne slid her gaze along the appearing treasure trail.

Dark hair lightly dusted his chiseled pecs and the base of his panty-dampening washboard abs, leading toward the heaven waiting for her below the beltline. Her eyes widened as the bulbous head of his thick cock peeked out from the spreading gap, standing at full attention as his clothing dropped.

Now she remembered why she'd been a bit hazy on the details of his physique after their previous encounter: she'd entered the pool before him, swimming a few needed laps to clear her head before he'd joined her. Even then, in the dimly lit chamber, he'd approached her from behind.

Here, now, in the warm glow radiating from somewhere in the vaulted dome ceiling, she got a good look at him—and it was breathtaking.

More importantly: he was all hers.

What moron would have passed up this? she thought as he languidly stroked his massive shaft, dipping the head to rub against her naked, dripping core, and she was too hot to care what had happened to her clothes. Grateful to be rid of the barriers, Evainne wrapped her fingers around his cock, leading him to the juncture of her thighs, body quivering with rapt anticipation.

She captured his gaze and, with an expression that could only be described as possessive, Evainne tightened her legs around his waist, impaling herself on his massive erection. Swearing in heavy breaths, she immediately came, the sheer size and girth of his cock making her body weep. She'd never been one to be timid with lovers; she wanted him all—hard and fast.

Yet, ever the gentleman, Kahlym took his sweet time, easing out of her writhing core until only the tip remained before dipping back in to gain another glorious inch. Sweat beaded on her skin, adding slick heat to their rising passions. She arched her back, offering up her sensitive breasts as another wave of pleasure threatened to overtake her.

She dug her nails into his shoulders, hiked her legs higher around his waist. She needed more.

"More…"

KAHLYM DEEPENED HIS THRUST, careful not to injure her with the heat of his passion, not to mention the size of his swollen member. Her sheath had placed a strangling grip on him, and he dared not pick up the pace.

Yet, with her one moaned syllable, she demanded he do just that.

He dragged his eyelids open to study her. Evainne's flushed ivory skin shimmered with a thin sheet of perspiration, and her blood-wine hair swirled as it framed her sweet face. A runaway drop gathered momentum, trailing down her neck, headed toward her firm breasts. Unwilling to let the temptation pass, Kahlym captured the stray bead with his tongue, lapping at the salty trickle. He didn't stop until he suckled her pebble-hard nipple.

She cried out as her body bucked beneath him, hips rising off the bed to meet his next stroke.

"Please," she whispered, "more."

Shifting his attentions to her other fleshy mound, Kahlym nipped at the succulent bead, earning a keening groan. He released the engorged nub with a pop, worked his way back to her kiss-swollen lips, then dropped his head and, bowing his back, inched farther into her tight channel. She tilted her ass and dug her nails into his arms, all the while murmuring and pleading for more.

Though hesitant to give in to her demands, Kahlym wanted to satisfy her, so he picked up his pace, driving deeper with each powerful thrust. With one final stroke, his hips slammed into hers and the impact caught him by surprise. He backed off for an instant, lifted his head, a question regarding her condition poised upon his lips.

She never gave him the chance to voice his concern. Instead, she mashed her face into his, her kiss hungry and primal. His jaw slackened, and she shoved her tongue into his mouth while her body writhed in encouragement beneath him. On instinct, he met her physical desires, stroke for stroke, until the erotic sounds of their damp skin slapping together filled the air.

Her needful sighs blended with his guttural groans, and he clung to her hips to keep up the furious pace. She thrust her chest up to meet him, back arched as the top of her head burrowed into the soft bedding. Her sheath quivered and pulsated, and her cries grew to a fever pitch, the fist-like grip bringing him so close to his own release.

Unsure how much longer he could hold out, Evainne presented him with all the encouragement he'd need: after a sharp intake of breath, she screamed out as dampness flooded the spasming channel.

"KAHLYM!"

The sheer pleasure of hearing his name fly out from the lips of his lover while deep in the throes of passion was all the trigger he needed, and Kahlym threw his head back and roared, the power of his own orgasm nearly rattling the windows. He remained taut as his seed spilled deep inside of her, muscles clenching and trembling until the last drop had been released, and as his spirit gradually returned to his body, the room began to spin slightly. Dropping his head onto the damp sheets, but careful not to smother his angel, he forced great gulps of air into his burning lungs to avoid passing out.

After a couple deep inhales, he rolled onto his side, and his heart soared as he drew Evainne into the shelter of his arms. He gathered her limbs and tucked her close, her rapid breaths tingling his sweat-drenched skin. Never before had any lover placed such enthusiastic demands on him, her hunger all-consuming and her response exquisite. The damp bedsheets remained pinned beneath them, and he was not eager to move from this treasured moment.

Even if he could move.

As a lazy, satisfied grin curled his lips, Kahlym caught a distinct, disturbing sound, and he froze to listen carefully to the stuttered breathing of his companion. His gaze snapped down and fear gripped his heart.

Dear Ishtanti, what have I done?

EVEN THOUGH SHE'D egged him on to pick up the pace, Evainne still hadn't been prepared for the force and power of the mother of all orgasms. The minor tremors that had thrummed through had just been teasers, whetting her appetite for more. And damn— feeling his entire size splitting her and filling her had completely pitched her off the edge.

His name had ripped from her lips as her body exploded in a dazzling array of chills and tingles, sensations zipping through every part of her like lightning racing along her blood and ice cascading over her skin. She'd felt as if the whole of her had shattered in one perfect moment, and somehow, she'd never be the same again.

But that was already true, and not just because everything familiar was light years away. Since she'd met Kahlym, she'd ceased to be the Evainne who stood apart from the world and hid in the shadows. No longer was she cast aside or reviled as less than she should be; here, in the arms of the only man who didn't seem bent on fixing her, she discovered the true meaning of the word "love."

It was both terrifying and beautiful.

Tears driven by this deep knowledge pooled at the edge of her eyes until too many emotions had gathered there, causing them to course down her cheeks. She struggled to suck in air, hoping the much-needed oxygen would settle her frazzled nerves. Instead, she only managed to pull the heavy, exotic scents of their lovemaking deeper into her being. And didn't that just kick the waterworks into high gear.

God, she thought she was so strong. In fact, she prided herself on her ability to dismiss the emotional outbursts that seemed to rule the rest of her gender. But she had to be honest now: the feelings from which she had so stupidly shielded herself did not make her stronger; rather, it weakened her. Her internal walls had shut her off from the world and from life. She'd asked him to consider her as a source of strength, not a point of weakness.

Perhaps she needed to believe it herself before expecting it from another.

The heart beating beneath her ear stuttered, its steady rhythm growing more frantic, and she wriggled out of his tightened embrace to raise up and capture Kahlym's panicked stare. Apprehension and unspoken apologies lined his beautifully handsome face, and she shook her head, tossing her damp hair violently from side to side.

"Kahlym," she said, "you can't ever put yourself in danger, you get me?" His eyebrows pulled together, and she rapidly blinked away the falling tears. "What we just did, how you just made me feel…? I don't ever want to lose that—not ever. So you have to promise me you'll never do anything stupid. I can't lose you. I don't want to think about what a complete piece of shit my life would be without you in it."

Her voice, once so strong and clear, creaked before it broke, thick emotions stifling the air needed to give power to her words.

"I mean it," she continued. "Don't you dare let me fall in love with you, only to have it all ripped away because you don't think you're good enough for me. I don't want anyone else. Promise me you'll never let us go."

She could no longer see his face, vision blurred by her unending stream of tears; a human-shaped wall of copper loomed as it closed in, its radiating heat offering much needed comfort and solace. She wrapped her arms around Kahlym's chest and sobbed in earnest.

The exact words "I love you" hadn't quite made their grand entrance, but as she replayed her blubbered tirade, she did recall hearing the "L" word slipping into part of it. Was it possible to love someone she barely knew, just because he just rocked her world?

Her pragmatic self sat in mute silence; no snarky quips or barbs to deflate her spirit. For once in her life, the voices in her head were all in complete agreement. She'd fallen madly in love with Kahlym.

Yup, her heart belonged to a sexy space vampire captain. But the more she considered the whole "vampire" thing, the less she believed that one—those pearly whites of his hadn't drawn any blood from her, so she'd stick with "sexy space captain."

A strange calm settled into her loose limbs, and soon, her tears tapered off. She sniffed back the last bout, then curled deeper into his embrace. The strong arms around her shoulders hugged her close, while soft kisses were pressed into her hair.

Certain she wasn't going to get all weepy again, Evainne swallowed past the lump in her throat and pulled back enough to see his face.

His tourmaline eyes sparkled, and the smile on his devastatingly handsome face took away what little breath she had. She opened her mouth, prepared to explain, only to freeze as he cradled her face into his hands. He wiped away the tear still clinging to her lower lashes, the smooth pads of his thumbs soft against her sensitive skin. With her gaze transfixed on his chiseled features, darting from his intoxicating eyes and down to his full mouth, his ragged voice washed over her, buoying her flailing mind and anchoring her timid soul.

"I will do all I can, with my every breath, to see that nothing comes between us."

She sucked in the corner of her bottom lip between her teeth to tamp down another threatening round of tears, and a compassionate smile crossed his face. He lowered his head, touching his cool, damp forehead to hers, and her eyes drifted closed as she gave in to his tender care. With a kiss brushed atop her hair, the world slipped into a reclined position.

Wrapped safely in the circle of his embrace, Evainne laid her head onto his chest, his strong and steady heartbeat lulling her to sleep. Maybe it was exhaustion talking, but she could have sworn she heard singing before slumber claimed her.

Chapter 8

A soft beep gained gradual volume, yanking Kahlym out of his dream, and as he pried open his eyes, confusion fogged his reasoning. A light flashed in time with the pestering sound from the vid terminal across the room. He lifted his head from his pillow and was halted by the perturbed groan from the angel nestled against him.

He brushed a kiss atop her tousled tresses, unleashing a flood of memories into his waking mind: he'd hummed melodies from his childhood and from more pleasant times until she'd finally drifted off to sleep in his arms. With the true message of her passionate words running in dizzying circles in his head, Kahlym had wept tears of pure joy in the silent darkness and his heart soared as he cradled her against his chest.

Careful not to disturb her, he'd rolled off the near edge of the bed, his movements smooth and slow, and with only a couple of mumbled protests, he'd crawled beneath the scattered sheets with her still in his arms. He'd cut the lights with nothing more than a thought and kept vigil over her until he could no longer remain awake. Never before had he slept so soundly.

Until life had decided on this droning disruption.

"What?" he croaked, then coughed to clear his throat and waited for a response. Another muffled sigh seeped from the bundle at his side, and his body jumped to attention as she rolled her ass against his crotch, coaxing a possessive rumble from deep in his chest.

"I apologize for waking you, Captain, but the Lady Khundyl has arrived and will be expecting to speak with you before Last Repast."

Right. The mechanized male voice sounded anything but sympathetic for the intrusion. Kahlym moved his free arm to rub at his eyes, the other pinned beneath his still-sleeping female.

"Thank you," he growled less than pleasantly. "How much longer before the meal begins?"

"Service will begin in one hour."

Another snarl, and he flopped onto his back.

"We will be there."

A click signaled the end of the conversation, and Kahlym let out a heavy sigh. The ceiling offered no escape, nor would sleep return. So, dragging his fingers through his knotted hair, he gingerly stretched through his shoulders, gradually waking his body fully.

"Five more minutes," Evainne murmured as she rolled to face him, hands tucked under her chin as she rested her cheek against his chest. He smiled and wrapped his freed arm around her, her silken skin warm beneath his fingers.

"You are more than welcome to remain here, *ziat'xahn*." He traced lazy circles along her ribs, marveling at the soft, sweet breath against his skin. So entranced was he by the tender moment, Kahlym almost missed her sarcastic scoff.

"Ha. Fat chance, bucko. I'm not letting you out of my sight."

He laughed, hugging her close, and placed a kiss atop her head as her sultry, sleep-laced voice continued. "Besides, I can't remember the last time I ate. Granted, my ass tells me I could stand to skip a meal or two, but I am kinda hungry."

Kahlym frowned at the implied negative tone and sat up enough to look at her face. A soft smile had graced her lips, while dark crescents still fluttered on her ivory cheeks.

"Do you mean to say you believe your body is in need of improvement somehow?" he asked.

Evainne chuckled, a wry grin tugging at one corner of her lush lips. "Hon, I'm female," she replied, "and where I come from, that means we always think our bodies are in need of improvement."

"Evainne, you are more beautiful than someone such as I truly deserve," he said, and she opened her eyes, turning her sleepy, brown orbs to him. "You will never be anything less than perfect to me. You asked me to see you as a strength, then I must ask you to do the same of yourself, *ziat'xahn*."

Her long, dark lashes beat like butterfly wings, and a timid blush painted her high cheekbones. But her smile, rivaling the brightness of the twin suns, made his heart melt.

His mouth watered, hungry for another taste of her addictive sensuality; the mere thought of her enthusiastic response to his passions had made his hardened cock weep with anticipation. Desire burned in her eyes, and soon, only a narrow ring of deep brown remained visible as she smiled wickedly at his tempting invitation.

"If you keep looking at me like that, I don't think either of us will make that meeting, sweetie."

Fuck. She was right. If he gave in to his desires, he wouldn't leave their room—ever, future be damned.

With an exasperated groan, Kahlym threw off the light sheet, which she scrabbled for, growling as she struggled to remain cocooned. She rolled onto her back.

"Once again, *ziat'xahn*, I must bow to your undeniable logic." He brushed a chaste kiss on her forehead before sitting up and, with some effort, swung his legs over the edge of the mattress to wait for further motivation.

Her lighthearted giggles drew his gaze back.

"Another convert to the cult of my awesomeness," she mumbled. "I rule!" And Kahlym shook his head as she punched her fist toward the ceiling.

"Yes, you do, my angel. Come. We do not have much time to waste." He extended a hand. With a tired smile, she dropped her raised arm and clasped his fingers, and an equally forlorn grin matched hers as he helped her out of the tangled sheets. Hand in hand, they covered the short distance to the room's narrow bathing station.

He tapped open the door and motioned to the tight space. "I will wait until you finish."

She frowned, her gaze swiveling around the small room. "Well, hell's bells. So much for showering together. All right, I'll be quick." And she gave him a light kiss on the cheek before stepping inside. The door slid shut as he stood, stunned, face tingling where her lips had just been.

She continued to bewitch him with her open acceptance and tender purity. Just hours before, she'd welcomed him into her body, had taken him closer to the heavens than any vessel could travel. And even now, her thoughts focused on them as a pair, as a team. Since their first encounter in the rejuvenating pool with the slick friction of the added water, he'd wanted nothing more than to take her once again.

But the ticking clock of duty clanged in his head and dragged his raging body out of its decadent desires. An angry growl slipped from his clenched jaw as he stalked woodenly to the closet. A formal Stria uniform befitting of his rank hung next to flowing robes of the softest silks, the deep blues and golds of his jacket and breeches a stark contrast against the pale pinks and earthy peaches of her regalia.

He reached out, fingers trembling as he caressed the gossamer fabric.

"Oh, hell no."

Kahlym spun round to Evainne, who shook her head with a disapproving frown. One fist rested on her cocked hip, her naked skin flushed from the recent warm water. Kahlym blinked in mute amazement.

"You've got another thing coming if you believe I'm gonna wear that." She stepped past him to search the confines for another option. "I've never gone anywhere in a pink dress before I got zapped here and deified, and I'm sure as hell not going to start now."

Kahlym watched in rapt awe as her backside swayed from side to side as her quest continued.

"But, I had hoped to present you as—"

He arched a curious brow when she snapped her head around and pinned him with a serious stare.

"No, Kahl. I cannot be 'presented' as anything." She yanked out a plain gray uniform jacket ensemble. "I know you all think I'm some sort of mighty thing, but I gotta tell you, the idea of being paraded around just paints a bulls-eye on my forehead that I would rather not deal with."

Kahlym stood in somber silence as she donned her new attire.

"You do not trust me?" he asked.

KAHLYM'S soft voice struck a nerve, and Evainne stopped after zipping up the pants. Going commando was getting to be the norm here, so she figured underwear was only a human thing. She sighed heavily and, dropping her shoulders, reached for the jacket to complete the ensemble.

As she turned to face him, her heart cracked at his crestfallen, puppy-dog look. She drank in his purely male nakedness, realizing that not only his body stood revealed, but emotions also poured out of him as he waited for her to respond.

She shrugged on the ensemble's top and crossed back over to

him. His gaze never left hers as she approached, his expression wary and apprehensive. She offered him a comforting smile and took his hands. Kahlym looked down at their intertwined fingers before lifting his bi-colored eyes to her.

"I trust you with all my heart, Kahlym. But I don't know these people. I know there's so much I still need to learn about this whole new world I've stepped into, and I'm sure I'm gonna be pissing off people left and right until I can get my bearings. Please understand, I'm not trying to be difficult." She gave a sheepish shrug. "Okay, so maybe I am being a little difficult about the whole 'pink' thing. But that's not the point."

He relaxed at her playful tone. "If I were to find you robes of a different shade, would that make you happier?"

She tugged her eyebrows together, confused. "What is it with the dresses?"

He released her hand to trail his fingers along her jaw, his growing smile patient. "Because in our world, in public, it is customary for females to wear gowns. No male worthy of any respect would allow his female to be seen by others dressed in any other fashion."

"Oh." Embarrassment crept across her skin, her cheeks burning, and she lowered her head. She did have a lot to learn. "I'm sorry, hon. I just thought that—"

His rich laughter poured down her back as he hugged her. "You have nothing for which to apologize, *ziat'xahn*. I can understand your concern. I, too, have my doubts about our hostess."

Evainne felt him tense up a fraction, and she pulled back, looked up into his handsome face, encouraging him to complete his thought.

"The presentation I was speaking of was to present you as…"

Her breath quickened. "As…?"

Kahlym swallowed and caught her gaze with a starkly open stare. "I was going to present you as my female."

She gaped, stunned, her jaw swinging on a hinge as words

escaped her. Heat returned to her cheeks, replacing the cold chill from her earlier panic. His dazzling smile stole away her remaining brain cell as she nodded mutely. His lips descended toward her, and she leaned in, her body responding to the instinctual pull of his bare skin and demanding presence—

Until a loud beep shattered the mood.

Evainne jumped, a tiny squeak slipping out in surprise. The sexy, bi-colored eyes before her vanished as Kahlym heaved a frustrated growl.

"Yes?"

"A thousand apologies, sir, but the Lady asked me to keep you informed of the time."

"Please tell Khundyl that I have been able to tell the time since I was a child and have not forgotten that basic skill." He shook his head, then placed a light kiss on the tip of Evainne's nose before striding into the single rider shower stall. His departure gave her a phenomenal view of his perfect ass, as well as a peek into the truth of his life; pale scars crisscrossed his magnificent back, creating a detailed map of hardship and battle—some were long and rough, while others splatted like drips of paint on the canvas of his body.

Another voice filled the room, this one haughty and definitely feminine. *"I also know that punctuality is not a trait you choose to cultivate on a regular basis."*

Evainne screwed up her face, about to give the bitch a piece of her mind, only Kahlym's easy laughter lightened her incensed streak. "Khundyl, still ever-present to point out my shortcomings, I see."

The door swished closed, leaving her in the room alone with the faceless voice. Or, at least she thought the voice was still around. She hadn't heard a disconnecting click. Should she say anything?

Her mind pulled out an appropriately similar scene from forgotten pop culture: the image of Han Solo fumbling through an impromptu dialog with an unseen officer of the galactic empire. Unsure of any listening ears, Evainne moved stealthily back to the closet to give her outfit another try. As she stood in front of the open doors, hands resting upon her hips, she couldn't believe she was seriously contemplating wearing a pastel pink gown.

"If you prefer garments of a different shade, please do not hesitate to request your choice."

Shocked, Evainne slammed her hand flat against her exposed boobs, and her gaze flicked around the room, searching for telltale red lights.

"What the hell! Are you watching me?" She tugged the uniform's lapels together, shielding her remaining nakedness, and stumbled toward the center of the room for better surveillance.

"You misunderstand, Char'ann. Your companion informed us of your displeasure with the selected attire. If you would be so kind as to tell us the hue, we will have the garment delivered straight away."

Evainne continued to search for cameras, unwilling to let down her guard. "Uh, if you have something in a dark green, that would be nice."

The voice vanished with a click an instant before a soft ping sounded from inside the closet. Frowning, she tiptoed back to the half-open door.

There, hanging on the rack, was a dress of so many shades of green, blending and flowing, from a deepest forest to hints of sage and spruce. *Damn! This place gave customer service a whole new definition.*

Remembering their time crunch, Evainne stripped out of the inappropriate pants and jacket and slipped on the whisper-soft gown. To her gratified amazement, she found a pair of short briefs, the cut reminding her of trendy boy-cut shorts from a couple of fashion seasons ago, and with a relieved grin, she stepped into the undergarment just as the bathroom door slid open.

Kahlym halted after one step, wafting steam silhouetting his purely male physique. He smiled appreciatively as he resumed his trek toward her.

"Yes. This color does suit you much better." He twisted a lock of her loose hair around his finger, the sharp black talon trailing a teasing line of shivers along her exposed arm.

"Please tell me you did tell them about my dislike of pink?"

A wry grin curved his sensual mouth. "I did. Would you rather I had not? It was only my desire to see you attired in what made you happy."

God, every time he spoke, his words were an intoxicating blend of societal formality and sexual innuendo. And the combination had her scissoring her legs beneath the concealing layers, her body eager to take him up on his veiled offer. She bit the inside of her cheek to curb her appetite and stepped away from temptation.

"Hon, we really need to work on your vocabulary choices."

Still unconvinced of their complete privacy, Evainne wandered around the room, giving him her back. Nothing popped out to her as obvious cameras—no flashing red lights or reflected lens glints.

His hands wrapping around her shoulders jolted her; his silent footfalls had been muffled by the thick carpet.

"You have nothing to fear here, *ziat'xahn*. All those who find shelter within these walls are given the highest level of privacy and seclusion."

She turned around, then gave him an appreciative whistle. "Wow. You sure clean up nice." Grinning, she marveled at the regal figure standing before her. He looked to be the lofty officer in his sharp uniform, the deep blue drawing out the bright green tones in his eyes, while the gold braids and trim highlighted his coppery skin.

The tourmaline pools swirled and darkened. "I believe I could say the same of you, my angel." He tilted his head slightly, dipping his chin yet still holding her gaze.

Damn, how the hell did she get so lucky?

He winked at her, and that devilish smile again appeared on his face. Warmth pooled low in her gut and high on her cheekbones, and he chuckled, offering his hand to her.

"Come. I fear if we remain in this room any longer, Khundyl will be proven right about my inability for promptness."

Joining in with his laughter, Evainne threaded her fingers into his and followed him to the door. "We can't have that, now can we?"

The door slid open, and she stepped out into the hall.

"My dear," he said, "you have no idea how long the memory of an Achtillian can be."

Chapter 9

Gha'jahn M'Uubair, Grand Emperor of the Seventh Quadrant, stared daggers over his steepled fingers, his deadly wrath aimed at the assembled group studying the inlaid tile mosaic on the floor of the throne room. The recent commander of Skirnahn Station, the focal point of the latest catastrophe, shook like a leaf, fidgeting from foot to foot as he stood next to the assassin hired to tidy up the mess, a female reputed to be the best. Yet the missing Divine was not among the gathered faces.

Alongside her stood another Praxxiran pirate, an insider who would allegedly assure him that a certain thorn in his side was dealt with—permanently. Panza M'Uubair, Gha'jahn's own blood heir, had joined the others in their disgrace. At least his son had the balls to look him in the eye. He'd drilled that lesson into all of his children, even the females.

Own your failure, or success will mean nothing.

"So, am I to believe we do not have any idea where she has been taken?"

"There are so many places that—"

The sharp raising of one finger silenced the mewling excuse of a ranking station liaison. Did the man not realize the massively intricate network of informants and loyal operatives he owned? The emperor had spies placed in even the farthest corner of the Seventh Quadrant—puppets and pawns who overheard every whispered word and reported to him without fail.

Yet a handful of rebels had somehow managed to blast out of a station protected by two squadrons of supposedly well-trained forces, taking with them the only female Divine of child-bearing years. Unbreakable security protocols had been decimated, and all his soldiers had to show for it was one body, a useless Ninoxian male who bore no recognizable markings or tags.

If the situation was not so dire, he might have been impressed.

His time, however, was ticking down to a close. If he did not find the brood bitch and have one of those old doddering fools get her with child, no telling how much longer his hold on the Dantaran galaxy would last. His family had ruled for so long because of the undeniable and unassailable support of the Divines. Yet, in the recent past, fewer and fewer races had been gifted with the birth of any of the Revered Four, and a Divine Fury had not been seen in a star's age.

"You say there is a way to track the ship, yet you have not given us the important information as to how this feat will be accomplished." The emperor scanned the standing figures, his amethyst stare burning through each one in turn.

"P-p-perhaps, an ion scan could point to s-s-some possible destination," said the commander. It appeared he might possess a shred of usefulness after all. Gha'jahn swiveled his glare toward the feeble man, as though to bore an irate hole through the top of his head.

The lone female lifted her blank gaze to him. She would never offer excuses, or long, drawn-out explanations. That was not her method.

"I request another contract," she said.

There was his assassin. A vicious grin curled Gha'jahn's lips, and the hint of amusement shifted the expression of the others, replacing their earlier embarrassment with fear.

"As I knew would, dear Kaxxahn. Perhaps this time, you will bring this unpleasantness to a more satisfying fruition."

He waved a dismissive hand, cutting off the bristling turncoat, mid-word. The throne room's overhead lighting dimmed, officially ending the audience, and footfalls shuffled in the darkness, growing fainter.

"Panza, you stay."

One pair of heels halted. A sliver of light from across the room cut a gash though the darkness as the exiting shadows vanished. Alone with his son, Gha'jahn rose from the uncomfortable seat of power and descended the dais, the room brightening with each step. He moved toward the inset cabinet to the left of the throne, focused on his need for refreshment.

Gha'jahn knew, from the deepening silence, that his son was formulating his pathetic defense. While he waited to hand down the well-deserved wrath, he grabbed the crystalline decanter and a glass from the shelf, then filled the latter nearly to the brim with the strong drink.

Should he care that his family legacy of brutal control and unyielding supremacy was slowly slipping through his fingers, all because of one elusive female? He took a long swallow as he pondered the answer.

"Panza," he said, "I am curious. When the gathered Divines punched a hole through the fucking universe to bring back the only genetically matched female, did you believe that this one breeder was something common and easily replaceable?" He kept his back turned to the object of his disappointment, lest he hurl the glass at his son and waste the alcohol.

"Father, I—"

Gha'jahn spun, leveling an enraged stare at him. "Do not use that title in this room with me, boy. In this place, I am your emperor, and you would do well to remember that if you wish to keep a tongue in your head."

The face before him blanched before ingrained military training snapped his son's spine ramrod straight as he jerked to attention. His head bobbed once in sharp reverence.

"Apologies, sire."

Gha'jahn stalked up to the rigid statue, careful not to spill the precious contents of his glass. The young man reminded him much of himself in his younger days—cocky, self-assured, and eager to prove his worth. His own father had taught him these lessons well. Perhaps too well, as the man had discovered too late.

As with so many other emperors before him, Gha'jahn had earned his succession with his blade plunged deep into the old bastard's chest. The man had grown weak and witless, and in order for Gha'jahn to maintain control of the Rimmarian Empire, he did the only intelligent thing: he slaughtered the man in his sleep. The news report stated that the previous emperor had died of heart failure during the night.

Well, it was true. The heart did tend to stop working when removed from the body.

Now, after a hundred cycles of passing judgment from the Obsidian Fire Throne, Gha'jahn stood before his own heir apparent. He'd heard rumors of Panza's cruel streak, but had yet to see any true evidence for himself. Though, from time to time, reports would cross his vid screen: limbs broken, plus other, less conventional injuries sustained during missions and interrogations led by his son.

But Panza was sorely mistaken if he believed himself ready to ascend to the throne.

Time and the lack of constant physical exertion may have softened the ruling emperor, but Gha'jahn still had a few tricks left up his sleeves. Keeping his ambitious son off guard was one. It never ceased to work to perfection.

Gha'jahn took a sip as he crafted his words carefully, baiting the hook with just enough to get him to bite but not give away the entire plan.

"I fear we must work quickly. Ishtanti only knows how much longer Divine Haseunn will survive, and that doddering old fool, Qi'tan, spent half a day trying to heal the couch. If it comes to it, we can save their seed until the bitch has been recovered, but the joining is in jeopardy of not taking root if the act is not consummated."

The telltale tugging of his son's brows told him his aim had been true. With Panza's curiosity piqued, he dangled the lure a little longer, waiting to see if his intuitions were correct.

"Do you have any ideas of where they might be?"

The question took Panza aback, and he blinked rapidly as he directed his respectful gaze back to Gha'jahn. No fear clouded his Panza's matte green eyes, but apprehension creased his brow. Gha'-jahn's urge to tap his foot or shake the boy until an answer fell out of him like coins from a pocket vibrated the tense muscles under the thick royal jacket. His patience paid off, though, and a soft cough broke though the silence.

"The crew member we recovered—the Ninoxian from Outer T'chan—I would guess they might look for sanctuary with the family of their fallen comrade."

Smiling, Gha'jahn relaxed his arms and took another drink, finishing off the dregs. He turned and strode back to his seat of power.

"Then I suggest you take the next available transport," he said and ascended the three steps on the dais. The ornately carved chunk of rock glowed in the focused starlight; ribbons of blackened crimson cut channels of gleaming red through the heart of the black stone. He traced one of the bloodlines that ran the length of the armrest, until the sound of retreating boot heels on the tile floor dragged his attention back.

"Oh, and Panza?"

He lifted his chin, the curved polished surface reflecting back at him the distorted image of his waiting son, the inset ruby veins adding a scarlet halo around the reflection.

"Bring her back, or do not bother returning."

Chapter 10

Kahlym wiped his perspiring hand onto the leg of his breeches again as he escorted Evainne toward the formal dining hall of the royal palace of Raedyn Septicon. He forced his feet to plod forward, his mind awhirl with possible scenarios awaiting him and his companion just beyond the massive double doors. He'd forgotten how uncomfortable the officers' uniform could be, until he'd fastened the lapels closed across his throat.

Now, he stifled the urge to tug at the confining collar as his gaze drifted to the beautiful female by his side. Multi-hued shades of green swirled around her, bright emerald melting into deep forest green as she kept pace. Her feet were wrapped in dainty sandals, the leather straps climbing up her shapely legs, with the slender, elevated heel giving her added height. Her bloodwine hair fell in waves, secured back in a series of jeweled clips along one side of her head. The cascading tresses tumbled over her shoulder and the ends brushed the perk tips of her breasts.

She was stunning as she walked beside him, and pride welled in his chest as the approaching door swung open. If she could bear her discomfort with grace and poise, he would do the same.

Her gasp combined with a bone-crunching grip on his hand snapped his focus to crystal clarity. He leaned over and brushed his mouth against the exposed shell of her ear.

"Do not panic, *ziat'xahn*. I will be right by your side."

She relaxed her hand fractionally. "Yeah, easy for you to say. You know the rules here. I'm terrified I'm gonna end up eating the centerpiece decorations by mistake."

He pulled her close, forcing a weak chuckle past the lump in his throat, as his drive to protect her kicked in. "I am certain you will perform well," he reassured her, his voice even and calming.

Please do not think less of me after this evening is over.

He immediately stamped down the serpents of doubt roiling in his gut. Coming here was a risk, but his crew needed a safe haven to recuperate, and if that meant he must suffer some indignities, so be it.

A condescending sniff from the open door chilled his blood, and Kahlym rose to his full height, squaring his shoulders as he met the sneering face of Ryghan, Khundyl's manservant and unofficial consort. Regal, vibrant jade eyes peered out at him from behind the veil of pale blond hair that swept across his forehead. His skin shimmered in opalescent contrast to the rich black of his high-collared tunic, gold threading catching the focused starlight. Androgynous features masked a harsh, cruel heart and a wicked, hateful tongue.

Perfect. Why couldn't the fucker be on some other calling this night?

A sinister grin tugged at the corner of the pouty mouth before him. <*And miss out on all the fun? Oh, my dear, I would have gutted my mother with glee to see this moment.*>

"Well, well. Will wonders never cease? You can arrive in a timely fashion, Kahlym." Ryghan's mocking tone was not lost on Evainne, and she cocked her head, lifting one eyebrow under her furrowed forehead.

Kahlym locked his jaw to prevent a snarling retort, and instead, tilted his head in feigned respect.

"Ryghan. Please inform your ladyship that—"

Ryghan rolled his eyes, lifted a lazy hand, and Kahlym swallowed the rest of his request, as well as a good chunk of his pride.

"Yes, yes. Come along. We don't have all day. I don't know why she even bothers hearing your mewlings, kagg'naeh. But who am I to judge?"

Kahlym notched his chin up a fraction, both to prove to the insubordinate lackey that his foul words did not hurt him and to ease Evainne's growing concern. The heat of her confused stare singed the side of his face, but he could not meet her eyes.

This behavior wasn't a surprise. Even citizens ranking beneath his lofty family stature looked upon him with disgust and repulsion, his mismatched eyes announcing to the whole universe his genetic defect.

A tug on his jacket drew his gaze away from the back of Ryghan's head, and his angel's incredulous, offended expression hit him like a fist to the gut. He clenched his jaw and, giving a fractional shake of his head, placed her hand atop his arm. Her beautiful features pinched together, though she said nothing. He bit down on the inside of his cheek as Evainne rubbed the corner of an eye with an obviously extended middle finger. Her irreverent gesture broke the growing tension and they continued on in silence down the narrow foyer, the cushioned ground muffling their footfalls.

The trek was mercilessly short, and soon, their path led them to a closed room. Ryghan rapped once before triggering the door, and Kahlym took a moment to seamlessly slip on the necessary façade.

With an exasperated scoff and an exaggerated wave toward the opening from their guide, Kahlym ushered Evainne inside. Starlight and candle glow illuminated the parlor, chairs, and small tables arranged in conversational clusters. With a gentle hold on Evainne's elbow, he led her toward the lone figure lounging in the shadows.

Ryghan hustled past him in a huff, then made deliberate care to honor the hidden occupant with a deep bow. "Milady Khundyl, your guests will soon be arriving. I suggest you make this meeting brief. Wouldn't want you sullied in the eyes of the aristocracy."

A snide smile curled the thin lips of Khundyl's fuck toy, knowing the barb had stricken true. Kahlym feared his clenched teeth would shatter as he held in his rage. This was not the place, nor was the slimy little shit worth his time and energy. This was for the good of the cause. Khundyl was a powerful ally who could protect Evainne should he be unable to handle the task alone.

For that, he'd suffer a couple more moments in the male's company.

"Thank you, dear. That will be all. I will be there shortly."

A regal voice issued a casual dismissal, and Ryghan wiggled his fingers at Kahlym before nodding respectfully to the reclining figure. Kahlym sucked in a sharp breath as he watched the asshole leave. Once he was alone with somewhat kinder company, he relaxed a fraction as laughter fell like broken glass, shattering the lingering tension.

"He only baits you because you are such an easy mark." Lights flared to life to reveal the Lady Khundyl in her resplendent glory. She slid her shapely legs from the divan and rose to her full height. Dressed in formal finery, with jewels dripping from her ears and cascading down her open throat, the scant excuse of a gown barely covered her ample assets, the deep ruby red material contrasting in perfect harmony against her pale, shimmering skin.

"But I suppose you do need to keep up appearances, acting the little prince." Large, almond-shaped eyes the color of fresh grass regarded him from beneath half-closed lids. Her white-blonde hair spiked up in a tidy, wide strip down the center of her head, the feathery ends trailing along the floor.

To all the males in the Seventh Quadrant, she was the ultimate female with unequaled beauty and legendary passions. Sheltered by the long-standing power of her homeworld's Ruling Hand, she was above reproach in the eyes of the Rimmarian Empire, which made her a knowledgeable ally.

Kahlym nodded stiffly as she approached, her narrow hips swaying in practiced temptation. "Your ladyship," he said coolly. "Thank you for granting us the honor of your audience." The mood shifted as dangerously seductive pheromones thickened the air. Not long ago, he would have craved her attentions, begged to be taken by her, his mind helpless against her promised sexual lure.

Now, the cloying fragrance made his stomach churn, his heart no longer a slave to his baser instincts. In truth, he only desired to reach out and pull his angel closer, yet that action would only raise questions that could put her in the midst of a battle she would not understand.

Khundyl's painted lids lowered sensually as her gaze traveled down his body before rising to meet his. "Spare me your pointless praise, child. The cause is enough for me to answer even your requests," she purred, sauntering past him to the large table in the center of the room. "Now, tell me why I am aiding you this time."

Relieved for the return to some civility, Kahlym relaxed his guarded stance, coughing lightly to cover the unladylike growl that bubbled up behind his back. He offered a timid brush of his fingers against hers in assurance, unsure whether her response was from Khundyl's blatant attempt at seduction or from her lack of any comment or regard. After a quick prayer to Ishtanti for strength of heart, he closed the vast distance between him and their host. "We need a place to lie low for a short time. One of my crew has betrayed us all. Qaen…" he balked as the image of Brel's nearly lifeless body flashed before his open eyes. Gritting his teeth, he pressed on. "Qaen has shown his true colors, and Lozzan has paid the ultimate price for it."

The hint of a frown pulled Khundyl's perfect brows together, compassion flashing across her serene features before vanishing in a blink. "I am sorry to hear of the loss. Am I to believe that you are now down two crew members?"

He nodded. "Falka can handle the duties of nav, but that leaves us light on tech and code hacking." His mind spun as he fought the urge to reveal the secret standing behind his back. Training and skills drilled into him from a young age kept the truth of his companion safe from unfriendly eyes.

She swatted away his request. "Yes, yes. I will see if there are others up to the task. But I do recall warning you about an alliance with the Praxxiran. They do tend to be ruled by their drive for destruction."

"I just felt perhaps—"

"And speaking of the flair for chaos, your father has sent a message."

Kahlym's blood ran cold. "He sent word here?"

Khundyl sighed, folded her arms beneath her up-thrust breasts and, with her palm cupping an elbow, rested one long, graceful finger against her cheek. "Not entirely. It seems he is quite eager to talk to you and has contacted every possible station that might offer you shelter. Do you have some reason for him to seek you?"

The earlier chill doubled, locking his body with ice in his veins. "I have something he wants."

Khundyl scoffed. "That much I'd gathered from the wide net he cast. Perhaps if you were a bit more specific in this rather broad statement?"

The moment of truth had arrived. Did he dare trust her?

She cocked her head, waiting patiently, and he opted for a more private line of communication. He opened his mind and focused a narrow stream of thoughts at Khundyl.

<The Emperor is searching for Divines to replenish his dying ranks.>

Khundyl pinned him with a bored stare. *<And this is news, why? This is common knowledge.>*

<He inadvertently found a rather powerful one, and I kidnapped them.>

She leaned back, expression impressed by his direct words. *<We could use him for our own gains. Turn the tide. Is he safe?>*

Kahlym fought to keep his eyes trained forward, to not glimpse over his shoulder to his silent companion. *<For the moment. But things are getting…complicated. With Qaen now fighting against us, Gha'jahn knows by now we have the Divine.>*

He'd never had to censor his thoughts to such a degree; if he were to give out the exact details, though, things might turn deadly in a heartbeat.

<If we can't use him, then we will kill him. Take away the possibility of letting that bastard get his hands on another Divine.>

"Out of the question!" Kahlym growled, puffing out his chest.

A droll stare pinned him. "Why you were ever given a ship of your own is beyond me." Condescension dripped like melting ice from her disappointed words. "You have always allowed your emotions to weaken you—friendship, family, loyalty. Love." She'd spat out the last on the list, the tender sentiment sounding more like a curse than a gift.

With a scoff, she pushed away from the table. "Leadership is forged in fires of pain and honor, not in useless drivel like peace and love." She sauntered toward him, stopping so close, the heat from her skin brushed his cheeks. Force of habit held his gaze mercifully averted, though he could still feel her eyes locked on his every move.

"But then again," she said, "with you being an outcast, I suppose it is easier to wish for what you will never have."

THAT DID IT.

"Now wait just a goddamned minute."

Evainne stepped out from Kahlym's shadow, propelled by her bristling anger. Granted, she only came up to the bitch's crotch, but Khundyl was about to find out how dangerous it was to insult her man.

She wedged herself between the cat's whisker of a gap between Kahlym and Ms. Big Tits. Craning her neck to look up into those standard, Area 51-sized alien eyes, their neon green shade weird and daunting, she reached down, and found her courage. Her vocal cords finally kicked in.

"Look, I might not know all the rules here, but where I come from, it's not cool to insult your guests."

An amused smirk cracked Khundyl's smooth features. "So," she said, "the shadow has a voice after all. And here I thought she was simply a mechanical companion. My apologies. I meant no disrespect." She splayed a hand across her chest, angled her head in feigned homage.

Rage boiled in Evainne's gut and the desire to smack that sneer off of her perfect face was crippling. But she tipped her chin up, even as her fingers curled into tight fists. "Really? Your words seem to tell another story there, sweetheart." She locked gazes with the woman.

Oh, she knew her type: the silver spoon set of her childhood. All of the world's luxuries placed at their feet, creating a disgusting sense of entitlement, made her skin crawl. In Evainne's mind, circumstance did not define the worth of any person; only action spoke to the truth of anyone's character.

Suddenly she realized why she had such an instant dislike for the woman: she reminded Evainne of her mother. Her sanctimonious air of superiority and her ingrained belief that she was better than everyone else bled from the woman almost as thick as that sickly-sweet perfume she must have bathed in before they'd arrived. Growing up, Evainne had dealt with so much of this, and judging by Kahlym's unflinching demeanor, he was clearly used to this treatment, as well.

"Reject" was what Qaen had called him. Bhaan had told her of the disgrace of his alleged disfigurement and of the whispered rumors of his illicit conception. Only now did she realize how similar their stories were.

Despised by the world for no other reason than simply breathing and their stubborn refusal to stop.

A warm, comforting presence brushed against her back,

followed by a hand upon her shoulder.

"Khundyl, I had hoped to make the presentation under other circumstances."

The bitch cackled, tossing back her perfectly coiffed head, though her outburst lasted only a moment before she regained her snobbish demeanor.

"Presentation? Surely you must be joking." She scoffed, her hand pressed to her chest in dramatic disgust.

Evainne's shocked expression must have conveyed a different message, however, and a growing sneer traced an ugly line across Khundyl's fashion magazine quality looks. "You would do better than this mongrel for a male, whoever you are."

Evainne opened her mouth to retort, when those giant eyes snapped up over her shoulder. The staticky silence crackled, and she bounced her gaze between the intense stares of Kahlym and their hostess. The muscles along his rugged jaw twitched and jumped, and she quelled the urge to brush away the angry tension.

But, just as quickly as it had begun, the blanket of quiet was yanked off, and Evainne dragged in an easy breath. She shifted her gaze up to the large, green eyes, still searching for answers. Whatever had transpired between her and Kahlym was now over, with her practiced resting bitch face once again back in place.

Evainne tapped her sandaled toes impatiently. "Someone mind letting the other kids in on the secret here?"

"Kahlym has taken a shine to you, female, but that is all it can ever be." Khundyl's dismissive tone took Evainne aback. "For him to present any female other than the Empress as his intended would be construed as an act of direct insurrection, which would endanger his entire family."

Evainne blinked slowly as the words sunk in. Oh, yeah. The whole "arranged marriage" thing. Confusion tugged her eyebrows together, and she spoke up.

"Now, hang on. I thought that was null and void."

The thick, platinum mohawk waved as Khundyl shook her head. "Nothing, save death, can annul a royal betrothal."

Perfect. Just fucking perfect. Evainne tossed her hands up in mute frustration.

"No," Kahlym said, "she refused me and chose Xandar as her male, altering the marriage contract. I know my father still holds out hope to cement the bond between our house and that of Rimmarian Ruling Heart, but unless he's willing to stick his dick in that witch, he is not about to get any help from me."

Kahlym's voice sent chills down her spine. She was just beginning to know him—the scant days they'd shared were only a blink of an eye in the span of life—but she could sense, thick in his words, the venom of a buried pain. She threaded her fingers through his, offering her acceptance and strength to him.

Khundyl sighed, standing tall. "So you believe, and quite innocently too, Kahlym. That 'witch' is still tied to your family, and until she has her match, I would suggest caution making public any such affections."

Evainne swiveled her head between the now-silent aliens towering over her. Tension pulsed from her lover, and she nodded in understanding. With a final squeeze, she released his hand and took a small step to his right, using the distance as a safety cushion for him.

"I will see what I can do about the replacement of your missing crew members," Khundyl said. "Until then, you must excuse me. I do have guests to attend to, and I am afraid that neither you nor your...female would be welcomed."

Evainne gaped, but Kahlym's expression showed no offense. In truth, he gave their host a practiced smile and a respectful nod. "Many thanks for your time, your ladyship."

Chapter 11

Confusion radiated from his angel. So many layers of intrigue and half-spoken truths necessary to keep everyone safe from prying eyes or unsympathetic ears must have her head spinning. Khundyl was deeply entrenched on both sides of the battle, always playing the shifting odds. He had hoped, foolishly, that this meeting could have been in complete privacy. Perhaps later, their conversation could continue, without double talk and harsh jabs.

A door to their left opened wide, and light and music spilled out into the formal dining hall. Elaborately arranged flowers and cages decorated the massive room, while the heady aroma of steaming platters filled the air as servants scurried around to put the finishing touches on the lavish setting.

His knotted stomach had little to do with hunger. The aristocracy on the other side would only pose deadly questions about his appearance and, as his host was also friendly with the Thrall hierarchy, Kahlym chose the path of shadowed survival, opting to forego his appetite. Food could be obtained by other means.

He guided Evainne back the way they'd come, much to her

grumbled protests. Once they'd cleared the threshold, he placed a soft kiss atop her head.

"I promise not to let you go hungry, *ziat'xahn*. Not after you defended my honor." His cheeks ached from the smile that had burst across his face as they strolled back to their room.

"This has nothing to do with food," she said. "Okay, so maybe it does, a bit." She shrugged as they continued down the quiet hallway. "I thought you said this place was safe."

He paused and placed his hand on the small of her back to steer her toward an alternate route. "It is." She skidded to a halt, and he glanced down at her. Sarcastic disbelief had wrinkled her brow, and he chuckled at her expressive face. "Trust me on this, angel. Khundyl was actually on her best behavior today." He brushed his thumb over the deep furrow crossing her forehead and trailed his fingertips into her loose curls. "She will see to replacing our needed crew members, and that alone is reason enough to deal with some… unkind words."

Reluctant, Evainne narrowed her eyes, but said nothing more. Kahlym offered his arm and an encouraging smile. With a nod, she accepted his chivalrous gesture, and they resumed their journey.

Not even his birth mother had shown such a protective streak. So long had he spent with only his brother and his crew at his back, and he had long since resigned himself to life without love. He never expected to find such a fierce warrior in such a beautiful package; his female was a true force to be reckoned with, and soon, the Thrall would find out just how powerful she was.

She snaked her arm around his waist, leaned her head against his chest. "But as someone who's had their fair share of verbal beat-downs, I know what it feels like to have to bite your tongue for sake of keeping up appearances. I just couldn't stand by and let that… that woman talk shit about you."

A passing servant, whom he recognized from previous visits, gave him a shy smile and a nod before vanishing down the linked corridor. "Khundyl also must maintain certain airs when unfriendly eyes may be watching."

Back at their room, Kahlym opened the door and ushered her inside, where food had been laid out waiting on the small, octagonal table near the bed. The fare was not as elaborate as the dishes of the formal repast, but it would do. He surveyed their selections while unfastening the strangling collar.

Evainne shook her head. "Sorry, hon, but she was enjoying those digs too much for me to believe it was all a front. I know you might trust her, but—"

An incoming message interrupted her most astute assessment, and raising a finger, Kahlym tapped the buzzing comm link. "Go," he said.

"*Gee, miss you too, kherdes.*"

Kahlym strolled through the doorway, dropped his shoulders, and chuckled in relief. "Apologies, Brel, but it has been a strange day to be sure."

Laughter on the other end of the link sounded no less strained. "*It could be worse. You could be at this mockery of a dinner party.*"

Kahlym sighed, shaking his head as he sat in the nearest chair. "I was informed that my presence would only bring questions our hostess was not willing to entertain. Seems dear old Dad has been spreading the word that he wants me found."

"*And here you thought he didn't care.*" Voices bled through the link before fading into the background.

"Well, I would prefer going back into the ranks of the invisible in the eyes of that bastard," Kahlym said. His gaze wandered around the room to settle on Evainne perched on the edge of the bed, legs hanging down as she fiddled with her sandal straps. The teasing flash of bare leg made his mouth water for a different kind of feasting.

"*No such luck today there, kherdes-xahn. R'uan has heard that Gha'jahn has enforcers scouring Outer T'chan for you. It's only a matter of time before he figures out exactly where you are.*"

Damn. That was quicker than he'd expected. And as soon as the emperor realized his error, the number of safe havens will diminish exponentially. Time was not on their side.

Knowledge of his next destination took hold, trailing icy fingers down his spine. Seems they would be stopping at Raedyn Primus after all.

"Thank you, *kherdes*. I suppose I should be grateful we didn't have more gear to repack. He chuckled, hoping to lighten the mood.

Faint footfalls grew in volume outside the door as Brel's harsh whisper broke through.

"*Shit. Kahl. Move. Move now!*"

Kahlym jumped to his feet as the door buckled inward and a full contingent of Khundyl's personal guard poured into room, filling the space between him and Evainne.

"EVAINNE!"

His reflexes kicked into high gear and he trained his weapon on the ten muzzles pointed at him just as heavy gas filled the room.

***

EVAINNE WAS FIGHTING with a knot in her long leather shoelaces, eyeing the plates of food, when light flooded in from the busted-down door. She ducked away from the flying shrapnel, rolling off the side of the bed and crouching for cover. Immediately, she slapped at her legs and waist. No weapon. Dammit.

Note to self: Never visit the alien bitch hostess unarmed.

Smoke filtered in. She waved off the noxious fumes, coughing, calling for Kahlym…until everything went black.

***

MURMURED VOICES PULLED at the cotton in her ears, and Evainne struggled to raise her head. "Kahl?"

She'd squeaked out the word, nearly hacking up a lung trying to kick-start her vocal cords, and someone hidden in the blackness shushed some others around her. She pushed herself up from the soft surface, the faint fragrance of surrounding flickering candles giving the place a scarily church-like feel.

As she gingerly raised to sitting, she caught the flutter of falling robes. When her eyes had adjusted to the muted light, she discovered she was encircled by prone figures.

"Fuck. Me."

"A thousand pardons, blessed Divine." A voice from just beyond the circle of light drew her narrowed gaze. "Why did you not make yourself known upon your arrival, *Dym Char'ann*? Lavish would have been the feast to celebrate your visit."

"Where's Kahlym?" she snapped, and with an angry growl, Evainne swung her legs off of the bed, nearly tripping over the grovelers. Her stomach rebelled at her hasty movements, and she swallowed hard.

One figure stepped out from the shadows, head bowed in reverence, obscuring the face, but she'd recognize that bleached blonde mohawk anywhere. "Great are the blessings that we beseech of the—"

"Can it, sister." She cringed, rubbing at her temples as the effects of whatever knock-out gas they'd used slowly wore off. "Answer my question. And get off the fucking floor."

Confused mutters whispered, and she ignored them, beelining straight for Khundyl. Although the bitch kept her eyes trained on the ground, she still managed to keep the sneering tone in her voice. "You needed to be set in a place more befitting your stature. Please do not think ill of us for not honoring you with the proper offerings sooner."

Evainne shook her head angrily, folding her arms across her chest. "Uh-uh, sweetcakes. You treat me like a dog, then want to kiss my ass? Blow me. You're not weaseling out of this one." She stood directly in front of the still-bowed figure, tapping her foot until a pair of terrified neon green eyes looked up. "Where. Is. Kahlym."

Watching Khundyl's perfectly unwrinkled face as she scrambled for a response was almost comical. "But he is unworthy of—"

"If you enjoy breathing, you might want to rethink the rest of that statement." Evainne narrowed her eyes, and the room cooled a degree or two. "I'm really sick of hearing about all this 'unworthy' shit. He's my friend and I want to know where he is."

Stunned confusion painted the aliens' features, and the genuine depth of the emotion took Evainne aback.

"Divine, you do not understand. You are not to be touched by any but another Divine."

This time, the temperature dropped severely as Evainne threw back her head in mirthless laughter. "Not bloody likely. I've heard this master plan, and anyone who thinks I'm gonna play along with that can just eat a bowl of dicks."

Evainne glanced around, taking in the gaping jaws of the still-kneeling monks. "Yeah. Surprise? You wanted a Divine?" she said. "Well, tough shit, kiddies. You got me instead. And if I don't see Kahlym or the door out of here—and I mean right-fucking-now—you're all gonna find out just how 'Divine' I can be."

At least the bitch had the good sense to look flustered as she backpedaled until her ass hit the wall. "You must not—"

That did it.

"If I hear the word 'not' come from your mouth one more time," she said, "I'm gonna start cracking skulls." And Evainne dug her fingernails into her arms to stop from wrapping them around a certain slender neck.

More jerky bowing, and Evainne caught the sounds of someone whispering into a comm unit on the wall. The swagger she displayed like a shield was nothing more than a ruse; beneath it, she was quaking in her high-heeled sandals. Sure, she was pissed beyond all reason, but her fear was centered on just one person.

If they had hurt Kahlym in any way with their dumbass religiosity, she would make good on her threat. The cool air stood the hairs on her bare arms at attention, but before she could wish for a jacket, the temperature evened out.

Fabu. Another one of those "Your wish is my command" rooms.

She had only a moment to register this, when the door slid open. "Lady Evainne?"

One word, and she launched herself straight at Kahlym, not caring about the number of prostrated speed bumps she stepped on in the process. He stiffened under her enthusiastic welcome, wooden and stilted. She rested her head against his chest, and after a moment, his arms encircled her shoulders, though the hug felt more pragmatic than passionate. She hoped it was because of the current audience, and her mind flipped through all of the snide remarks about Kahlym and his so-called defect.

She gripped onto his biceps and leaned back to look up into his eyes, his chin raised in rigid defiance. She might not be able to change things today, but, hell, she would give it her best shot.

"Are you well, *Dym Char'ann?*" He'd spoken without meeting her gaze, words flat and emotionless.

A soft smile warmed her lips, and she cradled his face in her hands, guiding his eyes toward hers. So many humiliations had been heaped upon him for something out of his control and still he stood proud and tall.

"I am now." She rose onto her tiptoes and kissed him tenderly.

His primal, possessive response took her by surprise but delighted her completely. He crushed her to him, the silky fabric brushing over her sensitive nipples, kissing her as though she were the very air he needed to live.

Deep chuckles from beyond the threshold brought her back to the present. "And here I thought you were going to abandon us for a life of leisure."

At Brel's amused statement, Kahlym broke the seal of their lips but maintained his vice-like grip on her.

To her surprise, Brel and R'uan stepped around the mute

guards, both beaming as they admired the room. Evainne laughed lightly, wiggling in Kahlym's arms for a bit of breathing room.

"Hell, had I known that being a Divine would've given us such an upgrade in room service, I'd've tattooed it on my forehead."

Shocked gasps reverberated through the robed masses, and Evainne rolled her eyes in irritation. "All right, that's it. Everyone out of the pool. Go on, scoot. Shoo!" She shook her head and waved the bulk of the unwanted guests toward the door, leaving her in relative peace with the people she called friends.

"Blessed Divine?"

Well, almost all of the riffraff was out. Evainne shifted her gaze, one eyebrow arching up to the trembling blonde figure still cowering near the door.

"What."

Khundyl shuffled a step forward, still staring at the intricate pattern on the floor rug.

"I pray for your understanding and forgiveness for your unacceptable treatment upon your arrival."

Evainne dropped her face into her palm, heaving a heavy sigh. "You don't get it, do you, Khundyl?" The use of her name drew their hostess' gaze up, bewilderment lacing her face. "Maybe next time you'll talk to people to find out the truth for yourself, instead of passing judgment because it's the politically correct thing to do."

The neon green eyes blinked in stunned contemplation, but showed no sign of comprehension. When it was clear nothing more could be said, Khundyl bowed one final time before backing out the door.

"And smart to boot? Damn, Kahl, what in the all the Seventh Quadrant is she doing hanging out with you?"

Laughter filled the room, and Evainne turned to face the two newly adopted, sure to be overprotective, older brothers. But as siblings go, she couldn't have picked better. She folded her arms and studied the two walking hulks as they checked out the room. They dwarfed the furniture. She was no shrimp herself, but even Kahlym had to be a foot taller than her, easy, and the back of her head fit perfectly between his pecs as she rested in his loose embrace. Brel had the typical, older sibling three inches on Kahlym at least, while R'uan and his brother, Dhaerin, rivaled Brel in both height and girth.

From the little bit she'd seen during their escape, they were fierce fighters, but the ferocity of their loyalty made them family. She remembered the deep grief on board after the loss of Lozzan, and the incredible outpouring of support to pick up the slack. She hadn't realized how small and tightly knit Kahlym's crew was until they had been put to the test. She'd offered to help, but her lack of any kind of skills needed in this world made it nothing more than lip service.

A quiet knock snapped her out of her revere, and the door slid open. Cart after cart laden with trays of food entered the room, servants moving them toward the large table.

Brel clapped his meaty hands together, then rubbed them in delight. "Thank Ishtanti. I didn't get to eat much before shit hit the fan at Last Repast."

R'uan scoffed as he grabbed a plate before the servant had finished setting down the feast. "Do not believe him. I saw him clear three plates."

"Hey, for me, that's not much."

The good-natured teasing continued at a dull roar, and Evainne felt the heat of a certain pair of tourmaline eyes on her. She blushed, glancing over her shoulder at Kahlym, then spun in the loose circle of his embrace and tilted her chin up to capture his gaze.

"Are you truly all right, *ziat'xahn*?" The shadows had receded from his eyes, and she again spied the man she'd fallen in love with reflected behind those hypnotic depths.

With a nod and a smile, she caressed his cheek. "A little freaked out by the whole thing, but yeah. I really am better now." She leaned into his chest, where the thumping beneath her ear centered her. The earlier tension fell away, so much so, her rebellious stomach decided to make its emptiness known.

Kahlym gripped her shoulders, held her at arm's length, a quizzical look skating across his face.

"Have you dined?"

His simple question froze the entire room.

"You're kidding, right? I just woke up and found myself on the friggin' sacrificial alter."

"What? Wait, you haven't eaten yet?" Brel stopped, hand mid-scoop as he stared at her. "Didn't you guys eat when you met with Khundyl?"

Kahlym only shook his head as he released Evainne. "No such luck. Seems our hostess decided it would be better if she weren't… what did that asshole of hers say? Oh, right. 'Sullied' with our company."

Evainne managed one step toward the food, when two plates were shoved into her hands, every variety and color of edibles piled so high, they started to slip off the edges.

"What the hell is her problem?" R'uan growled as she wobbled with the over-laden dishes, his quick reflexes saving the food and guiding her to the table at the same time.

All the food on the plates looked different from what she'd already experienced. Damn. This would be another experiment, and she wasn't in the mood to play Russian roulette with her menu. The knockout gas still had her head swimming, not to mention her stomach had done an uncomfortable flip-flop when the carts passed by.

Kahlym shook his head as he filled a plate of his own. "I wish I knew. I almost would've believed that she received the broad wave about our passenger, but with this response?" He sat down next to Evainne and, to her surprise, started dividing the heaped dishes into more manageable portions. "She has never been so openly hostile before. My money might be on Qaen. She did have a thing for him, after all."

Brel swung his leg over the low-backed chair before sitting down and diving into his food. He shrugged a shoulder as he loaded up his fork. "Kahl, you're talking about one of the galaxy's biggest walking erection. He had a 'thing' for everything."

"So why the change of heart?" Evainne chimed in, just as Kahlym finished portioning out a much more reasonable amount for her. Upon closer inspection, she found familiar shapes and colors divided into separate servings, and she smiled at his thoughtful act. She reached for his hand and gave his fingers a quick squeeze in thanks.

R'uan set down a tall glass of a rich red something in front of each person before joining them at the table. "Because if word got back to anyone at either Stria and Thrall command that she'd disrespected a Divine, she could get yanked from atop her pedestal."

Evainne coughed, then swallowed hard, forcing the food down the right pipe. She blinked back tears and remembered how to breathe. "Really?" she asked. "You're shitting me, right?"

Kahlym rubbed her back and offered her a drink. One sniff told her it was some kind of wine. Never a fan of the foofy stuff, she opted for a small sip. The heady liquid was cool and sweet, the burn kicking in on the way down. She could get used to this.

"Nope." R'uan answered while Brel stood and went back for more. "You wondered why Falka and Yhan'tu were so devout in their dealings with you? Here, if anyone disrespects a Divine, no matter their stature, they will be removed from their seat of power. Very rarely do the lowborn mingle with Divines, but their penalty is a swift death."

Evainne was happy she'd finished her mouthful of food in the midst of his explanation, otherwise she would have redecorated the table with her meal. Even so, her stomach still threatened to pitch the meager contents out.

"Good God, why? They're just people. What makes them think they can control other people like that?"

Brel paused, the fork just shy of his slackened jaw. "How do you worship the Divines on your homeworld?"

She swung her gaze over to meet their waiting eyes; pairs of exotic citrine, snowflake obsidian, and tourmaline all focused on her. "Uh…we don't?" With a shake of her head, she continued on. "Seriously. Where I come from, we have priests and prophets and other kinds of holy men, but nobody really worships *people*. Okay, so maybe you get adoration if you're famous and good looking. I mean, we believe in deities, but the clergy of every religion are still just people."

The thick, black brow over R'uan's black-and-grey eyes knitted together. "Then how were you trained?"

Evainne tossed back her head, incredulous laughter bubbling up. "Trained?" she squeaked out. "I didn't even know about any of this until I got here. But I guess I did have some help. I think my martial arts sensei was one of the clerics, like Yhan'tu. He had those same facials tats, and he taught me how to center my mind and focus the rage I felt." She took in a breath to organize her thoughts, and each of the brothers around the table waited patiently for her to continue. So many details about who she was before showing up on their doorstep were still a mystery to them. She owed them that much.

She set down her fork, meeting all the gazes in turn directed at her.

"I was a kid when I first started taking classes. It was a way to get out of my house and vent some of my…" She dropped her head to stare at the tablecloth, searching for answers in the gold lace. "Well, let's just say that your folks and mine learned how to parent from the same book. Anyway, our cook's son, Bao, took karate and lots of other martial arts, and I would watch him practice, so one day, I asked him if he'd introduce me to his teacher. It took some doing, but he finally agreed to take me on as a student. He taught me how to defend myself and how to focus when things… Well, when things went the way most of my life tended to go: to complete shit."

A bronze hand appeared in her periphery to cover her still fingers. She gratefully accepted the silent show of compassion and continued her tale.

"His teachings kept me safe, and sane, until my parents tossed me officially out two days after I graduated high school. I was eighteen, and since then, I've been trying to make my way in a world that's hated me." But Evainne shored up her pity party, then raised her gaze. "So, I guess you could say that most of what I've done has been flying by the seat of my pants. Call it gut instinct."

Brel lifted his glass, a proud smile on his face. "In that case, Evainne, I, for one, am grateful for your intuition."

"Well said, *kherdes*," R'uan chimed in, raising his drink as well.

Kahlym hoisted his glass and laced his fingers with hers. With a smile, he kissed the back of her hand.

"Welcome to the family, *ziat'xahn*."

Chapter 12

Family.

The word had tumbled around in Kahlym's mind long after he'd crawled into bed and wrapped his arms around his angel. With his father breathing down his neck in search of him and Evainne, and the rest of the Thrall not far behind, he might have to bring her home; bring the prey to the predator and hope he could still keep her safe.

He could continue to run and pray he outran the bastard, but where would they find shelter? If R'uan's report about Thrall forces being as far away as Outer T'chan, how many other worlds had already been pillaged?

Damn. The whole situation sucked.

Kahlym trailed his fingers down the bare skin of her arms. How could he let her know just how much she'd changed his life? She spoke from the heart, saw his world without prejudice. Her open, honest acceptance was refreshing, and it gave him hope. If a complete stranger could see through the long-standing hatred that had infected the Dantaran galaxy, maybe not all was lost.

Sleep had just pulled him under, when the lights flared to life.

Kahlym shielded his eyes, searching for the source of the disruption, as Brel grabbed his shoulder, jostling him fully awake.

"Falka just contacted us. They had to flee Outer T'chan." His harsh whisper had yanked Kahlym completely into the present, and he sat up as gingerly as possible, trying not to wake his still-sleeping angel. He tucked the sheet around her as she rolled onto her side.

"What? When?" he croaked. Glancing around the room, he found R'uan busily gathering their meager belongings.

"They only had a moment to inform Lozzan's family of his death, when enforcers descended like flies on a corpse. The shit hit the fan when Qaen showed his face. Guess they had to yank Dhaer out before he got killed trying to throttle the bastard."

"Great. So much for time to relax." Kahlym dragged his fingers through his hair, then scrubbed his scalp to help wake up his brain.

"But everyone got out, right?"

"Yeah. They are heading here to meet us, but we will have to make a quick getaway before those Thrall asshats figure out where we are."

Kahlym smirked at Brel's word choice. "Asshat?"

A proud grin split his brother's face. "What can I say? Your female has some pretty inventive swear words."

As if on cue, Evainne stirred. She blinked, a tired frown creasing her forehead. "What did I miss?"

Kahlym brushed his knuckles against the deep furrow. "Seems like plans are changing quicker than expected, *ziat'xahn*."

She jerked up, her beautiful brown eyes wide as she held the covers up under her armpits with practiced ease. "How much time do we have?"

Kahlym stared in stunned admiration as she clambered out of bed, ready to tackle whatever lay ahead. His shifted gaze caught the dropped jaws of Brel and R'uan before a blink of bare flesh vanished into the bath. Two sets of eyes swiveled in his direction, silence broken only by the flowing water from behind the closed door.

"Damn, bro. I do not think I have ever seen a female fly from a bed with that much speed."

R'uan jabbed Brel in the ribs, a grin on his face. "Only because you were asleep when they left."

Kahlym took a page from his angel's book and sprang to his feet. "She sets the pace for the rest of us," he said and opened the closet to grab the nearest gearsuit. "Brel, please tender our thanks to Khundyl for her hospitality. R'uan, see how quickly we can get transport back to the docking bay."

Brel nodded, crossing to the comm link on the wall, while R'uan conversed in hushed tones on his personal comm. Completely dressed, Kahlym crossed to the bath, arriving just as the shower stopped. He pressed his ear against the thin door, smiling and chuckling as muttered profanities came from the other side.

He rapped lightly on the door, then used his body to block her from the outer room as he handed her some necessary clothes. The warm blush painting her cheeks, as well as the rest of her bare flesh, deepened his smile. He winked, then left her in relative privacy to get dressed.

Brel grumbled at his back, and Kahlym spun about to find the doorway open with a contingent of Stria guards on the other side. He frowned, folding his arms across his chest.

"Oh, NOW you show up. Thanks, but we're just leaving."

The commanding officer stepped forward and gave him a sharp bow. "A thousand apologies, captain, but we only recently heard that you had arrived." The man's gaze darted around the room.

<Brel? Make sure Evainne stays out of sight. I don't trust this guy.>

Brel glared at the gathered soldiers before he made his way to the bath. *<She's gonna be pissed when it's me who joins her in there, and not you. Too bad she's not a Seer. That way, you could tell her not to beat the crap out of me.>*

Kahlym nodded, hoping it would be read as a response to the officer's lame excuse. "That might be, but the rest of my crew are on their way here and—"

"We heard you are traveling with a Divine."

R'uan's dark laugh filled the room as Brel stepped into the bath and swiftly shut the door behind him. "So that news made it to you, I see."

Kahlym scanned the doorway, assessing the size of the team. These were allies, yes, but something was off—they were armed to the teeth and looking for a fight.

"Is that why you're here? To see for yourself if the rumors are true?"

<*Bro, you are so lucky she's no dummy.*>

<*Is she all right?*> Kahlym sensed R'uan next to him, the Ontaxian glaring at the so-called friendly forces.

<*She said that next time she has to share a shower, she'd rather have larger facilities.*>

Coughing to cover up his surprised laugh, Kahlym quickly composed himself as all eyes watched on in curiosity. "So you now are believing rumors?" he said.

The commander's rapid blinks took on a different meaning. *Code?*

Kahlym nodded imperceptibly as he took in the message.

<*Brel? Get ready. The commander just informed me the men aren't all ours. It might*

get ugly out here.>

"Are you saying the Divine is not here with you?" the officer asked, relief in his eyes as he glanced toward four of the armed guards.

Kahlym shrugged and leaned his shoulder against R'uan. "I am afraid you are only moments too late. The Lady Khundyl requested a private audience. Perhaps you should wait outside her chambers."

The officer gave another sharp nod. "Thank you for your time, sir."

The room exploded in a rain of weapon fire as he turned away. Kahlym dropped to the ground, blaster in hand as he took out the guard to the commander's left. Brel busted out of the bath, running headlong into the surprised enemy, his fist connecting with the shocked man still fumbling with his holster, while R'uan let fly two short daggers, and the battle was over almost as soon as it had begun.

The odds once again in their favor, the relieved officer brushed the settling dust off of his jacket. "Thank you. I was hoping you remembered the old codes. Commander Mankaw." He extended his hand and gripped Kahlym's forearm.

"Can I come out?"

The feminine voice from the narrow alcove had sounded more annoyed than apprehensive. Without waiting for a response, Evainne stepped out, fingers twisting her bloodwine hair into a thickly woven braid. Her brown eyes reflected her perturbed state as she shouldered her way around Brel. "Now that I've missed all the fun?"

Kahlym motioned to his agitated angel, the officer's shocked expression adding to his growing unease.

"Commander Mankaw, may I present the Lady Evainne, Divine Healer from the Terran homeworld."

The stunned officer and the remaining soldiers started to kneel, only to be halted by a sharp, guttural sound and a shake of Evainne's head. "GAH! For fuck's sake, cut it out with all the friggin' groveling, okay? I've had it up to here with all the kowtowing," she said, gesturing to her forehead as she stalked over to Kahlym, who reared back slightly, unsure of her intention.

His concern was well founded when she balled up her fist and punched him in the meaty part of his shoulder. Not a powerful hit, but it did take him by surprise. "Is there something amiss?" he asked.

She glared, brown eyes sparkling with mischief, arms resting akimbo. "THAT'S for leaving me locked in the bathroom with Gigantor there."

Was she truly angered?

EVAINNE LOOKED up into the saddest, most gorgeous face she'd seen not on a billboard. Shit. She would have to teach him about her mood swings. Now she felt like crap for giving him a hard time.

She sighed, releasing some of her righteous indignation. "No, I'm not really that mad. But was that all necessary?"

"If I may speak up, blessed Divine," the guard at the door piped in. "I do believe it was for the best. This place is no longer safe and you must leave before reinforcements arrive." He turned toward Kahlym. "Her ladyship has been compromised. Her consort overheard the latest message from Commander Panza, and the reward was too much to resist."

"Reward?" She'd asked the question even though she'd already suspected the reason for a big payoff.

His answering nod dropped to the pit of her stomach, and Kahlym rested his own hand on her shoulder. "The Emperor has offered a seat in the Governing Counsel for whomever locates and returns the kidnapped Divine," the officer replied.

Evainne screwed up her face at that last descriptor. "Kidnapped? That's rich. Did he happen to mention that he was the one who'd kidnapped the Divine in the first place?"

"I do not know any details other than what I have heard." The new guy made a quick check of the downed soldiers, who were all dressed the same, except for charred patches in the center of three of the chests, the fourth having two blade hilts protruding from rather important body parts.

Well, at least it didn't look like that much of a fun fight.

"Come," the officer continued. "We must get you out of here now. Transport has arrived and will get you to your ship."

"So, I guess sightseeing is gonna have to wait?" she asked and smiled at Kahlym, hoping her light words would take some tension out of the room. When he answered with a shy smile of his own, she blew out her held breath. "All right, let's get this show on the road, then."

Kahlym clasped the commander's arm. "Thank you. Give us ten minutes, then you can let Khundyl know we declined her continued hospitality."

Brel and R'uan passed by, each offering the captain a warrior's handshake before stepping into the hallway while Evainne waited for her turn in the receiving line. When she finally stood before the man, his golden face drained so quickly she thought he might pass out. He made a move toward the floor, and she grabbed onto his shoulders.

"Please, don't," she said, stopping his descent. "I just wanted to say thank you, as well." She released him and extended her hand. His amethyst eyes blinked with deliberate slowness and confusion and, after a couple of heartbeats, Evainne sighed and prepared to drop the offer.

"It is forbidden to—" he began to stammer out, but an impish grin curled her lips.

"Trust me, sweetie, I'm not gonna tell anyone. Besides, following the rules was never one of my strong suits."

She read his apprehension in his bright purple eyes. At the edge of her periphery came the hesitant movement of his hand. If she gave him her normal, firm grip, that might freak him out even more. Deciding to err on the side of caution, she gave his hand a gentle squeeze.

She hadn't used that much force, but the man dropped to his knees, bowing low as he pressed his forehead against the back of her hand. Perplexed, she glanced to Kahlym for answers. All three boys were beaming at her, pride mirrored on each of their faces. Kahlym's eyes shone with something deeper, though, and a hot blush hit her cheeks like a slap.

"I think you just made a friend, *learom-xahn,*" Brel chuckled, elbowing Kahlym in the ribs before grabbing their meager belongings.

She glanced at the kneeling figure, whose his head had lifted, and a strange expression lit the soldier's face. She remembered images like this from news broadcasts when people witnessed miracles or met the Pope. Apparently, something deeply spiritual had transpired, and all she'd done was shake the man's hand.

"I will never forget this moment, *Dym Char'ann*, and I shall give my life to see you to safety."

Evainne blinked rapidly to clear the fog in her brain. "Uh, thanks?" Afraid things would start to get weirder, she released his hand with delicate care, just shy of dropping him like a hot potato and running, screaming, for the door. Would it always be like this when she met new people here?

Kahlym swooped in to save her once again, guiding her toward the door. "Until peace reigns, my brother." He thumped his fist against his heart.

Her new best friend rose to his feet and repeated the same gesture. "May Ishtanti lead you, captain."

Evainne followed Brel as he strolled purposefully down the hallway. R'uan had exited first, so she assumed he must have been leading the way, with her and Kahlym bringing up the rear. The men moved in synchronous harmony, their heads on swivels as they guided her through the maze of hallways and courtyards.

She glimpsed strange, exquisite gardens beyond the scattered floor-to-ceiling windows. Trees of orange bark and pale white leaves grew in neat rows; the ground was covered with the greenest grass she'd ever seen. A beautiful bird-like creature sat on one of the low-hanging branches, its long, multicolored tail reaching toward the manicured lawn. She watched in awe and admiration as the tail flicked, its kaleidoscopic plumage fluttering in the light breeze. She spied other people wandering through the opulent surroundings, their fine attire and flowing robes marking them as the upper echelon. They daintily sipped something from black marble goblets, too deeply entrenched in their conversations to pay much attention to the natural beauty just inches away.

No one seemed to take notice of their passing.

"One-way glass." The question had come out more of a statement, one that she'd asked to nobody in particular.

"I promise to show you the gardens on my homeworld, *ziat'xahn*, if it is what you desire." Kahlym's whispered breath was warm against her ear, and tingles raced down her spine. Her heart pounded, and it had little to do with the rapid pace of their exit.

She clamped down on the inside of her bottom lip to hold back a needy sigh. "We're gonna have to work on your choice of words there, hon."

His dark chuckle nearly caused her legs to buckle mid-stride, and his hand found her lower back to keep her on her feet. "Perhaps we can discuss my vocabulary later this evening."

She shifted her focus forward as two huge doors slid open, and the boys ahead strode calmly out of the massive structure, where crystalline gray sands stretched out as far as the eye could see. The sun drew near the horizon, setting the scattered pink clouds afire before it would eventually give up the day. Slender trees of shocking green lined the broad driveway, where a fleet of sleek black crafts sat in silent vigil about ten yards away. She blinked, awed by the beautifully alien skyscape.

Fears about the outside atmosphere suddenly gripped her mind, firing delayed panic through her body, and on instinct, she sucked in a sharp breath, holding it as she crossed the threshold.

One vehicle waited apart from the others, its side doors swung upward. R'uan was already seated behind the wheel when Brel had finished dropping their packs under the hood. *Huh, just like an old-school VW Bug*, she mused as she started to see spots.

Realizing she wasn't dead just yet, she exhaled in a huff, then panted to replenish her burning lungs.

Kahlym tilted his head with a curious frown. "Is there something amiss?"

The air tasted bitter, like a smoke-filled bar, and she coughed into her hand, shaking her head. "Just me being silly. I'm fine, I promise."

A graceful brow arched over one tourmaline eye as he stood beside the open door.

"STOP! DO NOT LET THAT TRANSPORT LEAVE!"

Her head jerked up. Two guards were rushing toward them, firing shots that kicked up dust at their feet, and Evainne sprang into action. Grabbing Kahlym's arm, she shoved him inside the transport and quickly crawled in after him. She reached up for the open gull wing door, dodging the incoming fire, and sealed them inside. The door clicked soundly shut.

"Step on it, R'uan!" she called over her shoulder.

The vehicle sped off, spraying rocks and debris toward the pursuing soldiers. Evainne pulled her legs under her ass and knelt in her seat to peer out through the rear window. In an instant, the guards were tiny, distant blips as the scenery blurred past.

She stared as they zipped farther ahead, her breaths fogging up the clear glass—short, panting breaths that created pretty circles that appeared and disappeared as the seconds ticked by.

"Everyone good back there?" R'uan's voice echoed through the small interior. A hand gently gripped Evainne's shoulder and turned her about. She unfolded her legs from beneath her to gaze up at Kahlym.

She had an almost overwhelming urge to throw her arms around him, or to check to make sure all of his parts were still connected. Instead, she gaped like a love-stricken schoolgirl. His tourmaline eyes bored straight down to her soul, and she thought she read a touch of anger in his smoldering gaze.

"We are fine, R'uan. Any damage?" Kahlym asked, his clipped voice filling the narrow confines.

"All good up here," Brel replied.

The longer she held Kahlym's unyielding stare, the more nervous she became.

"All right," she said. "What did I do wrong this time?"

KAHLYM'S HEART pounded so hard against his ribs, he feared it would jump out of his chest. Evainne's lightning-quick thinking had saved them and bought them some needed time, but her selfless action to pull him to safety, to place herself in the direct path of their enemy, terrified him beyond all reason.

"You did nothing wrong, Evainne," he said, hoping to temper his panic with compassion, "but you cannot endanger yourself. You are far too important—"

"Don't hand me that shit, Kahl. I'm not gonna sit back while you guys take all the risks. And gee, you know, a simple 'thanks for saving my ass' might be nice." Her beautiful brown eyes burned with an unexpected fire, venom lacing her angered words.

"You misunderstand—"

"No, sweet cheeks, it's YOU who keeps misunderstanding things," she said, leaning closer and thrusting her finger into his chest. "I don't care what you think I am and what you think I'm worth to your cause. I asked you to stop treating me like some fragile relic and see me for who I am."

"Trouble in paradise?" Brel chuckled from the front seat, and his angel snapped her gaze away from him for a heartbeat.

"Can it up there," she said, her fiery eyes finding his again, this time with a sheen of unshed tears pooling along her lower lids. "What do I have to do to get you to see me?" She'd punctuated the final two words with thumping taps against her chest.

The earlier ire in her voice was gone, replaced by a heart-wrenching plea for understanding. His mind traveled back to her passionate words as he'd held her in his arms: *Promise me you'll never let us go.*

He reached out to caress her cheek, but she spun away, giving him her back. Frozen in his seat, he lowered his hand with a defeated sigh.

<*She is right, Kahl. All of us are guilty of underestimating what she can do.*>

Brel's eyes reflected back at him in the rearview mirror. R'uan flicked his gaze from the control panel, concern lining his own snowflake obsidian orbs. Words failed Kahlym as he drew his eyes to his silent angel.

Until he had a better idea of what to say, he joined her in the silence. She was right, on all counts. She was smart and quick, mind sharp and spirit strong. She loved fiercely and spoke without guile. Then why did he refuse to acknowledge her strengths?

Because the truth terrified him.

Because without her, his heart had no reason to beat.

The journey to the private docking bay wound to an end when an explosion rocked their transport. The small vehicle pitched violently, then slammed into the ground, tumbling and rolling. Kahlym reached out for Evainne, but his head smacked against the door and his world winked out.

Distant voices yelled, and Kahlym struggled to regain his balance. While fuzzy figures moved about, he felt a great force yanking at his arm. He told his legs to work but the message seemed to miss its mark. A red haze surrounded the objects in his field of vision.

His fingers sought a firm hold on something, anything, when the butt of a weapon was slapped into his palm.

"Kahl! Kahlym, get up! We gotta go!"

Brel's voice pulled him back into reality. A handful of white-clad enforcers lay scattered around the flight deck. Kahlym squinted until his crew's recognizable faces came into focus. His ship was safe, Falka manning the door cannon and clearing the path for them, while Dhaerin charged the engines.

This situation was all too familiar, with one major difference: betrayal was the cause of this fire fight.

Kahlym shook his head and, dragging the back of his sleeve

across his eyes to clear his vision from the bloody veil, he frantically searched for one important missing person.

Evainne. Where was Evainne?

"Get her out of here, Kahl!"

A light burden was draped across his shoulder and a heavy hand pushed against his back. He ran as fast as his rubbery legs would carry him, one arm wrapped around the limp limbs dangling against his chest, while his gun blasted anything in his way. Together, with Brel and R'uan giving cover fire, they dashed the final distance to their waiting ship.

He had barely placed one foot beyond the ship's threshold, when the unconscious form in his arms vanished. Panicked, Kahlym spun around just as the landing bay door locked shut.

"NO!"

He clawed at the latch with desperate, terrified howls as the ground disappeared beneath them.

"Kahl! KAHLYM!" Brel's voice bled into his fear-laced mind. "We will get her back, I promise. But we have to go now or there won't be anyone left to mount a rescue."

Kahlym fought against the iron bands wrapped around his arms, kicking and screaming, struggling in vain to escape the vise-like grip of his brother. The words meant to calm his frantic mind offered little comfort, his soul shattering at having failed to protect his angel.

"Kahlym. Listen to me. We know where she will be taken. The forces who attacked us were assigned to Raedyn Primus." Honed by logic and edged with understanding, Brel's voice had cut like a blade through Kahlym's fear and the static of his thoughts.

Air burned as it raced in and out of his lungs. Then, knowledge slowly crept into his panic, evening out his heart rate as he regained control by small degrees.

"Seems Father has decided to do some searching of his own. She will be taken there before she is presented anywhere else."

Kahlym sensed the gradual release of Brel's grip, and he

stepped out of the brotherly cage, spinning round to the strong chiseled lines of a face marred by sorrow, sand, and blood. A deep cut slashed through his left eyebrow; his gearsuit was splattered with blast marks.

Brel placed his hand onto Kahlym's shoulder, and the two locked eyes, his brother's bright golden yellow reflecting the myriad of Kahl's emotions.

"We will get her back, *kherdes-xahn*. Don't forget, I have a blood debt to honor and I have no intention of leaving her in the hands of that bastard."

His limbs felt like lead as Kahlym rested his palm on his brother's strong arm. A devilish twinkle glinted in Brel's citrine orbs, and Kahlym leaned away, curious. "What's that look for?"

Brel chuckled darkly. "Just imagining what kind of damage that female of yours could do to dear old Dad if he tried anything."

Kahlym swallowed hard past the lump in his throat. "Let us hope it does not come to that, *kherdes*. I—" But he kept his fearful words buried deep inside his chest, hidden behind the dread in his gut.

I swear by the goddess, I will butcher him if he harms a hair on her head.

Chapter 13

Anaxar du'Jhuen stood at the foot of the med bay bed that held the female rumored to be the missing Divine. The ship carrying his disowned had escaped, but the prize had been obtained. He folded his arms across his chest, leaned in for a closer examination.

Several small cuts and a smattering of bruises marred her pale ivory skin; damage sustained during her retrieval. She was camouflaged in a young male's gearsuit, yet the confining material couldn't hide her lush, feminine curves—wide hips and an ample bosom would prove worthwhile for birthing the next generation of Divines. Her hair was a strange deep reddish shade with streaks of black interspersed throughout the thick woven plait.

He strolled around the table to study her hands resting atop the thermal sheet. He picked one up. Short stubby nails blunted her slender fingers and creases lined her palms. He let drop the cool limb, then moved to the cleric muttering over the samples in a corner of the room.

"Well?"

The rail-thin male glanced up from his analysis, the golden

geometric markings on the right side of his dark ebony skin glowing under the added sheen of nervous perspiration. His short, squat digits fumbled with narrow vials and flew over the buttons and dials on the med units.

"I-I-I fear we have no matching data on even her species, much less her as an individual."

Fool. Anaxar pinched the bridge of his nose and struggled to keep his composure. "Obviously, she is present in this room; therefore, she does exist and is breathing. All I want to know is: can she conceive?"

The cleric's spindly neck proved strong enough to bear his frantically bobbing head. "I-I-I-I believe she will, sire. We are fairly certain a child will hold in her womb. The Divine Seer prophesied the appearance of a faraway female who would save our galaxy."

Anaxar slid his gaze back toward the unconscious female. "Did the old woman say what kind of Divine she was?"

Silence met his question, so he turned to face the cleric, whose bald head shook back and forth. "A thousand apologies, sire, but that knowledge is yet unknown."

It is just as well, he mused. Judging from her vicious slashes, she was obviously not a Divine Healer. Any healer worth their salt would have bound those minor wounds in their sleep.

Pity. A Healer would have been a welcome addition.

Her eyelids fluttered as she stirred to wakefulness, and he kept a quiet distance as she blinked then shifted her gaze to him. Eyes the color of the darkest tree bark regarded him with fear. He puffed out his chest, stalking around the bed to stand beside the awakened Divine.

He covered his heart with his hand, dipped his chin in reverence. "Greetings, Divine. I hope you are feeling well rested and have sustained no lasting damage."

She scooted higher up the bed until she rested her back against the headboard, her eyes darting around the room. Fear oozed off of her, scenting the air with its heady aroma. His mouth watered in anticipation.

"Who are you?" she asked.

He remained bent over as she regarded him with eyes as wide as plates.

"You must have many questions after your arduous journey. My name is Anaxar du Jhuen, and I will do what I can to ease your mind."

"Where am I? What happened to the people who were holding me?" Her voice was soft and airy, timidity evident in each word. Perhaps the old coots had made a mistake. She didn't appear to have the necessary strength of heart to be a true Divine.

Anaxar slowly regained his full height. "You have nothing to fear from those thieves again. Did they harm you?"

She shook her head as she tugged the edge of the blanket up under her chin. "N-no. They kept me locked in a dark room and hardly spoke a word to me." She ran a quivering hand over her hair and curled her knees up to her chest. From the tight ball she'd tucked herself into in the far corner of the bed, she regarded him with a panicked stare. "They just dragged me around like a prisoner. I kept asking why they were doing this to me, but no one ever answered me. I don't even know how long I've been here. Please, mister, I just want to go home." Tears glistened for an instant, before slipping down her soot-smeared cheeks.

Anaxar gestured to the surroundings, forcing his pretense of calm and patient care. "You are safe now, blessed one, and on your way toward the royal palace on Raedyn Primus. From there, we will determine how best to return you to your homeworld."

His own patronizing tone grated on his nerves, but it seemed to keep her soothed. He perched on the edge of the bed, keeping a respectful buffer between them. "Do you remember your name?"

Confusion traced lines between her shapely brows and she trembled, heaving a sigh of relief. She bobbed her head in gratitude.

"Oh, thank you. Thank you so much. Yes, I'm sorry. My name is Alice. Are you really going to be able to take me home?"

Home. He sneered at her ridiculous plea. But until he could determine how best to use her, he'd pander to her mewling fears. Leaning over, he placed a hand on her blanket-shrouded foot and plastered on a kind grin. "We will take all possible steps to see that you arrive where you belong, Divine Alice."

The vapid female beamed at his false promise. "Oh, thank you. I-I just wanna go home." Tears welled in her big doe eyes, and she dashed them away with the back of her hand.

"You rest, and I will alert you when we reach our destination." He nodded to her before locking eyes with the waiting healer, who bowed and backed toward the exit, then held open the door.

Anaxar dipped his chin once again to the solitary female and left the room.

EVAINNE SAT IN FROZEN SILENCE, listening to the receding footsteps. She never thought she'd be so happy for metal floors and shiny boots. Assured she was alone, she dropped her shoulders and the ditzy airhead act.

Everything ached. Even her hair hurt. She touched her forehead and found some kind of bandage there. As she rolled her knotted shoulders, she gingerly tested all of her limbs, then sighed, relieved her whole body passed the "still living" quiz. With a groan, she undid her plait and ran her fingers through her hair, trying to piece together the missing events. The last thing she remembered was arguing with Kahlym about his lingering Cro-Magnon tendencies. She had just bitten his head off, when their cab was hit by something akin to a freight train. Everything after that was simply…gone.

When she'd opened her eyes, the face that hovered over her was definitely not the one she'd wanted to see. Similar, yet older and much crueler. Ruby red eyes had peered at her from above a hawkish nose, while angular features and a vicious mouth completed the picture. It had to be Kahlym's father. The man oozed power and the dangerous drive to get what he wanted. Plus, judging by the size of the swinging bat he'd been smuggling in his trousers, he hoped to sample her before dumping her in the hands of the real baddies.

Grateful for the ignorance of her captors, she'd opted to play up the bimbo routine. *And he bought it; hook, line, and sinker.* Now, head inclined, she was able to think in private. Any watchful eyes would assume she was crying, which was fine by her.

Would Kahlym know where to find her? Was he even still alive?

At this, the tears did fall.

More and more questions joined in, and with each new query, her fear ratcheted up another notch. She swallowed down the panic that threatened to turn her into a complete blubbering mess and reined in all of the rampaging what-ifs.

She stilled her mind, drawing on her old training, and sorted through her emotions. Losing it would definitely not do any good. The mini breakdown did relieve some of the built-up tension, but wallowing in self-pity wouldn't help her figure out a way out.

Okay, time to get to work. Back home, during her guided meditations, Evainne was able to perceive the entire contents of the room. At first, she thought it to be a game: her sensei, Toa, would move items around to see if she noticed. Now, although the stakes were much higher, the principle should still be the same.

She took in a deep, centering breath and closed her eyes. Then, with a controlled exhale, Evainne visualized the small room. Her earlier, covert surveillance had given her needed details: tools that could become weapons; the number of doors and their placements in conjunction with the bed. In the darkness, she created a full, 3D model of her current holding cell.

If I were a spy camera, where would I hide?

As if on cue, three tiny blue spots flared bright in her virtual room: one over the main exit, and two tucked in corners. Daring a peek, she cracked one eyelid open and peered up at the wall above the sliding door.

Well, I'll be damned. The edges of her lips lifted in stunned surprise as she spied the telltale shimmer of a lens focused on her. Its gleam was blueish, just as it had appeared in her mind's eye. Maybe this Divine Power wasn't a complete load of crap.

But were they just watching her? Or could they hear her, too? As she pondered how to test this theory, the door slid open to admit a bowing figure escorted by two armed guards.

"*Dym Char'ann*, we come to offer you food." It backed away, and a laden tray was carried in and placed on the extended table near the door. "May the blessings of Ishtanti be with you, and we pray the meal is to your liking."

She opened her mouth, about to grumble about the groveling but caught herself and quickly stepped back into the role of airheaded female. She blinked her eyes at the robed figure as it retreated.

"Thank you so much." The cleric snapped his head up, hood slipping away, shock painting his face. These Divines must really be a bunch of class-A assholes if simple gratitude was a rarity.

The tonsured head bobbed as the cleric shuffled backwards through the door. Evainne glanced over at the tray, searching for something familiar. Her mind drifted back to the last meal she'd had, the painstaking care Kahlym had shown by serving her things she'd already eaten and liked.

A tear slipped down her cheek, and she angrily wiped her hand across her eyes. Weeping and worrying over the unknown wouldn't help anything. She scooted off the edge of the bed and checked out the offered tray. Her stomach rumbled as the scents wafted up.

Could she trust that the food wasn't drugged?

Geez, paranoid much?

She was too valuable to poison, but maybe knocking her out for the trip back might be in the cards. Tentatively, she reached out for a burnt orange, pear-shaped thing, feeling the weight of eyes following her every movement. A large, mirrored wall dominated the space behind her.

One-way glass. Fan-fucking-tastic.

Time to put on a show.

She took a bite, and juices dripped down her chin. The fruit was sweet, the skin soft, the texture inside reminding her of eating a not-quite-ripe strawberry. More fruit-type things had been arranged on the platter, as well as thin, pale crisps. She picked up the tray and looked around for a cozier, less observed spot to eat. No other venue made itself known, though, so she crossed back to the bed and sat in the center, resting the tray before her on the blankets.

With each new morsel, she catalogued its taste as her palate searched for the tang of something not right, as if she could somehow envision that drugs would alter the flavor.

Like you'd know if it was wrong in the first place, bonehead.

Yeah, there was that, too. But she continued to draw on the lessons of her old sensei, the wise teacher's words only now beginning to make sense, almost as though he'd known she'd been destined for something other than a normal life back on Earth. While she ate, she shuffled through much of the training and the wisdom he'd imparted upon her.

"When you have fear, your body will tremble and your mind will quake. Only through

the calming of your thoughts can you see further than what you believe. Even when you believe you are alone, your centered thoughts will touch the hearts of the ones you seek."

Her jaw suddenly gaped, and she quickly recovered before drooling her latest mouthful into her lap. Did that mean what she thought it meant? At the time, so much of her old sensei's fortune cookie wisdom had gone over her head. She'd acquainted his broken English with his Asian heritage. Now, she realized he'd spoken with the same melodic timbre as Kahlym and his brother.

In fact, as she pulled up mind-images of her old teacher's face, she saw a chilling family resemblance. But Kahlym had said his other brother had died in a crash.

Evainne shook her head sharply, slamming on the brakes of that errant thought. So fixated was she on her lover, she of course saw him in every corner, reflected back to her on each shiny surface. She'd deal with that later. First, she would see if that cryptic message meant what she hoped it did.

She pushed aside the tray, then curled up in a tight ball. Hopefully, her audience would think she had simply fallen asleep. But, just as she had done before, she in took a long, slow, deep breath and closed her eyes, and instead of seeking out the contents of the room, she brought forth the face of the one she craved, the heart of the one she sought. She whispered his name in her mind:

Kahlym.

Chapter 14

Kahlym stared out into nothing, while all around him, his crew's voices rose and fell in a heated debate. After their narrow escape from Khundyl's trap, Dhaerin had steered them into the nearest hyperlane and they were off in a blink. Brel filled everyone in on the loyalties of the enforcers they'd battled, plus their possible destination.

Yet all he could do was force his legs to move mechanically from place to place, his thoughts spinning out of control, refusing to settle on any helpful guidance.

He'd failed her. These words sat like ash in his mouth, the charred remains of his shattered heart blowing away in the winds of despair.

<*You don't think I'm gonna let you off the hook that easy, do you?*>

He sat up, eyes wide as his angel's sweet voice filled his soul. "Evainne?"

Silence fell like an anvil as all heads swiveled to him.

<*Who else? Or do you have other women wandering through your head that I have to*

worry about?>

Kahlym laughed through a sudden spring of tears. "Only you, *ziat'xahn*." He glanced up, then rose to his feet, beaming at the relieved expressions that graced every face around the narrow table. "Are you safe?" he asked.

Chuckling, Brel dropped into his chair, running his hand across his face. "How many tricks does that female have up her sleeves?"

Kahlym tuned out the external conversations and focused his entire being on the beautiful voice in his head. He reached down the mental link connecting them and envisioned her sitting on a standard bed in some unnamed med bay.

<Yeah, for the time being at least. I met dear old Dad. He's kind of an asshole.>

Kahlym scoffed. "I do believe that is being overly generous to the man. Are you unharmed? Do you know where you are?" He caught Brel's eye and gave him a quick nod, mouthing one word: *Father.*

His brother's angry grumbles bled into the background. Then Brel stood up and tapped Dhaer on the shoulder, and the two of them dashed out. Kahlym was grateful for his crew's insightful teamwork. Soon, the ship would be speeding toward home. Who would arrive at that locale first, though?

<A little banged up from that crash. Some bumps and bruises, but I'll survive. He said he's taking me to Raedyn Primus to decide what to do next.>

Ice ran through his veins. "How much does he know?"

Her laughter filled his head, and he smiled, still awed by the knowledge that she yet lived and was able to link with him. In his mind, he trailed his fingers along her face, the remembered feel of her soft skin almost tangible.

<He doesn't know dick. I'm spoon-feeding him some bullshit story and he's eating it up.>

Caution tapped him on the shoulder, flaring to life his desire to protect her. "Take care, Evainne. The man is no fool."

<Sweetie, I'm a girl with big tits. Most men think I have the IQ of a

radish. So, I'll play the bimbo for as long as I can. Trust me on this. I might be crazy, but I'm not stupid.>

Another stray thought popped into his mind. "*Ziat'xahn*, did he mention the name of his vessel?"

<Uh, no. Hang on. Let me see what I can find.>

Her presence vanished, and his heart sank for a moment, when her warmth once again touched his thoughts.

<Sorry, hon. No such luck. I guess they don't put the name of the ship on all the utensils like the cruise ships back home, huh? Unless…wait. Does the word "Perredon" mean anything?>

Kahlym grit his teeth in checked anger. "Yes, my angel, it does." He rose and made his way down the corridor, following Brel's earlier path.

The *Perredon* had been slated to be his brother's ship in his father's armada. Instead, it looked like the bastard had decided to keep it for himself. Kahlym wasn't surprised. The *Perredon* had been designed to be the sleekest and the fastest warship—the crowning jewel of any fighting force.

If they were lucky, his father wouldn't expect such a swift retaliation, and they would make good time toward Raedyn Primus.

He reached the pilot cockpit and, leaning around Dhaerin, punched in the ID for the *Perredon*. The Ontaxian blinked, then let out a low whistle as he recognized the ship's markings. On the star chart display, a beacon flashed, pointing out the ship's location in juxtaposition with their current heading and speed. It seemed Ishtanti looked favorably on them. If they maintained their pace, they'd arrive before his father.

<So now that the necessities are out of the way, are you okay? Did anyone get hurt in the crash?>

A tender smile curled Kahlym's lips, and he patted Dhaerin on the shoulder, leaving the pilot area to make his way to his station, preferring both a more private setting and a more personal response before he answered her latest question. He sat in his grav chair and closed his eyes.

"Yes, *ziat'xahn*. We escaped with only minor injuries, as well. Their task was to retrieve you and leave no trace behind. Too bad they were unsuccessful in achieving both goals."

Within the stark intimacy of their link, he sensed her rising sadness, and he wrapped his mind around hers, cradling her as though she were in his arms.

<Kahlym, I'm so sorry for being such a bitch. I didn't mean…and I don't want you to think—>

Her grief tore at his heart. "Shh. As you have said, I do have much to learn about you. Perhaps, once we are together again, you will allow me the chance to study at your feet."

Her mood lightened some, and he poured his love down their connected path. "You need to rest, my angel."

<You better come back to me in one piece.>

He squeezed his eyes tight, hoping to hold back his tears. "I will find you soon, *ziat'xahn*. Stay strong."

Her voice slipped away, though the lingering warmth of her presence remained. He coughed to clear the thick emotions clogging his throat before tapping the comm link. "Falka, please tell me those engines aren't going to let me down today."

The silence lasted but a second, when the comforting roar of the engine room filled the air around him.

"Captain, today, she will fly as never before."

"Good." He glared at the distant, glowing green planet. "We need to beat Mordan to His realm in time to save an angel."

Chapter 15

Cool blue light bled into the silent dark that had cocooned Evainne ever since she had fallen asleep. So many weird things had happened, that her brain now struggled to sort dreams from reality. Remaining still, she opened her eyes, then blinked to take in her surroundings.

Yup, the whitewashed chrome still covered the walls, and that blue camera lens was still pointing right at her. She should have been defeated by that knowledge, though that would also mean her telepathic phone call to Kahlym had happened, as well. She listened carefully, tilting her head up to catch any trace of outside movement, any sound at all.

Nothing.

Had they stopped? The hum of the engines on board Kahlym's ship had been ever present, even when she snoozed, and the distant rumble had soothed her like a faint lullaby. Here, there was only a deep, all-encompassing nothingness. Another glance told her someone must have come in while she slept: the food tray was gone and a set of pale gold robes had taken its place.

Time to get this show on the road.

She took in a breath to steel her nerves and prepare herself to don her brainless persona. She sat up and stretched, arms reaching to the ceiling. Why hadn't she played the dumb blonde card in the first place? There she was, on a distant planet, for chrissake.

Oh, yeah. Kahlym.

From the moment she'd seen him, ray guns blazing, shooting the creeps about to blast her into smithereens, she'd been lost. Finding out he was a gorgeous sex god to boot had been icing on the cake. Aside from his overt hero complex, something disarming and undeniable surrounded him. Now more than ever she was grateful that he turned out to be one of the good guys.

A soft rap on the door stopped her musings.

"Yes?"

The door slid open to admit the cleric from last night. She recognized his stick-thin body. If not for his normal-sized head, he could have passed as Jack Skellington's brother, the tan robes hanging off his long, lanky limbs.

"A thousand apologies if I woke you, *Dym Char'ann.* I was sent to inquire about your condition. How do you fare this day?"

Geez, Louise! And she thought Yhan'tu talked formally. This guy gave C-3PO a run for his money in the etiquette department. She swallowed back her sharp retort and offered him a smile. Maybe she could get some help from him. After all, he was a holy man in some form, and they were supposed to be all about helping people.

"I am feeling much better, thank you." She climbed carefully out of the bed and crossed closer to her guest. She wasn't too surprised when he moved counter to her, maintaining a respectable distance.

He bobbed his head, though his gaze remained glued to the floor. "I am pleased to hear this news. I shall inform Commander Anaxar you are improved."

He started to back toward the door.

"Wait," she said, and her brain scrambled to ask her needed questions without raising too many eyebrows.

"Yes, Divine?"

She was grateful for his obedient, head-inclined stance, else he would have seen her rolled eyes at his gullibility. "Are we there yet?"

The hooded head lifted, and the golden tats on his cheek pinched and pulled as the cleric screwed up his face in confusion. "There, Divine?"

"Home," she replied. "Am I home now?" And she silently gagged at her required juvenile behavior as she bounced on the balls of her feet.

"We have arrived safely on Raedyn Primus, as promised," announced a booming voice from the door.

Kahlym's father. Crap, that man scared her. He had all the airs of her own father. A man accustomed to getting whatever he wanted, without a care of what it took or who it destroyed.

She maintained her charade, bowing to him, using the moment spent staring at the ground to help her get further into character.

"Huh? Is that what you call my planet?" she asked.

His forced chuckles raked at her nerves, ice dripping down her spine as he shook his head. "Oh no, Divine. We have reached *my* home. Remember, I explained we would stop here first, and after we are sure you are well enough to travel, we will find you a suitable way to where you need to be."

Gritting her teeth, she painted on a vapid expression, then beamed at him, nodding and grinning like an idiot. "Thank you, sire. Thank you so much."

He lightly gripped her shoulders, the mockery of a smile slashing across his hawkish face. "Your words of gratitude are not necessary, Divine Alice. It is the least I could do after the ordeal you have suffered."

"But you've been so kind to me." God, she felt trapped in the land of the never-ending soap opera. *Calgon, take me away!* She needed out of this room to see if she could reach Kahlym again.

Anaxar's crimson eyes glittered with dark intent.

Oh. Hell. No.

"Commander Anaxar?" the scarecrow to her left chimed in, saving her from what could have been a serious blow to her cover.

She stepped back and returned to the relative safety of the bed, resting her hands next to the laid-out robe.

Anaxar followed her with a predatory gaze, and her blood chilled. "Yes, cleric?"

"Do you wish me to complete the examination of her wounds, or would you prefer the palace physician to see to her?"

She smiled and tamped down her growing heebie-jeebies. "I'm fine, really. I think that sleep I got last night really helped."

Ruby red eyes narrowed to slits, and she felt like a bug under a deadly microscope. "Are you certain?" he said. "You could have sustained serious injuries of which you are unaware."

Like those that would make me useless to you as a baby factory? She was smart enough to go through the Lego ritual when she woke during the night; self-preservation had forced her to keep the visible wounds still in their healing phase, but everything on the inside was back up to snuff.

"Well," she said, adding a notch of panic to her voice, "if you think it's necessary."

His grin turned her stomach, yet she kept her face as guileless as humanly possible. "I believe it is of the utmost importance." He swiveled his crimson eyes away and spoke to the quivering cleric. "Contact the palace physician and tell him we bring a special patient to his care."

Friar Skellington bowed and shuffled out through the door, butt first. God, she'd be so happy once she was back with friendlies. Evainne lifted her gaze from the bed while the weight of Anaxar's focused stare clung to her body, raking her with his lascivious eyes. She choked back her disgust.

Right, get a good eyeful, pal, 'cuz it's gonna be all you're ever gonna get.

She composed herself, tucking away her repulsion, and turned to face him. "I'm gonna change into something more appropriate," she said.

His exaggerated bow also grated on her nerves, but she hid her visceral response from possible onlookers.

"Of course, Divine. I will return to gather you when you are ready." Once he'd regained his full stature, Anaxar didn't back out through the door. Instead, he graced her with one final lecherous grin before pivoting on his heel and striding out.

She swept the robes up into her arms and, moving to the door across from the mirrored wall, touched the door release, fighting the urge to flip off any observers behind the glass before the door shut. She sighed and allowed herself a full head-to-toe shudder, hoping to shake off some of the ick that coated her.

Ewww! Ewww, ewww, ewww!

She tossed the robes onto the sink as she started the water flow.

<Evainne? Are you all right?>

She let out a short cry of relief as she stepped beneath the soapy water, just as Kahlym's voice filled her head.

"Please tell me you're here, because if I don't get out of this place soon, I'm gonna castrate your dad."

Unmatched rage poured through their connection. *<Did he touch you?>*

Evainne quickly lathered her hair and rinsed her skin, unsure of how much time she'd have to get ready. "Not for lack of trying. Look, I'm not sure how long before he comes back. He said we're going to see the palace physician. Can you meet me there?"

<Greshon is a friend and loyal to our cause. He will not allow any harm to come to you.>

She captured a mouthful of liquid, swished it around, then spat it out. This whole shower/shampoo/toothpaste/blow dry all in one step sure made for a time-saver. The last of the suds spiraled down the drain as the water switched to air. "Fabu, sweetie, but I'd much rather see your handsome face there, if you get what I mean."

A phantom hand brushed along her cheek. *<We are heading toward the palace as we speak.>*

She reached up to cradle the invisible hand against her face, then smiled at her silly action. At least dressing was getting easier, the robes usually clasping over her shoulders. This outfit was slightly different, though, the small hooks connecting behind her neck with more of a halter top appearance rather than the togas she'd worn before. She tugged upwards at the loose neckline, hoping to cover more of her boobs. Last thing she wanted was for creepy Dad to think she was coming on to him.

"Good," she said, "I'll see you soon. And Kahl?"

<Yes?>

She stalled, unable to say those three little words. So she opted for three others just as important: "Don't get dead."

Chapter 16

Anaxar paced around the room as the opposing door slid open. He stopped, and turned. With her hair unbound and framing her freshly scrubbed skin, she was quite attractive. Many years had passed since he'd taken a concubine, and males did have needs. How would the Emperor react, though, to his wish to lie with the Divine? Her full breasts filled the loose-fitting, rich golden robe nicely, their ample excess peeking out from along the sleek fabric's edges, while the rest of her curves remained a mystery under the flowing skirt. Vanity, or perhaps naivety, had her fidgeting with the material as she emerged.

"May I say, Divine Alice, you look stunning."

She jerked her gaze up, and her cheeks paled. Her wide eyes were unadorned, her complexion sallow in the garish lighting.

She muttered something under her breath, running her fingers through her thick hair. He frowned, and she offered him a timid smile in return, along with a shy dip of her chin.

"Thank you," she replied. "I think I might not be as okay as I thought I was. I, um, nearly passed out while I was getting ready."

In two strides, he was at her side. "Then we must get you to the royal physician immediately. Are you well enough to walk?"

She paused, possibly contemplating her response, then gave a slight nod. "I think I'll be fine. Is it far?"

He tucked his arm beneath hers and escorted her out of the med bay. "It is very close by. We should arrive in a very short time. But if you feel too ill to continue, you will let me know."

They walked in relative silence to the main exit of the ship and, once upon the tarmac, he focused his eyes over his shoulder to the distant horizon. No tell-tale vapor trails announced the presence of any crafts other than the *Perredon*. Nodding, Anaxar led her to the entry gates of the Palace of the Ruling Hand of Jhuen.

"Is this where you live?" she asked, and the awestricken tone of his companion drew his gaze down. She stared agape at the spires and turrets that decorated the façade of the opulent mansion. On some homeworlds, he'd heard it said, Divines were forced to survive in poverty and piety.

This should make his conquest that much easier. As soon as the cleric gave her a clean bill of health, he'd reap his reward with her flat on her back.

He cleared his throat and nodded. "Yes, Divine. Perhaps once you have been declared well by the palace physician, I can show you the entire dwelling."

Her face lit up in childlike excitement, and she bobbed her head enthusiastically. "That would be amazing!"

The massive doors swung open, and the guards bowed low as they passed by. Anaxar caught her active perusal of the interior: she glanced down hallways, studied the ceiling, and even the floor gained her inquisitive attentions. He smirked in anticipation. She'd be so easy to manipulate, which would make her defiling that much sweeter.

All too soon, the royal physician's quarters appeared before them, and she staggered before reaching the door. Ever the gentleman, Anaxar held her arm to steady her wobbly legs.

"Shall I carry you the remaining distance?"

Her brown eyes sharpened with a gleam of unexpected intelligence as the muzzle of his own blaster pressed under his chin. "Nah," she said, "I think I've got this. But thanks anyway."

The door at his back swung open, and with a wink, she shoved him through, her gaze never leaving his. Anaxar snarled, baring his teeth.

"What is the meaning of this!" He stumbled in, tripping over the descending step into the med bay.

"This means you don't get to win today, asshole." She held the gun loosely, her index finger resting beside the trigger. "Sorry." Then she tossed back her head, barking out a mirthless laugh. "Just kidding. I'm not sorry at all."

Her gaze slid away from his, to a door opening behind him, and sneering, he growled loud enough to gain the ear of the emerging cleric.

"Greshon," he said, "call for the guards. This female is threatening your sovereign." The cleric was ancient, but hopefully the doddering old fool hadn't gone deaf yet. Anaxar notched up his chin but heard no shuffling toward the comm unit. Anger creased his brow, and he swiveled his gaze to the silent healer.

To his surprise, beside the physician stood his bastard son, Kahlym. Anaxar had fought to have Kahlym slain at his first cries, all the while protesting his lady wife's infidelity. But Ishtanti did not favor his prayers that day. Instead of tossing out Kahlym's dying body with the rest of the refuse, Anaxar was forced to endure the bastard's continued existence because some prophetic bitch had spewed some nonsense.

As time wore on, however, the family resemblance grew more and more undeniable, but Anaxar would never accept Kahlym as his blood heir. After the untimely passing of Xandar, his second son, Anaxar's hatred for his weak and simpering male accident continued to strengthen.

But the man who stood before him now was not the same spineless child who'd cowered in the shadow of his siblings.

"Kahlym." He'd spat out the name, suppressing the urge to wipe his mouth, lest the lingering taste remain on his lips.

As a boy, Kahlym would have flinched at the mere mention of his name. Today, though, the figure refused to bow and snivel. In fact, powerful arms folded across a broad chest—a well-practiced warrior stance that was almost convincing.

"Father."

"So, you have come home, have you? Do you expect to give the Emperor's prize to him yourself, in hopes for some measure of restored honor?"

A tic tugged at Kahlym's upper lip, while a dangerous fire lit those bi-colored eyes.

"No," he replied. "I came to rescue my female."

KAHLYM STOOD his ground as a tumultuous display of emotions contorted his father's face—rage and disbelief vied for supremacy on Anaxar's arrogant countenance, and had circumstances not been so dire, Kahlym would have found the whole thing entertaining. Only through sheer willpower was he able to stop himself from smiling at the man's torment.

But then again, why shouldn't he smile? The asshole often reveled in Kahlym's suffering during his childhood, even going so far as encouraging others to add to his torture. Disgrace, degradation, and hatred had been heaped upon Kahlym's narrow shoulders for no reason other than an accident of his birth.

A hungry desire to end the man made his fingers twitch, the urge to draw his weapon tempting him like the sweetest fruit, and Kahlym tried to convince himself he could suffer the stain of patricide on his soul. But his heart knew the truth, and that reason alone allowed the man to draw breath for another day.

"Brel?" he said. "Make sure he does not interfere."

His brother clasped him on the shoulder as he followed Kahlym inside the antechamber. "With pleasure, *kherdes-xahn*."

With a small jump, Brel descended the two steps into the lowered med bay. A self-satisfied grin broke upon his face, and he thumped their sire on the back, nearly driving the man to his knees. "Hi, Dad. Miss me?"

A flicker of movement caught Kahlym's eye as his angel dropped the retrieved weapon to her side. Her robe's golden shade did not flatter her as much as the deep greens she'd last worn, but nothing could detract from her heartbreaking beauty. She fidgeted nervously, the hint of a smile starting and stopping as her gaze skimmed the room.

Not daring to wait another moment, Kahlym bounded across the short span and pulled her tight, wrapping his arms around her and cradling her head to his chest. Something clattered to the ground, and soon, her fingers dug into his gearsuit. Kahlym sighed in relief, closed his eyes, and rested his cheek against her soft, flowing tresses. With a deep inhale, he pulled into his soul her soothing and familiar fragrance.

"What took you so long?"

Her strangled words had been laced with tears and a false bravado. Kahlym swallowed the rising tide of emotions and, placing a tender kiss atop her head, trailed his hand down her spine until it rested just above her curvaceous ass.

"*Ziat'xahn.*"

He took in one more breath to draw on the simple peace of her presence before he released his possessive hold. She leaned away and tilted her head back. Her full lips, quivering and slightly parted, were too much of an invitation. He devoured her mouth, his tongue tracing the soft edge of her plump lower lip before plunging inside, and she met him passion for passion, her fingers tugging eagerly at his hair as their tongues twirled and danced.

He swallowed her heavy sigh and gradually dialed down his

raging need. Breathless and hungry for so much more, Kahlym broke the seal of their kiss, then touched his forehead to hers, and a content smile replaced his earlier panic as he savored their stolen moment.

"Divine Alice, what is the meaning of this?" Anaxar demanded.

Kahlym reared back, confusion tugging his eyebrows together as he frowned at Evainne. "Alice?" he inquired.

Her sheepish grin warmed his heart, and the corners of his mouth lifted in automatic response. "Well," she replied, "I had to think fast, and she was the only other person I could think of who'd fallen down an even more screwed-up rabbit hole than me. It was either that, or Dorothy."

Kahlym could only shake his head at her continued ingenuity. "You will have to explain those references to me later."

She winked, eyes dancing with impish delight. "Gonna hold you to that." Then she swiveled her head to Kahlym's father. "You know, you were such an easy mark. All I had to do was bat my eyes and bounce my boobs in your general direction, and you bought the whole act. Damn, maybe I should think about a career on the stage."

Kahlym could only describe his father's look as priceless. "You lied?" he said.

Her body tensed in Kahlym's embrace. "You were going to hand me over on a silver platter to someone who wants to use me like a whore, so I protected myself."

Anaxar at least had the decency to look appalled at her accurate accusation. "But you are a Divine," he said, "and the ranks need to be replenished." He'd slipped back into his haughty demeanor as easily as donning a coat.

Evainne stepped out Kahlym's arms and closed the distance between her and Anaxar. "And so that makes it all right in your eyes? That justifies kidnapping me from my home, from my life, just because some ancient mucky-mucks can't pop out puppies anymore? Did you ever think it's just time for things to change?"

"NEVER!" Anaxar roared, and Kahlym snatched Evainne back into the shelter of his arms before the fingers on his father's clawing hands could grab her.

"Power must be maintained through the blood of the Divines," Anaxar hissed out, daring his sons to defy him. "The Emperor was right, and he will have his prize. But"—he sneered, shifting his ruby eyes toward Kahlym's angel—"since I am certain you must have also lied about that, I don't know what care it is of yours."

Kahlym tightened his embrace as Evainne tried to lunge forward. "No, Evainne. Do not take his bait," he whispered into her ear. "He seeks only to drag you into a fight." His gaze locked on to his father's smug crimson orbs. "I know his tactics all too well."

"As do I," Brel added, his meaty hand digging into Anaxar's neck to keep him firmly in place.

Kahlym looked over at the only quiet party in the room. High Cleric Greshon had stood like a statue during the unorthodox exchange.

"Is there somewhere he can be detained?" he asked.

The old man blinked several times as he continued to stare at the bundle in his arms. Kahlym frowned at the cleric's uncharacteristic silence. "Greshon?"

"Is she the One?" he asked.

Kahlym looked down at his beautiful angel, and a tender smile warmed his lips. "Yes, old friend, she is."

Chapter 17

Qaen swore in every language imaginable, and once he had exhausted the standard curses, he got creative. He threw his goggled eye-phones across the room as he paced circles in the nav chamber of his current ride. The tough, shatter-resistant lenses allowing him to peer into the vastness of space skidded harmlessly beneath the bed. The Emperor had been kind enough to give him one of his fastest cutters to search for Kahlym and that bitch.

So far, though, the only thing he'd discovered was the limits of his patience, as well as the truly vast expanse of the Seventh Quadrant. He'd managed to catch up with Dhaerin, Falka, and Yhan'tu on Lozzan's homeworld. He'd figured someone would stop by with news of what he'd done to that useless piece of crap. In fact, he'd hoped the whole lot of them had taken sanctuary on Outer T'chan. But no such luck.

Seems the goddess truly did favor that reject. He'd even be willing to bet that fucker was now screwing the Divine they rescued, the one the Emperor had such a hard-on for.

"Let her rot in Mordan's hell," he muttered, crouching down to retrieve the discarded lens. "I just want to see that snide bastard roasted over a bonfire."

"Talking to yourself?"

Panza M'Uubair smirked as he stood by the open doorway. Qaen graced him with an obscene gesture as he made his way back to his nav chair.

"Better company than you, M'Uubair. At least I know the responses aren't going to be complete shit."

He climbed into the suspended seat, pointedly ignoring his intruder, until his skin began to itch. Now under careful scrutiny, Qaen slipped his goggles back on and, as he angled the chair into a steeper incline, he growled.

"I know I'm fascinating," he said, "but I don't do boys. So either tell me what you want, or sod off."

Dark silence waited just beyond the moment, though Qaen could sense M'Uubair's lingering presence. Infuriated, Qaen yanked off the eye-phones and openly glared at the bastard.

His self-satisfied smirk pissed off Qaen even more.

"Thank you," said Panza. "I prefer to see your eyes when we speak. That way, I have a better chance of knowing whether or not you are lying."

Qaen grit his teeth, curbing his retort at the tip of his tongue. *Fucker, you wouldn't know the truth if it bit you on the ass.*

Erring on the side of caution, Qaen continued to stare at Panza. His current commander might have been the Emperor's son, but that didn't make him a leader by any stretch of the imagination. Qaen would rather follow Kahlym into Mordan's realm; that fucker was loyal to a fault, which made him such an easy target.

With an exaggerated groan, Qaen adjusted his seat back to vertical, then rested his forearms against his knees. "There," he said. "Happy?"

"Happiness will be achieved once I have the Emperor's prize in my possession."

Qaen threw his hands up and chuckled darkly. "What the fuck

do you think I'm doing here, asshole, playing with myself? Jhuen is not a complete idiot. He's not going to send out announcements to his secret hideout."

Panza's peridot eyes narrowed, and his moustache trembled in irate frustration. *Good,* Qaen thought. *Serves you right for being such a dumbass.*

"Could you at least tell me where he is not." Panza's hand shot up. "Aside from the obvious answer of 'inside this ship.'"

Smirking, Qaen snapped his fingers. "Oh, gee. And that would have been my first guess, too." He flopped back into the body-contouring cushions and stared at the outlying galaxy, whose vast, inky darkness was populated with hundreds of thousands of home-worlds all circling millions of glowing suns, surrounding by billions and billions of tiny pinpoints of twinkling stars.

Where wouldn't he go? *Good fucking question.* If he could eliminate those choices, it might narrow down the search.

"Well," he said at last, "Rimma is definitely high on that list, as well as any planet deep under Thrall control." He rubbed his jawline with the heel of his hand as he continued to ponder.

"What about his home system?"

"Raedyn?" Qaen paused, letting the idea tumble around in his head. "Not likely. Well, since he and his father are not on very good terms, Primus could fall on that list, too. But Khundyl has a soft spot for me. Maybe we should head to Septicon and see if he stopped there for supplies."

Panza's scoff broke his contemplation. "Is there any female in the Dantaran galaxy who does not hold a place for you in her bed?"

At least the asshole had the decency to leave in the wake of his laughter, amused by his own wit. The door slid shut, and Qaen donned his eye-phones once again.

"Only one," he muttered. "And when I get the chance, I will make that bitch beg for it."

Chapter 18

Evainne studied her fingers as they lay atop the thick, marble table that spanned nearly the entire length of the room. Yet again, a huge spread of food had been laid out —platters and tureens filled with exotic dishes and flavorful tidbits. She was finding her way around the fruits and the various finger foods with some success, but once the main course had arrived, the scent of the roasted meat had turned her stomach. It reminded her of burning tires. She watched the boys dig into the meal with gusto, Brel and Dhaerin in seeming competition to see who could clear the most plates.

All around, gazes followed her every move since it seemed the cat was now out of its proverbial bag. Whispers and nods seemed like shouts, and Evainne just wanted to melt into the high-backed chair.

After much discussion, Kahlym had opted to keep dear old Dad nearby instead of locking him in a broom closet as Dhaerin had first suggested. Once the plan of attack had been determined, they paraded him from the med bay to the main dining area, forming an interesting entourage. Servants who passed them did neck-breaking, comedic double takes before welcoming Kahlym and Brel with open smiles. A few went so far as to snicker at the plight of their patriarch.

The girls who happened by had a much different response. At first, they snubbed Kahlym and their group, pressing against the walls to avoid any physical contact. Statuesque and ridiculously beautiful, slender with perfectly proportioned curves, they glided through the narrow halls, their long, flowing copper or golden-wheat colored hair tumbling down their strangely metallic-hued skin. Every eye that sneered toward them were sparkling gems of the purest degrees.

But when they caught sight of Kahlym's fingers entwined with Evainne's, these runway rejects quickly changed their tunes. Eyelashes batted as hips swayed with each approaching step. Evainne muttered under her breath as the sycophantic females practically spilled out of their tops in their attempts to greet him.

She had to give him props, though. Their attentions were as surprising to him as they were to the rest of their party. R'uan glared at the gathered and giggling masses, and shooed them along, while Brel and Dhaerin offered to keep the stragglers warm if they were still in need of late night company. But their jibes were playful and without merit.

Others, namely the older women, would take her hand in reverent care. Evainne stood in bewilderment as they pressed their foreheads against the back of her hand before stepping back, eyes downcast. Words of benediction were murmured, but nothing coherent ever made it to her ears. She glanced to Kahlym for explanation, unsure of how to react, but his curiously stoic expression did nothing to calm the writhing snakes in her stomach.

Questions continued to fill her mind as they made their way through the maze of hallways until they reached their final destination. Would she be expected to pass some sort of test to prove her supposed Divine status? Would she be stuck living in a glass cage, set on display for all the universe to see? Thoughts churned as she recalled the snide comments regarding Kahlym and his supposed disfigurement.

Well, if she truly was something of a big deal in this world, then she would make some changes about judging people based on their looks alone. She tightened her grip on Kahlym's hand, grateful to have his strength while in unfriendly territory.

"This should be fun," Brel murmured as a pair a broad, jeweled doors swung open. Evainne turned her head, stunned, as a regal woman glided in, draped in robes of royal purple embellished with golden pearls. She scanned their ragtag group with thinly veiled contempt.

Kahlym nodded sharply, breaking the silence with one word: "Mother."

Evainne wasn't sure what had surprised the woman more: seeing her husband trussed up, or seeing her youngest son with a girl. The cruel beauty of her ageless features contorted through a myriad of emotions, until the cleric who whispered to all he encountered told Kahlym's mother who Evainne was supposed to be. At once, eyes like the clearest diamonds pinned her with all the delicacy of a kid staring at a plate of Brussels sprouts: disgust and revulsion curling her blood red lips at the bitter pill she'd have to swallow.

"Grand and wondrous be the blessings upon our house with your presence, Blessed Divine. A meal shall be prepared in your honor."

Apparently, manners dictated Evainne receive a formal greeting, but an unconvincing bow and a monotonous speech by rote was all the woman was willing to offer. To be honest, Evainne was tired of being treated like some sort of religious icon. She'd just broken Falka and Yhan'tu of their genuflecting habits. Now she had a whole new crop of grovelers to deal with.

For the first time since arriving across the universe, Evainne actually wanted to go home, wanted to go back to that blessed invisibility that she had once cursed while growing up. She never desired fame; being in the limelight was not her secret dream. She only wanted to have some friends, people she could call up on some random Tuesday night to get together for a couple of drinks, or to go catch the latest movie, or anything that allowed for social interaction.

But this?…She'd never wanted any of this, all those stares and the whispers as she passed by. *And this is only one house on one planet.* Granted, it was a friggin' ginormous house, but one place nonetheless.

What would she even expect if she let this whole crazy universe know what she was?

The coiling snakes spun faster as the temperature climbed up a notch or twelve. She huffed in air as she attempted to keep pace with her increasing heart rate. Saliva pooled in her mouth, and she swallowed hard against a rising panic.

Shit. I'm gonna puke.

Before she could embarrass herself, she jumped to her feet and, knocking the chair behind her to the floor, dashed out of the room. She pounded on door after door, confused and praying for some luck, until she found a way outside.

Sweet air kissed her cheek just as she threw up into a rather festive-looking shrub. The door's archway was still close enough to use as an anchor, holding her up on wobbly legs, but she didn't know just how much longer she could defy gravity. Tears blurred her vision as she wiped off her mouth with the back of a trembling hand.

"Is there something amiss?"

The prim and proper voice behind her wasn't the one she'd expected to hear.

Oh, great. Way to make a first impression with Mom.

Her mind raced for a viable response, her head both nodding and shaking simultaneously. Given the current knowledge of Kahlym's relationship with his parents and the horror stories she'd heard about his mother's lack of maternal instincts, Evainne was torn between spilling her guts and telling her to piss off. But, since she had already accomplished the first option in bright Technicolor, she opted to split the difference. Leaning back, Evainne felt the solid surface of the doorjamb at her back and slid down to a semi-dignified heap onto the soft ground.

"I'm…aw, hell, I am so far from all right, I'd need a pair of binoculars to even see it."

SO, this is the Grand Divine.

Jaleen ni'Jhuen hovered in the doorway over the sick child, who was most decidedly not the image of the all-powerful deity Kahlym's birthing midwife had spun. This female appeared barely old enough to be allowed out on her own. She hadn't spoken a word during the entire meal, her wide doe eyes glancing around in curious study. She hadn't eaten enough to sate a babe, yet now she was vomiting in the gardens.

Jaleen wasn't sure how long she'd have with the female before Kahlym came to her rescue. When the Divine had spoken, her voice was not what Jaleen had expected—it was deeper than she should have had, her tone filled with maturity and intelligence, and a surprising degree of hopelessness. Her choice of words had been a bit odd, but the message had been unmistakable.

Jaleen took a chance and reached down to touch the female lightly on her shoulder.

"Did the food not agree with you, Divine?"

The young woman shook her head, her loose hair shivering as she heaved a heavy sigh. "I wish it was that easy, although that might be part of it, yes." When she turned her face up, her cheeks' pallor gave Jaleen pause. She knelt closer, an odd, motherly instinct stirring deep within her heart.

"Divine," she whispered, "what troubles you?"

Again, the free-falling bloodwine tresses shook. "Please, my name is Evainne."

As Jaleen opened her mouth to rebuke the degree of familiarity, the young female raised her hand. "Yeah, I know. Kahlym's been trying to teach me about all the rules and regs, but I'm just done. And honestly, right now, I feel like complete crap and not like a divine anything."

Jaleen frowned at the blunt, casual language with no manner of protocol observed. The Divine even seemed to go so far as to assume some lesser level of formality. Was this a test to determine her degree of piety?

Caught off guard by the odd behavior, Jaleen could only sit in silence as she prayed for the correct answer to present itself. She studied the unique, alien face before her. The young woman's pale skin sat in fierce contrast to her deep brown eyes and ruddy burgundy hair. She was not overly small, her ample bosom barely contained by the open-sleeved gown. The golden fabric did not complement her coloring, adding to the jaundiced shade of her cheeks, and because the robe was gathered at the waist, Jaleen was able to discern the curve of the Divine's hips, much more pronounced than in the slender waifs common among the young females on Raedyn Primus. Her hands bore no jeweled ornaments, nor were her fingers tipped with sharpened talons. One plain, thick, silver band graced the thumb of her left hand.

Were the Divines of her race marked only by a single piece of jewelry? Were they forced into a pauper's role?

A sad smile crossed the young woman's innocent face as she started to her feet. "It's okay," she said. "Guess I just need to get used to it."

"Evainne!"

Kahlym rushed through the still-open doorway and dropped to his knees beside her, careful to avoid knocking over Jaleen in his exuberance. His behavior bordered on impertinent as he lifted his wary gaze to hers, and he hesitated a heartbeat, eyes cold as he gathered the Divine into his arms.

"How dare you—" Jaleen started to sputter, but to her utter

amazement, the female ignored her protestations and instead, returned his warm embrace, burying her face into Kahlym's chest. His mismatched eyes glared daggers, defiance painting a haughty expression. As he stroked the female's back, he offered a glass of water to the unconventional Divine who, with trembling fingers, accepted the gift. She rinsed her mouth, clearing her palate before draining the cup.

The tender moment was at odds with every lesson drilled into her since childhood: only the worthy were allowed in a Divine's presence, and to touch them in any manner was never permitted. Jaleen blinked repeatedly to assure herself that she was indeed seeing things as they truly were.

"I'm sorry, Kahl," Evainne said, her voice, thick with emotion, pouring from her huddled form. "I can't do this. I just can't."

Jaleen's mouth dropped open at their semi-private conversation, and her brows knitted together. *What is the meaning of this?*

Chapter 19

Kahlym held his rage focused on his mother until Evainne's heartfelt words had spilled out. He closed his eyes and pressed a soft kiss atop her head. Dear Ishtanti, how he wished he was back aboard his ship where he could comfort her in the way she needed and deserved. She trembled in his arms, her skin damp, cool to his touch, the acrid stench of vomit strong and near.

"I have you, *ziat'xahn*," he whispered into her ear, cautious of the present company, yet he could not sit by as Evainne suffered.

"This is..." his mother began, her voice like shards of ice cutting through the peace and warmth he only experienced with his Evainne. Her righteous indignation mirrored the exact tones of his father's words, their constant disapproval always weighing down his soul. Kahlym opened his mouth, prepared to return fire with a venomous rebuttal.

To his surprise, his beautiful angel beat him to the punch.

"This is what I've been trying to tell you," she said, "if only you could pull your head out of your ass long enough to listen."

He released his protective hold, and Evainne turned to look at his mother.

"I play by my own rules," she went on, "and none of them have ever included treating people like shit, just because some dumbass says I should."

His mother's stunned look was almost as priceless as the one that had recently graced his father's own countenance. But fear for Evainne's health and safety stopped him from reveling in her discomfort.

"Is this how the Divines on your homeworld behave?" Jaleen asked.

"No." Evainne shook her head, tucking herself further into Kahlym's embrace. "This is how I behave," she replied. "Back on my planet, I'm no one—at all. One in about seven billion. I'm not a blip on anyone's radar. I have no friends, no family, no…no nothing. We don't worship anything other than money and pretty people on the silver screen. Religion is either a business or a weapon. All of this"—she gestured to the surrounding lush gardens—"all of the bowing, and the looks, and the whispers…" She turned toward Kahlym, her beautiful brown eyes laced with heavy sadness. "I'm sorry, but I just don't think I can be what you need me to be."

Kahlym ignored his mother's sputterings as he trailed his knuckles along Evainne's cheek, brushing away the silvery tracks of her tears. "You have nothing for which to apologize, *ziat'xahn*. I believe you are exactly what you are meant to be. Already you have brought hope to so many—the crew of my ship, plus many of the palace's citizens are beginning to take heart once again. And they only saw you; they have yet to speak to you."

Her unladylike, but appropriate, sharp laugh drew up the corners of his lips. "Yeah," she said, "won't that be a swell time. Then they'll really get the full experience." He held her close as she shook her head, heaving a heavy sigh. "Don't listen to me, Kahl. This has just been one total clusterfuck of a day, and I'd kill for a long, hot bath."

"Wha—? How? Never have I—!" Jaleen continued to spew gibberish as he stood, guiding Evainne to her feet.

"What is the main cause for your concern, Mother?"

He looked down at her, her jaw agape with confusion twisting her regal face. He almost pitied her if the truth of his answer hadn't rung in his ears.

<*You are unworthy of*—>

"What do I need to do to prove my worth? You act as if I'd chosen to be born like this." He seethed but forced his arms to keep a tender hold on Evainne, the urge to strike out at his mother fierce and demanding.

Jaleen scrambled to her feet, hatred in her cold, colorless diamond eyes. "You should be grateful you were allowed to live beyond your first breath, *kagg'naeh*. If not for the meddling of that old witch, Shezheer, you would have been slaughtered while you wailed."

Kahlym bared his teeth at the insult, dangerous words of retaliation balanced on the tip of his tongue, when the air chilled without warning. He glanced around, searching for the sudden clouds from an oncoming storm as the temperature continued to drop, and he half expected to find ice crystals clinging to the nearby golden leaves. It took a second for him to ferret out the source of the surprise cold.

Evainne rose to her feet and stood tall, her intense stare aimed at his stunned mother. Although her arms hung loose by her sides, tension vibrated the space around her. Heat slipped off of her body as she stepped away from him, and the degree of masterful control of her emotions was a thing of absolute beauty.

"While I am around, lady, you might want to think carefully about what you say." Venom had dripped from her words, with the promise of violent repercussion apparent in the spaces between each.

His mother dropped to her knees, and only his knowledge of Evainne stopped Kahlym from doing the same. To incur the wrath of a Divine was an immediate and irreversible death sentence.

"Please, *Dym Char'ann*. I beg for your—"

"Beg all you want, bitch. Until you start treating everyone—especially your own sons—with some common decency, I'm not giving you the time of day."

She spun to face him, eyes ablaze with anger. "Get me out of here before I do something I'm going to regret."

"Where would—"

"I don't fucking care." She frantically waved off the rest of his question. "Just get me away from here—now."

Panic kicked his legs into gear, and he nodded sharply, whisking her back inside. The ship was quite a distance and he feared for her. Never before had he seen her so upset; as they headed toward his private rooms, she moved with an angry purpose, steps choppy as the golden gown fluttered to keep pace. He placed a hand on her back to guide her down each twist and turn, and they traveled in stiff silence, passing guards and servants until they finally reached their destination.

His heart pounded as he triggered the door, and she nearly ran inside. He followed her in, the door shutting at his back, yet he remained frozen. She stood two steps away, her head dropped into her hands. Hesitantly, he approached and touched her shoulder, anger blending with anguish radiating from her trembling body.

"Evainne?"

Even if he lived a thousand years, he would never forget the heartbreaking look of grief and disbelief on his angel's face as she turned toward him.

"How can people be so hateful?" she whispered, and he closed the scant distance between them, needing to comfort her. She remained statue-still as he wrapped his arms around her.

"Your parents, my parents..." she went on. "What the hell is wrong with these people, that they can't just accept us and let us be who we are?" Her rage was beginning to fade, but its lingering effects had taken its toll, her voice cracking with each word. "I never claimed to be perfect, or to be the best, but dammit, I did the best I could, and it was never good enough for them. Now? To come here and find that even in so-called advanced races, parents still treat their kids like shit if they're not what they'd imagined them to be?"

Kahlym closed his eyes, stroking his fingers up and down her spine as he cradled her. She took in a shaky breath, shoulders collapsing as she gave in to her sorrow. Offering her the warmth of his embrace, he stood guard over her as she wept, helpless to do more. He prayed his presence was what she needed. With each stuttered inhale, his drive to protect her grew.

"Shh, *ziat'xahn*. Forget about them."

He pressed kisses into her thick, fragrant hair, gliding toward the grav couch suspended near the picture window. She'd had an attentive fascination with the gardens at Khundyl's palace, and he hoped the view now would brighten her mood. Keeping a tender hold, he sat down, then pulled her into his embrace. The rush of angry tears had lessened during their short trek, and once she was nestled into his lap, head buried in his armpit, her breathing had evened out. In the growing silence, tension eased.

"Can we blast them all out the nearest airlock?"

Kahlym chuckled at her mumbled words and stroked his fingers through her thick, tumbling curls. Even in the tumultuous onslaught of violent emotions, she'd managed to keep both her wit and her wits.

"Don't tempt me. I cannot begin to tell you the number of times I'd planned their demise." He cradled her face in his palms, wiping away the tears that streaked her cheeks with the pads of his thumbs. Lost in her eyes, he sat in silence, her breathing the only sound. Her warm brown orbs shifted.

Gone was her anger and sorrow, and the soft hues took on a more sensual glow. He leaned in, intent on devouring her lips, when she turned away and scrambled out of his lap, shaking her head as an embarrassed laugh squeaked out.

"Umm, hang on. Don't move," she said.

Don't move? Kahlym blinked to reengage his brain as she searched the wall until she discovered the bathroom and vanished behind the door. Was she still ill? Should he call for Greshon?

The sounds of running water stopped almost as quickly as they'd started, and Evainne reemerged. His bewildered expression must have been more apparent than he realized. She smiled and slunk back, her lush curves barely shielded by the flowing gown.

"Sorry, just needed to, uh…freshen up a little more. I mean, I couldn't let you kiss me after…well, you know." A sheepish blush painted her cheeks as he put the pieces together. She'd thought of him; her actions had been directly for his benefit.

The setting twin suns cast a multicolored halo around her as she approached, and although he preferred the green dress that complemented her natural beauty, he had to applaud the cut of her current regal robe. Her breasts peeked out from the edges of the soft fabric, while the valley between them begged for him to sample. He had only scant moments to realize her journey had reached its end, and he trailed his gaze up from her eye-level assets as she sank down onto his lap.

Responding on primal instinct, he gripped her hips, grinding his straining, bound erection against the apex of her thighs. Her back arched as she dug her fingers into his shoulders, a heavy moan encouraging him. The sweet scent of her arousal filled the air, and he was unable to resist temptation any longer. With a hungry growl, he shredded the flimsy garment and devoured her bared breasts. She groaned in response, cradling his head as her legs tightened around his thighs.

"Please tell me you've got a fly on that suit of yours, hon."

He gave her nipple one more teasing lick before his eyebrows tugged together and he trailed his gaze up to her face. "A…a what?"

She tilted her chin down, mischief darkening her deep brown eyes.

"Just get those damned pants off."

Chapter 20

Evainne stared down into the face of her own personal hero, and her heart did a little somersault. Yet again, he'd swooped in to save the day, namely stopping her from tearing his mom a new orifice.

Now, she only wanted to feel him so deep inside her that she didn't know where she ended and he began.

She never needed sex before, but with Kahlym, it was more than just a physical act. With him, she felt empowered, invincible, and vulnerable, all at the same time. The depth of his attention to her needs and desires was a deadly addiction and she had become hooked.

Encouraging him to act, she reached for the triggering release on the collar of his gearsuit and peeled the skintight leather open.

His swirling tourmaline eyes burned with passion as his confusion melted away, a hungry grin serving as an answer. He slid his hands from her hips, making short work of the striptease and a heartbeat later, his bare flesh pressed against her inner thighs. The heat from his rock-hard cock drove all of the moisture in her body to the point of contact. Not wanting to waste another second,

Evainne slipped her hand between their bodies and gripped his shaft.

She captured his gaze, lost in its intoxicating beauty as she slowly impaled herself, while his fingers bit into her hipbones, guiding her with tender care. She flattened her palms against his chest, rolling her hips as he eased his massive erection into her damp channel, each inch gained bringing her one orgasm closer to a complete sexual meltdown. Her eyes drifted shut as she reveled in the sensation of the powerful male between her legs, his muscles tensing and flexing in his careful, loving invasion.

Love.

She'd fallen in love with him.

She clenched her jaw, the depths of this knowledge triggering a full-body shock wave and, crying out, she arched back as he penetrated the final inch. Shudders cascaded down her spine, and Evainne dug her fingers into Kahlym's shoulders to stay glued onto this plane.

Words she didn't understand spilled from his lips, and she returned to her body. She dropped her chin and dragged her eyes open to meet his expression, which she could only describe as "reverently terrified." Ancient, painful shadows haunted his beautiful eyes and panic had paled his cheeks.

Casting aside her fears, she cupped his face.

"I love you, Kahlym."

His breathing quickened, and the corners of her mouth tugged up.

"I'm sure that's no big surprise, but—"

His kiss swallowed the rest of her thought, along with any remaining brain cells, while his arms wrapped around her shoulders and his hips rocked, his slow thrusts stoking the raging fire in her veins. Evainne writhed, her knees squeezing his thighs as he milked another orgasm from her.

Oxygen became secondary; only the feeling of his skin and the touch of his lips was necessary for her to live. Lightning zinged through her blood, flying her higher and higher, his tender and loving pace shattering her control until her entire body trembled, her heart pounding like a jackhammer against her ribs.

Pinpoints of light danced along her narrowing vision, and her arms became like lead.

What's happening to me?

With patient care, air filled her lungs, and together, they breathed in time. Even her racing heart matched his in speed. As one, they moved, each pulse and thrust synchronized in complete harmony. She clung to him as her release inched closer—ecstasy; pure, terrifying, and all-consuming, drove her onward until it pitched her over the ultimate edge.

I LOVE YOU.

Her simple words had unlocked the final door to his heart, and on instinct, their soulbond was forged and the Joining had begun. With his shaft buried deep in her hot, gripping channel, his spirit sought hers, while the sweet friction of her hardened nipples cut into his chest and fanned the fires racing under his skin. He cradled her body against his, her damp, bloodwine tresses wrapping around his arms, and he lost himself in the moment. Her lips were like silk, her passions a delicious dichotomy of tender and fierce.

With each inhale, his hips surged forward, then retreated as the breath left him, flowing into her. Never had he dreamt of experiencing a true Soulcry, the deepest and most profound connection between any two beings, and his heart soared, even as a tiny corner of his mind warned him of the possibility of her refusal. He knew she could not know exactly what had just transpired between them, but he would deal with that later.

For now, she was his, and that was all that mattered.

A shudder ran down her body, and she tightened around him. Kahlym swallowed her erotic sigh as he came hard, her gripping sheath milking every drop from him. Soon, time resumed its slow trek until he was once again in his own skin and he carefully broke the seal of their mouths, giving one final chaste kiss to her slightly parted lips.

He lifted his eyelids to drink in her flushed milk-and-honey complexion. Rivulets of sweat glistened in the valley between her heaving breasts, her deep rosy peaks standing in dark contrast to her pale skin. Her lashes painted soft black crescents along her cheeks, keeping her beautiful brown eyes hidden from him. Yet it was the frown creasing her forehead that held his attention. He cradled her face and brushed away the tears as they coursed down.

"Evainne?"

His call was met with a silent whirlwind of thoughts, her emotions playing chase in her mind. He held her tight, resting his chin atop her thick curls. Even though their spirits had returned to their prospective bodies, a lingering trace of the powerful connection still tethered them together. Confusion bled through her skin, overshadowing the fading glow, and her body shook and trembled.

"Think on this later, *ziat'xahn*. Please, do not cry."

"I-I-I didn't even know I s-s-s-started." Her shoulders shook with her sobs as she crawled deeper into his embrace.

He threaded his fingers through her hair, swaying from side to side as he sought to soothe her. The grav couch was comfortable, but he needed to stretch out and sleep in his own bed. Sadly, that would mean moving.

With tender care, he eased out from her moist sheath, then slipped his arm beneath her knees. During their short trip to the bed, Kahlym whispered softly to her, each loving word followed by a feather-light kiss.

Her tears had dried up by the time he'd laid her down on the cool sheets, her breathing steadying, and he discarded the tattered remnants of her gown as well as his gearsuit before settling her in between the thin fabrics. Evainne dug her fingers into his biceps, her eyes wide as he crawled in beside her. Holding her worried gaze, he smiled reassuringly and pulled her close, curling his body around hers.

"I promise, *ziat'xahn*, I am not going far. Rest, my angel."

Her eyelashes tickled his bare chest, the long pause between blinks troubling him, and he stroked her back in soothing circles. His deep breath was answered by her responding inhale and he carefully guided her breathing, hoping to calm her fears as well as his own. After a few moments of silence, her tension melted as her eyelids fluttered down. Butterfly kisses, coupled with the steady rise and fall of her chest was all the incentive he needed to follow her into sleep.

Blessed Ishtanti, he thought, *tell me I did the right thing.*

Chapter 21

Anaxar muttered under his breath as he neared his bedchamber, entourage in tow.

Watched over like a common criminal in my own home.

After Kahlym had vanished chasing the skirts of that bitch of a Divine, Brel had chosen two palace guards loyal to their pathetic cause to escort him back to his quarters. Apparently, royal sentinels weren't good enough to ensure he arrived safely at his chambers.

My private chambers. Rage seethed, but his growls did not hasten their journey. They stopped just outside the threshold, and the guards took up their prospective places, ensuring that Anaxar's night would remain relatively undisturbed and blessedly unobserved. Long ago, his father had installed surveillance vids in every room, save one. In this one, secrets were kept secret.

Yet even that knowledge was of no comfort. The need for violence and retribution simmered in his blood. Anaxar slammed his fist against the control panel, then stormed inside to pace the room like a caged beast, arms linked at the small of his back as the door slid closed. The thick rugs muffled the sounds of his boot heels as he schemed in silence.

That bastard thinks he can just waltz in and command me?

He hurled the nearest object at the wall. The decorative goblet shattered and crystal shards rained down. Although iridescent flecks now peppered the thick ivory carpeting, the dazzling display did little to alleviate his dark mood.

"I take it, husband mine, you are not pleased by your son's return?"

He snapped his gaze toward Jaleen, who sat at her vanity table, removing her jewelry and makeup. She fiddled with the clasp on the ornate set of deep purple pearls at her throat as she eyed him in the mirror. In the prime of her youth, she was the most sought-after female on all of Raedyn Primus, and although the cycles had been kind to his wife, the creases around her eyes had deepened and the strands of white-gold that wove through her jet curls were more pronounced.

"I would be pleased to see that abomination strung up by his balls in the square." He strode over to her, his steps loose and predatory, and gripped the rounded chair back, imagining Kahlym's throat beneath his fingers. The wood creaked in inert pain. "You spoke to the female. Can the Divines have made a mistake?"

Her face drained, fear paling her copper skin. "No" she said. "She is a Divine; of that, you can be sure. The ease at which she wields her skills was terrifying. I do not believe the old fools have an inkling of her true abilities." Jaleen swallowed hard, the muscles in her throat rippling, and she turned around, mischief dancing in her diamond depths. "But neither does she, and I believe we can use this to our advantage."

His brow furrowed as he considered her proposal. "For anything to work, we need to get her away from that bastard of yours and any of those on his crew. They all seemed overly protective of her."

Jaleen waved her hand dismissively. "That is because they see her as a tiny, weak creature. It would be a simple thing to trade her to the Emperor to return our family's seat on the Ruling Counsel.

Perhaps, if she's properly motivated, she might even dispatch the old goat for us."

The corners of his lips curled up. "If the bitch can get with child, that would ensure the claim by our house."

Jealousy flashed across his wife's face. He'd never kept his dalliances secret from her, but no bastard had ever come from them, keeping her with the title of Mother of the House.

"You believe yourself to be up to the task, husband?" She'd spat out the final word before giving him her back to complete her nightly routine.

He grabbed her shoulders, his embrace tighter than a lover's, and glared at her reflection. "Do you doubt my skills to father a son?"

She snarled an erotic reply, her heavy sigh betraying the truth of her response. "I doubt your skills to steal the prize your son has claimed."

He dug his talons into her neck and, drinking in the rising scent of her arousal, he grasped her flowing hair and tugged. Her throat lay open to him, and he whispered hotly against her skin, "She will beg for me to take her, just as you will beg soon enough, wife."

Anaxar claimed her mouth with a ruthless kiss, grinning at her weak attempts to deny him.

I will get my way in this as well, boy. Mark my words.

Chapter 22

Kahlym gazed at Evainne as Greshon spoke to her, longing and uncertainty tugging at his heart. Dressed once again in robes, these of his family's regal blue, she lit up the gardens with her ethereal beauty, and his soul ached to taste her lips.

Two risings had passed since their Joining and nothing had been spoken of it. He'd barely slept that night, his mind spinning at the ramifications of his hasty actions.

He had made a grave error. He felt it in the very pit of his stomach. He'd assumed, with her words of love, she'd been prepared to accept the gift of his Soulcry. No deeper bond could exist between two hearts and he only wanted to show her how much she'd changed his life, but in his haste, he'd never asked her if she understood the significance and depth of their connection. Shame haunted his dreams, with self-loathing fast on its heels.

As if the goddess knew of his deep misgivings, She threw every manner of chaos his direction that next morning. His link had blown up as the first sun rose, and he'd sprung into action, eager for the distraction. Word had spread quickly throughout Raedyn

Primus of not only his return, but also of the Winterborn female at his side. The nobles had demanded an immediate audience with Evainne, while the clerics adamantly insisted she be tested and trained. Together with Brel, they ran interference, giving her space while pondering their next move.

Courtly intrigue had never been his strong suit, but to protect his love, Kahlym would learn those rules. During the hours away from her side, he wished for nothing more than to return to their bed and lose himself in her loving embrace. Yet, when he stood in her presence, his uncertainty crippled him, stealing his voice and his courage. He owed her more than his absence, but he did not even know where to begin with his explanation.

<You could start with the truth, kherdes.>

His gaze shifted to Brel's harsh citrine glare. Kahlym clenched his teeth, quashing his rising growl.

<What truth? That I fucked up? No, I have to figure out some way to—>

Brel gripped Kahlym's shoulder and dragged him toward the nearest escape. Safely inside the palace, Kahlym spun to face his only confidant, guilt churning his insides.

"Don't give me that shit, Kahl. You make it sound like you're some reject—"

"I AM!" he bellowed, shoving away his brother's needed counsel. "That's just what I am. I was never smart enough to see it before, and now, I've trapped her. And she's so much more than a Divine Healer." He stalked the secure room, grateful for the additional privacy measures.

"Tell me something I don't know. She's amazing, Kahl. We've all seen that. She's smart and—"

Kahlym waved off the rest of his litany of her qualities, shaking his head, and silence coated the room as he searched for the courage to say what he believed in his heart.

"What aren't you saying?" Brel asked.

Kahlym's nostrils flared, the sharp, shallow inhale echoing

through the chamber. He closed his eyes, sending a prayer to Ishtanti before he faced his brother.

"I…I think she might be a Divine Fury."

Brel's face drained and his jaw hung open.

And you consigned her to live with your pathetic ass for all eternity, added the self-deprecating words in his father's voice.

Kahlym prepared for a similar sentiment to fall from his brother's lips. What he did not expect, though, was the bone-crushing hug.

"That is the best news I've heard all damned day!" Brel boomed as Kahlym struggled to suck in air while being bounced like an infant. Rolling laughter spun around him.

"How…can this…be good news?" he said, forcing the words out with the remaining oxygen in his lungs. As much as he wanted to stay in his dark and foul mood, the infectious sounds of his brother's elation had lightened his despair. "Brel," he said, "can't…breathe… here."

The locked arms released, and Kahlym lifted his gaze. Joy unlike any he'd ever seen reflected in the citrine eyes above him.

"Don't you see, *kherdes-xahn*? She is made for you."

Confusion tugged Kahlym's eyebrows together. "How can Evainne's even more elevated status prove she was made for me?"

Brel continued to beam as he led Kahlym to the chairs beside the grand picture window. "The prophecy states 'Winterborn will control the Fates,' and there is a mention of fury in it as well."

Kahlym groaned at the cursed words that had spared his life and set his parents against him.

He collapsed heavily into the overstuffed seat. "But it didn't say I would find and fall in love with a Divine Fury."

"What does it matter?" Brel crouched to capture his gaze. "She is here, she is real, and she doesn't seem like the weak type. Hell, she put Father in his place, and I'm guessing she gave Mother the same treatment."

The hint of a smile touched Kahlym's lips. "Growing up, I

didn't think anything could ever scare that woman. Watching her cower and tremble at Evainne's feet was so satisfying."

Brel chuckled with a sly grin. "I wish I could've seen that. So was that when you'd figured she was more than just a Divine Healer?"

Kahlym rested his head against a nearby pillar, stared at the ornate skyscape mosaic on the ceiling. "No," he said. "Back at Graey's, she confided she had received training as an Adept."

Brel sat down, frowning. "Wait—I thought she said Divines were not worshipped or prepared on her homeworld."

Kahlym shrugged. "According to her, her skills were honed while she was in exile from her family, and these abilities were only meant to entertain or comfort."

Brel rested his forearms on his knees, gaze unfocused, and they sat in deep silence, lost in their own thoughts.

"You have to tell her, brother."

Kahlym cringed at the truth of Brel's simple statement. "Tell her what? Tell her she is destined to save our worlds? That a prophecy states you are supposed to love me, and because I was stupid enough to believe it, I made you mine without even asking if that was what you wanted, and now you're stuck with me until the stars go out?"

"Well, I have heard of more romantic proposals, but I guess that ain't so bad."

EVAINNE NODDED her thanks to the old doctor. He'd answered quite a few of her questions, and she only had to remind him about twenty times that she actually had a name. Things must have been improving.

The morning after the most frighteningly intense sexual encounter of her life, Kahlym was a ghost, appearing as a figure off in the distance or vanishing as soon as she turned her head. She knew this behavior all too well: the "morning after" avoidance. Once, during a college party, she'd watched couples form, dissolve, then re-form with other partners elsewhere all night long. Curious, she'd opted to stay overnight to see the social experiment to its fruition. Sure enough, in the light of day, the amorous gropers had been a bit more subdued and distant.

Yet there was something sadly different about Kahlym's attitude: a deeper sentiment that didn't have the same vibe as the horny students. It certainly wasn't juvenile embarrassment about a lackluster performance. No, this was regretful guilt—palpable and heart-wrenching. In the glimpses she had caught of him, he oozed pain and remorse. She'd awoken to an empty bed, and it had remained the same when she'd crawled into it at night.

The next day, she spent trying to learn as much as she could about her new digs. Stuck in another friggin' robe, Evainne walked the halls, setting each turn and new path to memory. She glanced through open doorways, peeked behind closed ones. And room after room, she studied the lay of the land, trying to remember what went where.

Shit, this place is a goddamned fortress. Walls were thick and doors were soundproof. Yet, as she wandered, Evainne sensed the surrounding presence of people, like the ghostly brush of fingertips against her spirit; when she passed by any room, the tiny hairs on the back of her neck stood at attention.

At first, she thought it was some kind of space-age air conditioning, a cool breath that tickled her bare skin. Drawn to discover more, she placed her open palm against one closed door … and gasped as the figures inside jumped into her view, as bright and as clear as if she were looking through a window.

Three children were laughing, while a small, three-legged creature romped and bounced around the room. Evainne turned her head to find two women preparing a meal, attentions fixed on the task at hand. One woman smiled and offered a taste to the other. A sly grin warmed the second one's lips as she tenderly cupped the offered spoon and sipped, never breaking eye contact with her fellow cook.

Evainne yanked away her hand, hot guilt singeing her cheeks for playing Peeping Tom, and the door snapped back to its solid state. The sudden reversal threw her off-kilter, and she made a desperate grasp for the nearest object.

To her surprise, her fingers gripped something rather limb-like and she swallowed back her rising bile, trailing her gaze along the line of an arm garbed in bright blue and gleaming gold fabric that suddenly calmed her frazzled nerves. A strange serenity washed over her. Sucking in a stuttered breath, Evainne straightened her spine and met the aquamarine eyes above her.

"Is something amiss? Are you unwell, *Dym Char'ann?*"

Relieved, she smiled weakly, then shook her head, grateful to see the friendly face of the palace doctor.

"As much as I'd love to say no, I'm not sure if that's the right answer. And you can call me Evainne, remember?"

Greshon offered her a physician-standard all-knowing nod and patted her hand, his shimmering golden skin bright against her pale ivory.

"Perhaps you are in need of a constitutional," he said and, with confident strides, Greshon led her toward the beautiful gardens outside. The door whooshed open, and Evainne inhaled the crisp, flowery air, which reminded her of a blend of a cool autumn night and an early spring bouquet. Two suns, one icy green, the other a bold pink, shone bright in the alien sky, blanketing her in a comforting warmth.

"What am I doing here?" Evainne wasn't exactly sure to whom she was asking the question: the stars, the universe, her companion, or herself. No matter the recipient, though, she didn't expect to get much of a definite answer. Just getting the words out of her mind was a good start. She dropped her shoulders and pondered her current state.

"If I were to say 'enjoying the fresh air,'" Greshon said, "would it gain a smile?"

Evainne chuckled lightly and returned her gaze to the older man. Everyone in this new world had eyes like gems, and the intelligent blue-green that met her reflected honesty and true willingness to help.

"Yeah," she replied. "Yeah, it would. Thanks." She took in another deep breath, allowing the surrounding peace to seep into her body, then exhaled with a huff. "This might sound like a really dumb question, but can you tell me exactly what this prophecy said? I keep hearing snippets of it, but nothing more. I know it has to do with some sort of end of the rebellion, or an uprising, or whatever the hell you want to call it, but that's it."

Greshon hesitated, caught off-guard by her direct tone, and for a moment, she feared he would begin the whole bowing routine and usher her back inside. Risking the possibilities, she covered his hand with hers.

"Please," she said.

Seemed the "magic word" had power in this realm as well. Greshon's expression melted, and he dipped his chin.

"As you wish, *Dym Char'ann.*"

She forced herself not to jump for joy and followed his gaze to a nearby bench. Together, they crossed the weaving stone path to sit beneath the shade of a massive magenta tree, its slouching limbs offering privacy within its shadows.

Evainne kept her hands in her lap as she waited patiently for him to begin. Her companion studied the skies so intently, she nearly followed his searching eyes, but instead, she gnawed on her lower lip, bouncing her leg in time with her racing thoughts. A faint breeze rustled the surrounding leaves, the sound and their sweet fragrance soothing. At last, Greshon spoke.

"The first prophecy was written in the Scrolls of the Ancestors and foresaw the birth of a child with twin star eyes. As with most ancient words, it was vague, and as such, misinterpreted. It spoke of great change to come when the child reached maturity."

Greshon paused to stare off into the distance.

Evainne coughed softly to clear away the fear coating her throat. "How long ago was this?" she asked, her rough voice drawing the doctor's attention. He turned to face her. Compassion and sadness had blended in his eyes. *Had he seen this happen? How old is he?*

She must have telegraphed her concerns and, judging by the round laughter that rolled from Greshon's chest, she was way off base. The steel gray shimmer of his skin still took her breath away. She was sitting with an alien, having a conversation. The concept continued to rattle around in her brain as another realization crept in. Not only was she surrounded by real life extraterrestrials, but she had also fallen deeply in love with one.

Greshon covered her folded hands with his, giving them a sympathetic pat. "You do me a great honor, Lady Evainne. I might be old, but the words had been carved into the stone tablets long before even my house came into being."

Evainne smiled sheepishly and, shrugging a shoulder, tucked a fluttering lock of hair behind her ear. "Sorry," she said. "That was kinda rude."

Greshon chuckled and shook his head. "No need to apologize, *Dym Char'ann.* I can sympathize with your confusion. There is much to understand and I will do what I can for you."

"So, what happened?" she said, hoping her tactful redirect would make up for her earlier faux pas. Greshon's smile wilted a fraction, the corners of his mouth drooping just enough to tell her the answer was not good.

"I did say the exact meaning was misconstrued, did I not? The ancient leaders feared the idea of any change and, in their haste to maintain the status quo, they proclaimed all children born without eyes of the purest color must be slain before their Naming ceremony."

Evainne stared agape, her stomach churning, and it took a

couple of heartbeats before her vocal cords finally got working. "Are you f-f-f...You're joking, right?" Some part of her brain had remembered her manners enough to censor her foul-mouthed outrage in front of the prim and proper physician.

"Power, once gained, is a dangerous addiction, and no leader is ever willing to risk losing their drug of choice."

Even as she shook her head in disbelief, her gut knew the words to be true. "What is wrong with some people?"

Two bushy golden eyebrows pulled together as Greshon blinked repeatedly. "Do your leaders not seek to retain their control over the populace?"

This time, Evainne frowned. "Well, kinda. But no. In my country, we have elections for our presidents, our leaders, every four years. Other places have royalty, or religious leaders, but most of the serious decisions are made by committees of people. Just about every system is corrupt as hell, since, kinda like you said, some people don't like to share. This, though..." Her voice failed, and she dropped her hands, along with her gaze, into her lap. "I remember hearing my Sunday school teacher talk about pharaohs and other leaders demanding the deaths of firstborn boys to stop prophets from threatening their reigns. I never really believed it, though. I thought there was no way anyone could be so cruel. No one would kill a child just because some great voice in the sky told them to."

"Perhaps our worlds are not as different as you think."

Evainne paused. Although Greshon wasn't too far from the truth, she refused to abandon hope. Not while good people were doing the right thing, even this far away from everything familiar. With fixed truth, her thoughts steered toward her lover.

Ever since she'd woken up on board Kahlym's ship, he'd shown her true kindness, while his crew had given her a sense of belonging she'd never known. Now, not an hour passed by without her thinking of Kahlym. Hour? Who was she kidding? Every second of every day. Images of him continually crept into the forefront of her daydreams, and she tried to convince herself she was okay with his current disappearing act. Maybe she was terrified of what had really happened between them—something deeply profound had taken place during their latest romp, and neither of them was ready to examine it yet.

Even as she sat in this palatial garden, the urge to run through the halls, searching every room until she found him, was strong. Whether it was to kiss him until she lost all reason, or to beat the ever-living shit out of him, she didn't know.

"Tell me about the newest prophecy."

"*Dym Char'ann*, do you need—"

"Evainne," she whispered hoarsely. "Please, my name is Evainne, and what I need are some answers. I'm tired of being a pawn in a game without knowing the rules." She dragged the back of her hand across her eyes, dashing away any sign of weakness before she turned back to Greshon. "I deserve to know what I've gotten myself into—willingly or otherwise."

The old doctor regarded her with a penetrating stare, and she fought the overwhelming urge to lower her eyes and contemplate her fingernails, praying for him to make the next move.

He sighed, relaxed, and nodded, a faint smile wrinkling the corners of his eyes. "Mayhap a fresh insight could shed light on this. At the birth of any son from a ruling house, a seer is present to cast their fate."

She quickly snapped closed her gaping jaw, but from Greshon's light chuckle, her unladylike gawking had already been caught. "This is not the way of things on your homeworld, I see. Needless to say, when Kahlym was born, his mother immediately ordered him to be killed, as tradition dictated. However, the seer fell into a trance and spoke the following:

'Eyes unmatched shall witness untold sorrow;
Through the lost traveler's heart shall great sadness be shattered.
Winterborn will control the Fates;
As one shall great tasks be carried.
Grief will prevail lest love and fury unite the divided.'"

A silence descended, so thick that even the breeze refused to disturb it. Evainne mulled over the words, hoping to puzzle out their true nature.

"Well," she said, "my birthday is on the winter solstice, so that's the easy part. And the traveler bit? Yeah, I guess you could say that makes sense, too." She tugged her eyebrows together as she deciphered more. "And I get Kahlym's part, but the rest? That, I don't quite get."

Greshon offered her a sympathetic smile. "Now you understand the truth of prophecy, *Dym Char'ann*."

She smirked, chuckling half to herself. "Yeah, but y'ain't seen me in action just yet. I love a good mystery and I don't give up."

Greshon arched a brow over a curious aquamarine eye, then placed his hand over his heart and dipped his chin. "There is much strength within you, Divine. I am honored to have this time to speak with you and to learn more of your spirit. Kahlym is most fortunate to be blessed with one such as you."

Heat rushed to her cheeks, accompanied by a silly grin. "Yeah, well, I don't think he's feeling the same way." A mischievous smile twinkled in the old man's eye, and Evainne paused. "What?" she said.

Greshon tucked his hands into the long sleeves of his flowing robes. "Why would you believe this?"

"Well." She scoffed, rising to her feet. "First off, he's treated me like a leper for the past couple of days. Since we got here, I think we've had five minutes without being yanked in fifteen different directions all at once." Her need for physical contact drove her to the tree's thick trunk, where she marveled at its deceptively smooth bark. Everything here was not what it seemed to be, including, and especially, her emotions. "It just seems that, well, lately, when he looks at me, it's like..."

When no other words fell from her lips, Greshon chimed in, "Like what, *Char'ann*?"

She shrugged, tracing the furrows and swirls on the soft bark.

"Like he's embarrassed or feels guilty about something, but I can't imagine what it could be. He's nothing, if not incredibly thoughtful. He swoops in to act like my own personal superhero, then he just…I don't know. I've never been good in any kind of relationship before this, so why should this be any different? It's probably just me being psycho about things. Even halfway across the universe, I'm still the same, no matter where I go."

"Is that not something for which to be proud?"

She shifted her attention back to the kindly man eyeing her with rapt curiosity. Feathery lines brushed the edges of his aquamarine eyes, and his short-cropped hair was an odd blend of ebony and gold. Like the rest of the planet's inhabitants, his skin gleamed like polished metal, its silvery sheen softened by yards of bright blue and pale yellow fabric. He reminded her of a storybook grandfather—the sage old man who spouted old-fashioned advice in every tale that started with the phrase: "Back in my day…"

She smiled despite her self-doubt. "If I weren't such a monumental screw-up, I might agree with you. What can I say? I'm a bad luck magnet."

Greshon stood and joined her. "I believe you are forgetting couples require two hearts to beat as one," he said.

From a close, yet hidden vantage point, a pair of tourmaline eyes followed her every move, and she could feel the weight of his stare as an intimate trail of invisible fingertips brushed along her exposed shoulder. Curious, Evainne lowered her gaze and glanced toward the door leading back into the palace.

There, Kahlym stood just inside the gardens, so close, only a couple of steps and she'd be in his arms. Yet, the distance in his stare tugged at her soul. She recognized that look, and it chilled her to the bone: Brel had lain bleeding out in front of her, and her lover had blamed himself for it. That same grief now haunted his handsome features, and her breath caught in her chest.

"But how do you convince someone of something you hardly believe yourself?"

She was lying to herself. She more than believed in love, and even after the strange solitude of the past couple of days, she knew in her heart she'd always love Kahlym. Did that make her stubborn or stupid? Evainne heaved a sigh as knowledge settled in her gut.

I am so screwed.

"*Dym Char'ann*, every journey must start with one small step."

As she continued to spy, Brel approached Kahlym and, after a very short conversation, dragged him back inside, out of earshot.

"Yeah," she said, "but who's to make the first move?"

A light chuckle drew her attention back to the kind cleric with his Cheshire Cat smile.

"Why, the one who has more to gain, of course."

Smirking, Evainne threw her arms around him, giving him a quick peck on the cheek. "You are absolutely right. Thanks."

Without waiting to see the cleric's stunned expression, Evainne strode toward the door leading back inside the palace, where she paused, fingertips brushing the handle as she eavesdropped on Kahlym and Brel's conversation. She didn't want to be rude and interrupt, but she also wanted to make it clear they weren't unobserved, so she opted to split the difference: she quietly turned the knob and slipped through to blend in with the growing shadows. The pair sat with their backs turned, both staring at the floor as if seeking answers in the grand mosaic covering the length of the long hall.

When Kahlym began to blather on about the reasons why Evainne should run screaming from his presence, she finally spoke up.

Brel wore a self-satisfied grin, while the one who held her heart looked like a kid caught with his hand in the cookie jar. An embarrassed blush painted his handsome face, and he ducked his head before he took to his feet.

"Evainne," he said, "it is not for me to—"

She closed the scant distance between them and placed her

fingers onto his lips. Standing in his massive shadow, Evainne smiled at his stumbled apology and looked up into his troubled eyes.

"Kahlym, as far as I care, I am only for you. You alone give me a reason to keep going in this crazy world. Somehow, in all this madness, you make sense. We make sense." He blinked rapidly, his tourmaline eyes damp with unshed tears, and she swallowed hard against her own feelings. "I don't have all the answers," she added, "but I do know I love you. Whether that's gonna be enough to save us, or this place, or not, time will tell. All my life, I've been told I wasn't good enough for anyone or anything. Now, I feel I'm never going to be able to live up to what you think me to be."

He started to speak, but a quick shake of her head stayed his tongue.

"When you look at me, I…I get confused. You see something I don't believe me to be. Just as I see something in you that you feel doesn't exist. I see a loving, strong hero; someone who protects what he loves and is worthy of so much more than a misfit like me."

Her voice cracked as the first tear slipped down her cheek.

"Dammit, Kahl. Just tell me you don't regret what we shared. That's all I need to know."

KAHLYM'S EYES FLARED OPEN, and he pulled her into his embrace. With one simple statement, her timid plea had reduced all of his arguments to dust. He brushed his lips against her hair, dragging her comforting scent into his frantic soul.

"Never, *ziat'xahn*."

She sobbed as she clung to his shirt. "Then stop saying all that crap."

Smiling in spite of the tears, Kahlym held her, reveling in her honest and direct words. She was right. For so long, he'd been trapped by prophecy and a looming fate. He had forgotten that life was meant to be lived and destiny should be met head-on. In his arms, he held the Winterborn Divine. More than that, he held his female, Evainne, whose soft touch and fiery spirit humbled him and brought purpose to his suffering.

"Can you forgive me, my angel?"

She leaned away, and to his surprise, popped him solidly on the shoulder. "As soon as you stop being a bull-headed schmuck."

A deep chuckle at his back reminded him they were not alone. "Even though I have no idea what that is, it didn't sound very complementary. That means, I'll have to agree with her on that one."

Kahlym turned, catching the open mirth in his brother's eyes and the honest smile that warmed the big Raedynese face. Throughout their trials and tribulations, Brel had never let him down. Before long, the laughter diminished, replaced with a somber light that shone in the citrine jewels.

With one arm around Evainne's waist, Kahlym clasped his brother on the shoulder. Brel returned the gesture, then leaned down, touching his forehead to Kahlym's.

"Enjoy this gift the goddess has blessed you with, *kherdes-xahn*. You have more than

earned the right to a bit of happiness."

In one perfect moment, he held the only things that made life worthwhile. The uncertain future made him quake in his boots, yes, but right now, he had a stolen instant of peace. Daring to dream, Kahlym closed his eyes and savored it, silencing the warning voice of doom.

Chapter 23

"Just focus, Evainne."

"Kahlym, I swear to Christ, you tell me one more time to focus and I'm gonna shove this whole friggin' palace up your ass."

Brel coughed and quickly shifted his gaze, lest he be the new target of her frustration. Evainne glared at him anyway, brushing her hair out of her face once again.

She'd been training for the last four days. Or that's what Kahl and Brel had called it. She, on the other hand, had other, more colorful terms.

Torment.

Aggravation.

A complete fucking waste of time.

At least she was out of those damned gowns. It had taken some doing, but she'd managed to convince everyone that training had to happen in something more sensible. She'd pictured it more like her martial arts classes, and the flowing fabric would have pissed her off more than necessary.

And she was still waiting to hit something.

Rolling her shoulders, Evainne narrowed her eyes at the recent bane of her existence: an innocuous square that looked more like an oversized shoebox than a hateful source of all kinds of evil.

Never judge a book by its cover.

Wishing she could push up the lengthy sleeves she was wearing, she took in a long, centering breath, closed her eyes, and tried to clear her mind. Yhan'tu had explained the mystery of the cube in such a way that Evainne pictured something akin to Schrodinger's cat: the answers to the universe were inside the box, but if you opened it, those answers vanished.

So she'd spent the last two days trying to "see" inside the box, using her Divine gifts. But did she see anything other than the stupid black square? Oh no, of course not. The hateful block just sat on the table, silently mocking her with its inert-ness.

"*Dym Char'ann*, you are not concentrating."

Evainne bolted up from her chair. "What the hell do you want from me?" she snapped, throwing her hand in the air. "I've been staring at this fucking…contraption for the past hour, and the only thing I'm getting from it is a headache." She paced the room, then paused at one of the floor-to-ceiling picture windows where, beyond the thick glass, the alien landscape rolled out before her.

Tall buildings cut smooth spirals and sharp cylinders into the strange purple skyscape, while tiny flashes of light zipped by in organized traffic patterns. Some dipped to perch on barely visible landing pads; others climbed into the heavens to vanish in a blink. Evainne still had a hard time believing her eyes, but the two setting suns definitely had a real quality. The icy, white mountains were capped with pale blue snow as they clawed toward the sky. Burnt orange grass blanketed the ground and brown and fuchsia trees danced in the breeze as they stood in perfect formation around the palace gardens.

Ever since she and Kahlym had mended fences, she'd only seen this same view, from this same window. She was tired of the stale air and the confining walls. She wanted out, and she wanted out now.

She splayed her fingers flat against the cool barrier. The temperature outside was beginning to fall. If she were back home, she'd think autumn was in the air. Here, though, she had no basis for comparison. For all she knew, this was normal; this could be hot for them, or as cold as it got.

"You have to keep trying, *Dym Char'ann*. There is…"

With a sigh, she dropped her forehead against the glass as Yhan'tu launched into the speech she almost knew by heart. Her muscles twitched, eager to move and fight. She seriously wanted to smash the damned box to kindling. Never before had she such a desire to destroy an inanimate object.

She sensed Kahlym at her back before his hand touched her shoulder.

"Do you need a rest, *ziat'xahn*?"

His soft voice, laced with concern, set her blood on fire, but she was in no mood to be consoled.

"No," she rasped, focusing on the gardens just beyond her fingers. "What I need is to get the fuck out of this glass prison and run naked through the flowers. Okay, so maybe not naked. That would be terrifying on so many levels."

The festive yellow flowers danced in the breeze, and envious of their happy ignorance, Evainne closed her eyes to banish the beckoning outside. She took a deep breath and lifted her head away from the comforting cool glass. "But a very big part of me just wants to know why the dumbass box is so friggin' important."

She spun and pressed her back against the window, then looked up into those tourmaline eyes. She'd just started getting him to treat her more like a normal woman, until the cleric began yammering about her needing to train as a Divine. If only she could simply test out of this part, claiming that on-the-job training seemed to be doing her all right.

No such luck, though.

Instead, she'd learned to read. Apparently, Divines were gifted with the ability to decipher any written language, in any format imaginable, from every planet in the Seventh Quadrant. Which might explain her interest in foreign languages during school. She'd loved her time in French classes and had found that even Russian and Gaelic came easy.

The various writings were unlike anything she'd ever seen, reminding her more of hieroglyphs than letters. Yet after a few hours of flipping through ancient tomes, familiar words materialized and meanings wormed their way into her brain. She wanted to attribute it to the universal language chip, but Brel assured her the program worked only on the spoken word.

Huh. Pretty cool.

She'd spent the rest of that day and most of the next learning about the vast history of the Dantaran galaxy, focusing on the bloody wars fought over to control the Divines. From what she gathered, every planet in the Seventh Quadrant had one Divine who acted as supreme priest, or Voice of the Goddess, for that race. But since each Divine could only control one of the different aspects, before long, races began to raid their neighbors for something better. People ruled by weaker Divines were soon conquered and subjugated to their usurpers' wills. During one of these sieges about ten thousand years ago, a Rimmarian Emperor decided the other worlds were too unstable and too primitive to hold the power of the Divines.

So, bent on complete control, he used the influence of one rare and twisted Divine Fury to coerce the entire collective of Divines, and under an unshakable leash of fate, each planet's religious figurehead had set down a horrific proclamation: Whenever a Divine was born unto its people, the infant would be delivered to Rimma for training and safekeeping.

She'd scoffed when she'd read that part. Her social studies teachers had struggled to make the Holocaust or the Crusades sound less like blatant evil. The Thrall, as the proclamation had been christened, still held sway over this part of the universe.

The books, obviously written by the victors, had only given her a small hint of the truth. Giant gaps in some of the texts meant erasures or corrections regarding events and loyalties in others. *Guess the drive to rewrite the past is universal.*

When things settled down, she'd ask Kahlym about their more recent history. But between his Stria captain duties and his attempts to keep an eye on his treacherous parents, coupled with her enforced education, they'd been afforded little downtime; stolen moments were squeezed in before he crashed out in the early hours of the day. During those precious times, the last thing on her mind was a recap of current events.

No sooner had she mastered the written word, though, the next set of trials had begun. And that test still sat across from her, unopened for the past two days.

Yhan'tu huffed and waddled over to her, shaking his big blue head, light shimmering off of the gold geometric tattoos on the side of his face. "Lady Evainne," he said, "it is vital you learn to focus your skills to see beyond what is visible."

"What if I don't want to see more than I can, huh?" She pinned two of the healer's four eyes with a serious stare. "Didn't anyone think of that?"

Yhan'tu dipped his chin, dropping his gaze to the floor. "A thousand pardons, *Dym Char'ann*. I did not wish to offend you."

She groaned, hanging her head into her hand. "Shit, Yhan'tu, you didn't offend me. But can't I just beat the crap out of it? That, I can do."

Brel snickered again, sipping a cool, tasty-looking beverage. These aliens made one hell of a good cocktail, and she would much rather have been enjoying a drink than stare another second at that fucking puzzle.

"You have to be able to channel your abilities on command, *learom-xahn*," he said. "What were you thinking of when you demonstrated your gifts to Jaleen?"

Evainne's hackles raised, and she narrowed her eyes at the

mention of their mother's name. That bitch had been nothing but a sycophantic suck-up since their initial meeting.

"I was pissed," she growled, and she gnashed her teeth to keep from saying more. Every room in the palace was bugged, and she was circumspect with her word choice when in unfriendly territory. But that woman had gotten under her skin and refused to budge.

"Maybe that's the key," Kahlym remarked.

Evainne screwed up her face, then shifted her eyes to meet Kahlym's open stare.

"Great," she said. "So I need to stay pissed off all the time? Fabu. Hell, if that's the case, I should've just stayed at home." Angry at everything and nothing in particular, she shouldered past Kahlym to storm out of the room, in no mood to be focused or to say anything to hurt the only people she cared about.

Her choppy steps wound her around the maze of corridors, no destination in mind, and coming around a corner too sharply, she ran straight into R'uan. The big Ontaxian juggled a fragile-looking dish as steaming liquid sloshed over the edge. Her anger vanished. Frantic to aid in saving both the bowl and the lunch inside, she reached out quickly, giving him a hand, and between the two of them, his meal was saved.

"Oh, geez. I am so sorry. I just wasn't looking where I was going. Are you okay? I mean—"

His warm smile stopped her mindless blathering, and he shook his head, his black-and-silver mane bristling in the fading daylight.

"No need to apologize so profusely, *learom-xahn*. No lasting damage has been done." Then the edges of his toothy grin drooped as his eyebrows knitted together. "But perhaps I should be asking you the same question."

Evainne forced an unconvincing smile and shrugged sheepishly. "I guess I'll be all right."

R'uan arched one bushy brow, his droll stare more effective than any of Yhan'tu's lectures and a tiny whine snuck out as her shoulders sunk.

"Yeah, I know. I suck at lying," she said, and she paced, her steps tracing jagged lines on the broadly swirled tile floor. "Why can't I just be me? What's wrong with me as I am?" A well-placed bench waited quietly along the far wall, and she plopped down. "First I'm all that, then I'm not enough, and part of me gets that I have a lot to learn, but sometimes I feel like all I'm learning is the limits of my own patience. And it's getting really close to the breaking point."

"When did you last eat?" R'uan asked.

The simple question kicked her empty stomach into overdrive and, reacting a heartbeat too late, Evainne wrapped her arms around her grumbling midsection, giving R'uan an embarrassed smirk.

He chuckled before joining her on the bench and offering her a spoon. "Then I suppose it is lucky you ran into me."

"Literally," she added, and with a heavy sigh, she accepted the utensil. "Too bad I gave up believing in luck a long time ago." She dropped her hand into her lap, searching for answers in the green-and-silver spirals beneath her feet. "Sometimes, I swear, since I didn't fuck up enough on my own planet, I got my ass shipped out here. It's like the universe just wanted to see how much deeper it was possible for me to get into shit."

Silence said much more than words, and she cringed, shook her head. "I know, I know. Get off the cross, someone else needs the wood."

"I see no cross of which you speak," R'uan remarked, peering past her with a curious grin.

She frowned. "It just means I need to stop feeling sorry for myself and do the damned job."

The thick, heady scent of the broth hit her nose, and her mouth watered in hungry anticipation. R'uan pushed the bowl farther into her range of vision, and a weak smile touched her lips. She sampled a mouthful of the steamy soup, resigned to her bad mood. Both savory and sour, the flavors blended into a strange, liquid BLT that comforted her tired emotions. Another spoon joined hers in the broth as she gave in to her need for food.

The shared bowl emptied at a lazy pace, and Evainne reveled in the peaceful serenity of her silent dinner guest, while her mind spun like a frenetic hamster wheel, no thought standing still for longer than a heartbeat.

Everyone was counting on her and she was terrified she would fail. Back home on Earth, she dreamed of a time someone would notice her. She didn't want fame or celebrity-level recognition, but a real friend would have been nice. Even that, though, had been a feeble hope.

Growing up a ghost in her own home, Evainne had only wanted to hear someone call out her name with a sense of joy. Her mother had whined it; her father had roared it with disdain; the help hadn't been allowed to refer to her by her given name, only "young miss," an archaic throwback to a different time. She'd lived in a mausoleum, surrounded by stuffy Victorian sensibilities, in the middle of modern-day Boston.

Yet even after all of the tutors and the boarding schools, after the failed attempts to make her into a lady, Evainne still craved the one thing she'd never had: acceptance. She never understood why she couldn't make her parents happy. She'd tried to be a good girl; she'd forced each smile and had done her best to follow the encyclopedia of conflicting directions—her dad said *run*, while her mom said *stay*, and both orders would arrive within a heartbeat of each other, leaving her with no right answer, ever. After it was apparent that even her breathing was a disappointment, she'd given up trying to believe others and instead focused on protecting herself.

"Come back to us, Evainne."

A gentle hand on her shoulder jerked her out of her maudlin memories. The once warmly lit hallway shivered in the strange, gray darkness. She blinked rapidly, and the daylight returned.

"Perhaps the next step in your training should be shielding."

"Huh? What?" she stammered as she met R'uan's comforting

smile. Sunny heat had driven away the summoned chill, and Evainne glanced around, finding no source of the sudden shift.

"Many things in our world are psycho-reactive, and with the added push of your Divine status, you will find even the suns respond to your mood."

Her jaw dropped open at this new tidbit of information.

"Why the hell didn't someone tell me this?" she squeaked, embarrassed by the potential ramifications of her unconscious directions. "Omigod—have I been screwing things up all over the place, or is it just where I am? Shit." She recalled Bhaan's sanctuary, the ease at which her dreams and desires had been fulfilled. Panic cranked up her breathing a notch or two and the temperature rose to keep pace.

R'uan quickly set down the bowl and knelt before her, wrapping his hands on her shoulders. "Slow down, *learom-xahn*. You have nothing to fear. You have done nothing wrong. Breathe, Evainne. Just breathe."

"But…Oh shit, oh shit. Dammit, I'm so sorry," she said, her earlier brooding replaced by blazing mortification as she dropped her face into her hands.

Gentle pressure on her forehead called to her, centered her frantic thoughts.

<Can you hear my voice?>

She snuffed back the frustrated tears and nodded weakly.

<Shielding is a simple skill. Think of them as walls to protect your inner-most secrets.>

"I don't get how I'm—"

She flinched as a phantom hand brushed against her psyche and, recoiling on instinct, Evainne shoved away the unexpected touch to hide behind a newly materialized door.

<That is amazing. You catch on quick.>

"Well, you have someone tickle your brain, and we'll see how fast you figure things out."

A soft chuckle drew her back inside her skull. Before her stood a thick, wooden barrier with nothing on either side. Emptiness stretched out above and below as well, and she studied the ornately carved structure, frowning.

"Okay, so this is great for this moment, but what about everything else? Do I have to fill my head with a bunch of…doors? And what if I want to, I don't know, see what's going on?"

<*This is your mind, learom-xahn. You may create the shields in any fashion you desire.*>

Spurred on by curiosity, she visualized glass, and the wood shimmered into crystal clarity. Behind the window stood R'uan, a warm smile on his leonine face.

"So, what now? Do I have to stay in here?" she asked, and he shook his head, gesturing to the whole outside world.

<*Not at all. If you wished, you could banish me from your mind and there would be nothing for me to do about it. Though untrained, your will is incredibly strong. Already you have gained more mastery of shielding than a novice cleric.*>

She ventured closer and reached out. The surface offered no resistance and she pushed through, touching the Ontaxian on the shoulder.

"Well, hell's bells," she said. "What good is this, if a sneeze can penetrate it?" She frowned, drawing back her hand. But it was his quizzical expression that caught her eye. "What?"

R'uan smirked and took several large steps backwards. Confusion tugged her eyebrows together, and she parted her lips, about to ask where he was going when, without warning, he roared and charged. She cringed, preparing for the freight train to hit.

Instead, the speeding tank bounced off of the thin barrier, the impact throwing him back several feet.

Aw, crap.

Evainne's eyes flew wide open, and she pulled away from the grinning lion. Drops of blood trickled from his nose, muddying the ash-and-ivory fur around his mouth.

"Omigod. What the hell just happened? Are you okay?" She searched around for some kind of napkin or towel, finding only the sleeve of her form-fitting garment. Apologies tumbled from her lips as she meekly blotted his bloody nose with her fingertips.

R'uan captured her hands, held her still until she stopped her attempts to help. "Again, you have nothing for which to be absolved. Your shields are powerful and will keep out any unwanted intruders. They will also protect your thoughts so you will no longer project your emotions and wants so openly." Then his smile wavered, his snowflake obsidian eyes serious, concerned. "I did not intend to frighten you."

Evainne let out a staggered breath and, leaning back, rested against the wall. "No, you didn't…Well, actually, you kinda scared the crap outta me, but not in a bad way," she hastily added as he dropped his gaze to the floor. "Please," she said, "I didn't mean to make you feel bad. If you want to know the truth, you're the first person who's really given me anything useful."

An impish smirk tugged at one bushy brow, and in a blink, a girlish blush heated her cheeks. Evainne groaned and rolled her head, letting the weight hang down.

"Fuck, that came out all shades of wrong."

R'uan chuckled, then settled in next to her. "I admire the speed of your mind, Evainne. It is one of the reasons you were able to deflect my attack so easily. Your open honesty serves you well and provides you strength. Your skills will continue to grow, as long as you do not lose sight of yourself. That which makes you unique gives you power to accomplish all that you desire."

Evainne lifted her gaze. No veiled admonishment sat in his expression. Instead, a trace of pride hovered in his lingering smile. Her mind slipped back to the early morning conversation over a cup of coffee with Bhaan and she could see the strong family resemblance between R'uan and his more reckless brother, Dhaerin. But now, in this quiet moment and in his simple actions, she saw R'uan's sage father.

Brain still reeling, she opted for a better solution and, with a relaxing huff, she hugged him. His big body jolted, tensed, before a large hand splayed across her back, his movements wooden and stilted. She laughed weakly at his hesitant response.

"I guess you guys aren't much into hugging here."

"Not if one wishes to retain certain parts of one's anatomy," he replied, but his dry tone only encouraged her to squeeze him tighter, giggling before she released him.

"I promise I won't let anyone geld you. Where I come from, hugs aren't only for lovers; they can just be between friends or family. Just a way to say things when words don't seem to cut it."

"Are all the females on your world so physical with their words?" He tilted his head, brow furrowed as he considered the possibility. Her smile faltered, truth deeper than his teasing tone.

She shrugged. "Actually, most of the girls back home are probably more open than I'll ever be." She sunk back into the bench. "I was never one of the popular kids. Too heavy and too stubborn. Not a good combination in a superficial society."

"But of immeasurable value to those who can see your true worth."

"Aw, shucks," she joked, popping the big Ontaxian playfully on the shoulder. A comfortable silence settled in and she drew in a long, slow breath. As she huffed it out, she took to her feet.

"All right," she said, "I think I'm ready to take on that damned box."

"But you have already mastered it, Evainne."

Her eyebrows tugged together as she jerked her head around to Kahlym, who stood just beyond her reach, his tortured expression sending a strange blend of embarrassment and guilt straight to her gut. His cheeks were flushed as if he'd just run a marathon, while a flash of sparked panic coated his words. She hadn't sensed him approach. Staring at him, she realized she hadn't even felt his presence in her head, as she had grown so used to in such a short amount of time.

Had these new shields of hers blocked him, too?

He stepped closer, yet remained out of arm's reach as she struggled to hold his elusive gaze.

"Only moments ago, the challenge cage simply vanished. That could only occur if the riddle had been solved."

No. Something was wrong. This wasn't good. Not to mention, her lover refused to meet her eyes.

"What? How? What did I do?" Her heart pounded, and she reached out to him. He stood ramrod still, his beautiful bi-colored orbs veiled as they studied the floor at his feet.

"Baby, you're scaring me," she said, but as soon as her hand touched his, she was blasted with a wave of swirling emotions. The storm was brief, lasting a matter of seconds before the soothing warmth of relief blanketed her as he wrapped his arms around her. Her breathing slowed, locking onto his powerful rhythm, her frantic heartbeat quickly falling into line as well.

"Forgive me, *ziat'xahn*." His rough voice ruffled her hair, and he kissed the top of her head. "You disappeared from my heart the same moment as did the cage from the room. I...I feared the worst."

She held him so tight, wishing she could crawl under his skin. "I'm sorry. No, nothing bad has happened. I'm here, baby. I'm right here. I'm sorry."

Why she was apologizing? Because she was seriously freaking out over knowing she'd upset him so deeply, and without thought. Tears pricked her eyes and she squeezed them shut to hold back her uncharacteristic urge to weep.

One large hand cradled her head against his chest, its steady, hypnotic thumping centering her rattled thoughts. "Shhh...No, I am the one who should apologize. I was so focused on honing your skills, I neglected to see to such a basic task as teaching you shielding."

"She is a quick study, *kherdes*. And I believe the fault here is mine. I did not realize you two had forged a soulbond." One of Kahlym's arms released her, but she wasn't ready to let him go just yet. So, opting to split the difference and retain a bit of her waning dignity, Evainne turned in his embrace enough to look at more than just his chest.

R'uan wore a sheepish grin as he locked forearms with Kahlym. *All this over me?*

But, shoving aside her childish melancholy, Evainne found her backbone and shook her head, sniffling to hold back any threatening waterworks. One step opened her to both stunned expressions, and she dashed her hand across her eyes.

"Gah! Okay, enough," she said. "No more apologizing, from anyone to anyone for any reason. Unless it's a serious crime, like murder or stealing the last doughnut, got me?" She swiveled her gaze between the confused, remorseful looks from the two guys big enough to each bench press a Buick. "I mean it. No one did anything wrong." *Except maybe me.* Kahlym circled his palm against her back, helping her to dismiss her self-accusatory thought.

Evainne placed a hand on R'uan's arm, unable to reach his shoulder without standing on her tiptoes and ruining the moment.

"You helped me with something that is really gonna come in handy, not just here, but outside this place, I'm sure."

After a light squeeze, she turned toward Kahlym, her personal hero. R'uan had said an interesting phrase: forged a soulbond. She'd teased Kahlym about his less-than-romantic proposal days ago. Seemed she needed some serious answers.

<Soulbond?>

Kahlym lowered his head, and she leaned into his chest. *<It is the strongest pledge two hearts can make.>* She ducked her own head, sneaking into his field of vision. *<Normally, the ceremony occurs after much preparation and both people enter willingly into the union. Yet, when we were together, I…>*

Now that it had a title, Evainne realized how much deeper than a marriage it truly was. But instead of this knowledge frightening her, it gave her strength. Their connection was alive—it breathed and grew and fed her spirit, and she knew she'd never feel whole unless Kahlym was part of her life.

His panic melted and a reticent smile tugged up the corners of his sensual mouth as he gently clasped her fingers and lifted her hands. With profoundly reverent care, Kahlym brushed his lips across her trembling, upturned palms.

<*First, you held my bloodbond. Now, ziat'xahn, you hold my soul. I pray to the Goddess I continue to prove myself worthy of your loving care.*>

Evainne swallowed hard past the lump in her throat. Her vision blurred, and she responded in the only way that seemed fitting: she cupped his face, drawing his gaze up from the floor, and kissed him, pouring all of her devotion and adoration into one tender moment.

A tingle crept along her skin, feather-light and intoxicating, with their joined lips the ignition point. The only thing that stopped her from ripping off his clothes was the presence of an audience, and even that little nugget took a while to sink in as she reveled in the taste of her lover.

At her random thoughts, a shy smile broke the seal of their lips and a silly giggling fit bubbled up from some very tired part of her psyche. She opted to blame exhaustion for her straying brain cells, but she'd already let the cat out of that bag, and now, she would have to explain herself.

"Did I miss something amusing, *ziat'xahn?*"

Kahlym's quiet question fanned her cheeks, his breath warm and enticing, and her eyelids fluttered down.

"Promise you won't laugh?"

He pressed a soft kiss to her nose. "Only if you say something intentionally humorous."

Evainne inhaled deeply to squelch her silly streak before launching into her query. "Well, you have that really cool thing you keep calling me. And don't get me wrong, I do love it. But I don't really know what it means, and…" She gnawed at her lower lip in momentary respite. "And, well…I don't have anything that sexy to call you. All my friggin' Earth speak sounds so blah."

A gentle nudge under her chin encouraged her gaze to rise as he whispered, "It means 'little one,' my angel."

God, he was beyond beautiful. All the adjectives she could think of paled in comparison to the reality of her Kahlym.

Hers.

"How about if I just call you mine?"

His smile rivaled the two suns outside the thick window at her back, and he cradled her cheek with his warm palm.

"That, *ziat'xahn*, would suit me just fine."

Maybe once, just this once, the universe could give her a break. She didn't know what might lie just around the corner, but she was going to savor this peaceful moment.

Chapter 24

"You are certain the female is the Divine we seek?"

Grand Emperor Gha'jahn M'Uubair gazed out through his high palace window, the glow of his amethyst eyes reflected in the smoky glass. He laced his long fingers behind the small of his back, primarily to stop him from throttling the surprise messenger standing in his receiving room. The volatile nature of Anaxar and Kahlym's relationship was well known throughout the realms, but perhaps he'd misjudged the depths of their hatred. Betrayal of blood, especially between males, was a capital crime. Granted, his own hands were far from clean. Yet, even he was taken aback by the vicious streak in his long-standing opponent.

Perhaps the man may not be as weak as I first believed.

"She has great power, but she is inexperienced. Her abilities are wild and without training or focus."

The emperor glanced at the stoic spectral image. Anaxar, he had to admit, had balls. He'd give the man credit for the daring move. If the others of his house learned of this clandestine meeting, the man's head would truly be on the chopping block. Regardless, a foe bartering for a truce proved his original suspicions: his Divine was in the hands of his enemy, and now, to get her back, negotiations must occur.

"She will only be of use if she can bear young. Has she been tested?"

His projected guest scoffed. "If I could get her away from the little shit and his overprotective crew for enough to shove her against the nearest wall, I could give you that answer."

Curiosity piqued, Gha'jahn turned around. "Do you believe your son has claimed her?"

Another growl, and Anaxar curled his lip, shaking his head. "That fucking *dren'tah* is too set in the old ways. My guess is he's too afraid of the consequences of defiling a Divine. Not that it hasn't stopped him from following her around like a pathetic whelp."

The emperor crossed the room to settle into the massive high-backed chair behind his desk. "So you are saying she is well guarded at all times?" he asked and stroked his bearded chin, sifting through possible retrieval scenarios. Diplomacy might need to take a back seat in order to procure his much-needed puzzle piece.

"If you are contemplating a full-frontal assault, I would strongly advise against that."

Gha'jahn lifted his stormy violet eyes to regard Anaxar's cocky red orbs. He arched one brow, creasing his forehead as he glared through space at his holographic visitor.

"And why is that, would you say?"

Ghostly arms folded across an opaque chest as the smug smile grew. "Because if you try to take her by force, I will make her useless to you and watch as your empire crumbles."

Gha'jahn drummed his fingertips on the console, staring daggers through his pompous caller. The bastard was right. Without his having the upper hand, violence could very well bring about a catastrophic end.

"What is it you want, Jhuen?"

"I want my seat on the Ruling Counsel once again."

The air crackled with greedy energy as hunger glowed within the glaring rubies. A smirk tugged at his lips. *Ah, the truth will out.*

"I believe that can be arranged," Gha'jahn said. "But I sense there is more."

If only the man were here in the flesh; much easier to read true intentions with a corporeal form. Prudence, however, had dictated this meeting be as secret as possible. Devious deals were best made without transit vouchers.

"Kill Kahlym."

The emperor blinked slowly, digesting the unexpected request. "Why not simply do it yourself? Ah, yes…" he said, nodding, "the prophecy. Yes, I can see how that could make things, shall we say, 'problematic.'"

Tension vibrated from the shimmering form, which lost cohesion for a heartbeat, gone in the blink of an eye.

"That blasphemous farce has saved his skin for far too long," Anaxar said. "I see no need to devote any more resources to an old wives' tale. Personally, I prefer the current status quo and would much prefer the universe be without that abomination. I am including the shield codes. Try not to muck up the place too much. I do have to live here, after all."

Gha'jahn rose, ran his hands along the front of his regal golden tunic, then stepped around the desk. The hologram swiveled to keep eye contact, leery apprehension oozing off of the three-dimensional replica.

"In exchange for the safe return of the Divine," Gha'jahn said, "we will ensure your station as Prime Ruling Hand on the Ruling Counsel. We will send our recovery party by the current full moon rise, and during these recoveries, accidents have been known to happen."

The image winked out, but not before giving a curt nod.

Gha'jahn chuckled darkly, staring at the now-vacant space in the center of his receiving room.

Yes, Anaxar. Accidents have been known to happen.

THE IMAGE of the emperor vanished, and Anaxar was once again alone in his bedroom. He gloated at his success, certain of the only unobserved palace chamber's secrecy. He would soon be rid of the thorn that had festered too long in his foot.

Prophecy be damned. Never once had the goddess granted himself power. Everything he controlled, he'd earned. He'd clawed his way to great heights, spilling his blood and that of all who'd opposed him, to retain his supremacy.

Time to choose a side. Time to declare, once and for all, that Raedyn would rather stand with the Thrall than suffer under the weak-willed outcasts governing the Chandaran Stria.

"And it is well past time to clean the gene pool of that walking abortion."

Chapter 25

*A*nd *things had been going so well.*

Kahlym closed his eyes and, dragging his palm across his face, berated himself for his overly optimistic viewpoint. He couldn't wipe away the rage that simmered beneath his skin, and he knew peace on his homeworld would be short-lived.

"I'm sorry, Kahl."

Blowing out a fraction of his anger, Kahlym shook his head, then lifted his gaze to his sheepish tech. "I'm the one who should be apologizing. I should have seen this coming, Ka." He slumped onto the garden bench. "I might have just sealed all our dooms, staying here as long as we have."

He'd hoped the choice to leave would have been his. He hadn't truly fathomed the depths of his father's deceitful, contemptuous nature.

With so much of his energy focused on Evainne, he'd assumed his father had been angrily sulking in his chambers. How did he not see this?

<Kherdes, none of us could have seen this.>

Brel's sympathetic voice did nothing to diffuse Kahlym's temper. He opened his eyes and glanced at his crew. Less than an hour ago, Falka had come to him in a panic, and her words still spun in his head.

"All right, Ka, it's your story. I know I'll screw it up, so how about you tell it." Kahlym rested his elbows onto his knees, heavy head hanging from his knotted shoulders. Falka's footsteps shuffled around the space as she recounted her observance.

"I thought we hadn't heard anything from your parents' end of the palace for a while, so I decided to take a short stroll. The guards were still posted; that was a bit of good news. But as I started back down the hall, I heard two voices coming through the far window." She shrugged. "Okay, so maybe I had to really put my ear to the wall, but that's beside the point. The only reason I stopped to listen was because both speakers were male." She paused, and Kahlym lifted his head. "It was your father speaking to the Rimmarian Emperor. I would know that voice anywhere. Kahl, your father has given the entry codes to the Thrall and they're on their way here now, to take Evainne——"

A thunderous explosion of expletives interrupted her recitation and, lifting a hand, she settled the angry energies. Then she swiveled her gaze, locking eyes with Kahlym. "And to kill you," she said. "We have to leave—now."

Dhaerin took to his feet to pace tight circles in the narrow corridor.

"That fucking bastard," he hissed, and his orange-and-brown eyes flared wide, snapped toward Kahlym. "Sorry, brother, but it's the truth."

"You're not going to hear any argument from me," he sighed in reply. Scanning the gathered faces and doing a mental head count, Kahlym sat up straighter. "Wait. Where is she now?"

Falka piped in, "I saw her last with Yhan'tu, and they were in the central gardens."

Kahlym nodded, mapping the most direct path from their

current location to the landing bays, with a side trip to the center of the palace.

Crap. There is no direct path.

He cursed himself again for not keeping her within arm's reach. Evainne was safe with Yhan'tu, but for how long, he wasn't sure.

Nor, for that matter, did he know how long any of them had.

He paced the secluded corridor, legs powering through his rampant emotions.

"All right," he said, "if my calculations are correct, a strike team leaving from Rimma would be here in under three hours. But if they were sent from somewhere else…"

His words dried up, unwilling to voice the thought that chilled his blood. He dared not begin to ponder that possibility. They could have anywhere between three hours or three heartbeats.

Ishtanti, what do I do?

"I say we get the hell outta here, and quick," Dhaerin said as he pushed away from the wall and closed the distance in two long strides. "Why are we even talking about this?" And his shaggy head swung from side to side, including the gathered crew members in his statement. "We could find safe haven on Ontaxa. Once there, we call the other captains to a meeting to let them know about Evainne and how she's—"

"No." Kahlym's single harsh word brooked no discussion. "She will not be used as a pawn."

"Would you rather see her used as a whore?"

Kahlym's fist connected with Dhaerin's jaw before any thought finished crossing his mind, knocking his friend off of his feet. Swearing under his breath, he shook out his throbbing hand and paced away from his crew. The tingles in his fingertips abated as he snapped his wrist, blood flowing back in the right direction.

Silence blanketed the hall. Even the walls waited in anticipation.

Then Kahlym spun toward his stunned friends, a dangerous mix of anger and embarrassment heating his cheeks.

Brel shook his head, whistling low. "Kahl," he said, "none of us want to see her hurt—"

Kahlym growled and glared at his brother. He slammed his hand onto the unicomm link. "Yhan'tu, how quickly can you get Evainne back to the ship?"

"Back?" The quizzical tone turned his blood to ice. *"But, captain, I am on board the ship."*

"With Evainne?" five speakers called out in rapid fire.

"No. She and I parted ways a while ago. Why? Is something amiss?"

Proximity alarms sounded in the distance—a general call to quarters for all non-essential palace workers. Company was arriving much sooner than expected, and depending on the ships along the borders of their space, they might have seconds to act.

"We could send her home."

The quiet voice had slashed through the hush with deadly accuracy, and all eyes swung around to the pensive Ontaxian. R'uan sighed heavily and, joining the group, clasped Dhaerin's hand to guide him back to his feet.

"As I was teaching her how to shield her mind," R'uan said, "I stumbled upon the location of her homeworld. I know it's not ideal, but it would not be too difficult to tune a standard biotransfer link to the coordinates."

All of the air vanished from the room, and Kahlym gasped to stay conscious. *Send her away?* At this thought, his soul screamed, panic and fear vying for supremacy over his reasons to keep her by his side. After all, she was his heart and without her, he'd be lost—a broken, empty husk floating adrift on the turbulent seas. His chest started to ache, the pain of her absence already creating a void that nothing but her could ever fill.

But could he protect her here? With Qaen still hunting them, and now news of the Thrall pounding on their doors, Kahlym's head reeled with frantic thoughts. No matter how fast they moved, not getting her out in time colored every possibility.

The battle for his soul raged as his crew patiently waited. He searched their faces, their own sympathies and heartaches reflecting back, and his spirit crumbled even more. He clenched his teeth, praying for the strength to make the right decision. No choice—to keep her safe, he had to keep her out of the Emperor's reach.

"She won't go easily." Kahlym's brain warred against his mouth as the words spilled out.

Brel scoffed, folding his arms. "She's a fighter, little brother. She won't go at all."

Kahlym ignored the murmurs of agreement and directed his next question to R'uan. "Can we bring her back?" This solution hinged on his reply, and in the waiting silence, the sound of blood thundering through Kahlym's ears was deafening.

"Whoa, hold on." Dhaerin stepped into the center of the tense circle. "You can't seriously be considering this, right?"

Kahlym raised his hand, cutting off any further rebuke from his bristling friend. His heart screamed the same question, maddened by the prospect of losing his only reason for living.

R'uan balked, then offered a noncommittal shrug. "I think so?"

Kahlym flung his arms up, a mirthless laugh ringing off the walls, and his heels clacked along the sleek floor as he paced to quell the urge to strangle his friend. With no help immediately visible, he dropped his head back, looking to the heavens for answers.

"Oh, gee, thanks, R'uan," Brel chimed in, giving voice to Kahlym's racing thoughts. "That's real comforting."

Kahlym dragged in a long, slow breath, running a shaky hand through his hair and praying for guidance as conversations spun into arguments, reasons pro and con vying for maximum volume. He gave a couple of tugs on his hair, hoping the sting would set his mind into action, and closed his eyes to calm his frantic brain. In the surrounding dark, he listened carefully to that deep part of his soul a certain beautiful angel had unearthed and encouraged to crawl out of the shadows, when he felt the prick of tears behind his shuttered lids.

Lost in silence, her laugh buoyed his spirit as he imagined her sexy, crooked smile, the scent of her hair wafting through his memories, her invisible fingertips trailing along his arm.

He couldn't doom her to fall with him. Not with a death sentence on his head. Sending her far away would keep her safe, keep her alive, and he forced the bitter truth into his breaking heart. For as long as he lived, she would hold his soulbond. Perhaps one day, she might even forgive him, though he would never be able to forgive himself.

He remembered the shrill noise Evainne had made to silence the room, and he swallowed back his sorrow, squared his shoulders, and blinked away his moment of weakness, turning back to his crew. More family than friend, all had welcomed Evainne, adopted her into their tight-knit fold. Plus, the Ontaxian brothers were fiercely protective, and that gave him the courage to continue.

"Okay, okay, listen!" He waited until the murmurs had died down. "We think of that as an absolute last resort." Shouts began again, and he glared daggers. "Only if we cannot return her to the ship. I can find her, but I need the rest of you to get the ship prepped for a quick—"

Words were flung at him, all offering to aid in the search, but with a single gesture, he silenced the impending altercation. "If everyone goes off in different directions, we're all screwed. If there were any other way, I'd choose it, believe me. But time is running out, and she is far too precious to fall into the hands of the Thrall. R'uan," he shot the word over his shoulder, "follow the south corridor to its end."

Brel grabbed on to the burly black-and-gray Ontaxian before he could even move two steps. "No, Kahl, wait. There has to be another way. All of us must look. Divide and conquer. The palace is a huge place."

His brother's tremulous voice nearly crippled his resolve. Both truly owed her their lives, but keeping her here while their enemies closed in was far too dangerous. *And I'm not that lucky.* No matter how Kahlym assessed the situation, he could find no winning scenario.

The weight of all eyes rested on him, hopelessness bleeding from his friends, yet he refused to give in to any useless emotions. He was about to send his angel away to save her life. From a dark corner of his mind, her sweet voice whispered from a distant memory: *I need to know I'm your strength, not your weakness.*

If he were honest with himself, she'd become so much more. She was the best part of him. Without her stalwart love and open acceptance, he wouldn't have had the strength to face the army racing toward them. If she remained, though, he wouldn't have the strength to place her in lethal danger.

And leaders did not hide.

He nodded, masking the defeat in his heart. Kahlym lifted his eyes and, casting aside his internal pain, met the troubled gazes of each crew member. She'd asked to be his strength. He would honor her wish.

"I made a promise to keep her safe, and—" Sirens screamed down the corridor, and the entire palace shook, swallowing them all in darkness. They waited for the backup generators to kick in. *Damn, that was too quick.*

"Safe might need to be far, and we don't have much time," Kahlym said, the words tumbling out rapidly, and he was surprised by the confidence in his own voice. "R'uan, the transfer station near the docking bay."

Now, for the hard part.

He laid a hand onto his brother's shoulder and a heartbeat passed before Brel dropped his arm, shifting his troubled citrine eyes to him. Desperate agony had contorted his brother's features, and Kahlym was tempted to take back his earlier orders but, digging past his own fears, he instead gripped Brel's tense shoulder. Words of comfort would be meaningless and the thought of lying to his only family made him ill.

Seconds slipped by while he and Brel stood in silent contemplation.

"*Kherdes-xahn,*" Brel said, "are you sure about this?"

Kahlym clenched his teeth, gave a weary nod. "Brel, I can't let her get hurt. Again. Trust me. I will do all I can to get her to the ship."

A second explosion, this one louder, closer, rocked the foundation, and the gold pools before him sharpened in a flash. Then Brel jerked his head and shouted over his shoulder, "You heard him. Let's get moving."

Kahlym stared at the statue gallery. "Falka, you go with R'uan. Be sure to configure the transport to recall the final destination."

Two sharp nods and his orders were followed. Kahlym turned to Dhaerin and Brel, both faces reflecting his own churning torment. His resolve faltered, until another blast steeled his spine.

"If this backfires," he said, "I give you permission to remind me of this moment for the rest of my miserable life. Right now, I need to you to trust me. Get the ship ready, and pray."

Dhaerin eyed him cautiously, hesitating a heartbeat before clasping Kahlym's forearm. "May Ishtanti give you speed, *kherdes.*" Bound by a warrior's oath stronger than blood, the big Ontaxian bowed his head.

"Well, we'd better hurry. If I've learned anything about your Divine, she's not going to stay out of the fight for long."

A dark chuckle slipped from his stern lips, and he dipped his chin. "Not going to argue with you on that point, Dhaer."

Kahlym spun, preparing to nudge Brel into action, only to find him already halfway down the hall. With a growl, he followed, as the alarms continued to clang. Dread quickened his pace, and soon, the three were racing through the halls, dodging frightened servants and attendants stumbling away from the encroaching smoke.

Don't let this be a mistake.

The words pushed him faster toward his angel.

Hopefully he would reach her before his enemies did.

Chapter 26

Thick, noxious fumes poured out through the open windows and filtered into the waning sunlight while Evainne groaned, rolling her eyes at her current attire. Why did she let the friggin' doc talk her into one of these stupid gowns? Foolishly, she'd believed things to have settled down and that today's training would consist of simple meditation and centering techniques. The morning had, in fact, gone smoothly. So much so, she'd sent her shadow away. *What could possibly go wrong?* she'd thought as she'd wandered through the palace's intertwining corridors.

No one had said anything about a fire drill, or running for her life.

I would've worn better shoes.

As it was, her strappy sandals offered minor support as she gathered up the hem of her swirled cream-and-forest green robe and ran to find the source of the commotion. Shouts and cries had blended into a cacophonous wail beneath the mechanical screech of the sirens. The stench of burnt wood and overcooked meat nearly gagged her, her long, flowing sleeve serving as an impromptu face mask.

She coughed and, squinting through the haze, tried to spy a familiar face. She didn't find a face, but saw a recognizable someone: white-clad enforcers shouldering their way through the chaos. Evainne's stomach dropped.

Fuck me sideways.

A fist came out of the smoke, and she dodged on instinct, limboing under the swinging arm. She whipped around, swept her leg out for a vicious side kick, and immediately regretted the action.

"They wear armor, you twit," she muttered as she rubbed at the growing knot in the meat of her thigh, hopping to regain her balance. Even though her kick had caught the edge of the unyielding thick chest plate, her attack had still managed to drop the enforcer to the ground. She slammed her elbow down between the base of his skull and his shoulder blades, and he crumpled, down for the count.

Her quick search found one discarded blaster but no blades —*Better than nothing*—so she scooped up the gun and took to her feet. At once, the hairs on the back of her neck stood up and she spun, praying her aim was true. Three tugs on the trigger, and three enemy guards landed in multiple pieces. Shouts rang out in the haze, and she rushed toward the sounds of a skirmish.

Enforcers swarmed the halls, shoving through the confused crowd. From their catch and release actions, they had a target in mind, and judging from their search of only women, she suspected their intended target.

Shit.

Her gaze darted and she ducked into an open doorway, grumbling as the door slid shut. She pressed her ear against the cool surface. Never before had she wished for old-school hinged doors. Unable to do more than listen intently, she closed her eyes, concentrating on every sound beyond the slick metal.

But the alarms still blared, blocking out a good portion of any subtle information: numbers, how heavily armed, how close—all keys for survival. A little voice in her head dragged her back to her earlier incarceration, and she smirked, took a deep breath, then exhaled, picturing the corridor beyond in her mind.

The wall vanished and she was surrounded by the frantic throng. White helmets stood out, far too frequent for her tastes. *Damn.* She came back to herself and tapped her foot, gnawing on her bottom lip.

<Ziat'xahn? Where are you?>

She huffed out a relieved breath and dropped her shoulders. "Baby, you are totally asking the wrong person. You make it sound like I know where I am in the first place."

Focusing on the strength of their connection, she felt his approach, the tug on her heart pointing her in one direction.

"Okay, hon, you're getting closer. Go about another thirty feet. I'm the door to your left."

Once he was within touching range, Evainne slid open the door and yanked him inside. The lock clicked at her back, and a pair of strong arms wrapped around her. She inhaled deeply, her nose buried in his chest, and relaxed. Smoke had charred the air and he smelled like he'd just stepped out of a bonfire, but she didn't care. She wedged her hands between them and reveled in his embrace.

As peaceful as this moment should have been, she sensed a disquieting vibe. Kahlym was hiding something, and it was bad.

She eased out of his strangling hug to peer up into his tourmaline eyes. Ashy soot had smudged along his cheeks, and his deep burgundy gearsuit bore the evidence of a hard-fought battle to stand before her now. The bi-colored orbs that usually turned her insides to jello were haunted, with grief shadowing the fuchsia and jade depths.

Panic gripped her, and her heartbeat kicked up a notch. "Kahl, what's wrong? What happened? Is everyone okay?"

Kahlym tucked her trembling hands close, shook his head sadly. "I underestimated my father's treachery. He has given us up to the Thrall."

"Oh, God. Kahl, I'm so sorry." Evainne threw her arms around him, hugged him for all she was worth. Like herself, he'd been cast aside like garbage, and it angered her to have him feel the same betrayal.

He patted her back, the gesture stilted, and her eyebrows drew together in confusion. She leaned back, narrowing her gaze. He'd focused on some distant point, sadness hanging on him like an anvil. She chalked it up to his father's actions, but that little voice told her it was something more.

When he shifted his eyes to her, a cryptic smile weakly touched his face. He brushed his lips across the top of her hair, the tender gesture frightening her even more.

"Come," he said, voice cracking, "we have to go." He took her hand, moving toward the door.

Her knees locked and she skidded to a halt. "To the ship?"

Kahlym turned and grazed her cheek with his knuckles. "There is not much time before we are found, and I do not even want to consider what will become of you in their hands. Please, *ziat'xahn*."

She leaned into his gentle touch, her fear threatening to spiral, and she clung to his arm, trying to read his enigmatic expression. Divine or not, she was terrified of losing him, or losing any member of *Tiamat's Revenge*. They were the only family she'd ever wanted, and she'd die before she let anything tear them apart.

Mustering the courage her friends were counting on, Evainne buried her unease and stood tall before her savior. She owed it to him. Gripping his hand, she gave a sharp nod, and Kahlym turned away too quickly for her to read his expression. He slid the door open a fraction and peered down the hazy hall.

Evainne yearned to make him tell her what was on his mind. Even the optimist in her was screaming out something was wrong.

The walls shuddered and cries echoed through the smoke, redirecting her thoughts onto the task of staying alive.

Stop freaking out and keep your head in the game.

Kahlym only gave her his back as he threw open the door and ran down the corridor, the sound of their furious footfalls lost in the surrounding chaos. Her heart threatened to choke her—whether from the sprint or from the smoke, she wasn't sure—but with Kahlym in the lead, they navigated the maze of twists and turns, switching hands repeatedly during their trek as her palms got slick and clammy.

Soon, the familiar silhouette of *Tiamat's Revenge* appeared in the diminishing haze, and relief washed away her apprehension. The thought had barely crossed her mind, when an explosion too close for comfort shook the walls, collapsing part of the ceiling. Glass and shrapnel rained down, and Evainne squeaked, diving to avoid a large chunk of rock while wearing Kahlym as body armor.

Coughing, she lifted her head, then groaned. The recent blast had blocked off their current path. Evainne disentangled her limbs from the trailing tendrils of her silken gown and climbed to her feet. Kahlym rose by her side, coughing as he dusted off his hands. A glance in all directions shoved her heart into her gut. Enforcers poured in through the rubble, barring their way from any angle.

"Please tell me you have another escape plan," she whispered. With a nod as his response, he took her hand and sprinted away from the fracas. Once the ship was at their backs, he slowed and opened a door at the end of an unexplored corridor. Another loud, distant boom, and Kahlym sealed them in quick.

Evainne's earlier anxiety returned and tiptoed down her spine as she spied only one other crew member. Had the rest been captured?

R'uan turned toward her, no joy or mirth in his snowflake obsidian eyes, his face serious and taut.

"Time's running out, Kahl. We have to move—now."

Kahlym swung her to face him. His gaze darted over her face, and she bobbed and weaved to maintain eye contact.

"Now?" she said. "What do you mean 'now'? Where? The ship's out there and—"

His mouth slammed into hers with a frantic kiss. She clutched at his thick biceps, her brain shoving him away while her body begged to keep him close. Desperation oozed from his embrace, his arms wrapping like a vise around her.

<Kahlym? What aren't you telling me?>

She enjoyed the tender moment, yet her heart pounded in confusion. He broke the seal of their lips, then pressed his forehead against hers, his racing breaths fanning her cheeks while her lungs forced in air, if only to stop from passing out. Through sheer willpower she stood on wobbly legs, his palms cradling her face.

"I can't let you get hurt, Evainne."

Strong words and snappy comebacks flooded her mind, each witty tidbit vanishing before she could get her jaw to work. Even her eyelids rebelled, unwilling to lift. She covered his hands, her fingertips trailing down his arms as she prayed for her tongue to kick into gear.

He placed his trembling lips on her damp forehead.

"R'uan?"

Another set of hands steered her away from her lover, and she backpedaled, tripping over the flowing tendrils of fabric, her gaze never leaving Kahlym's tortured face. She'd managed two steps before a cone of light surrounded her. She reached up, palms flattening against the surprisingly solid barrier.

"Wait. What…Kahl? Kahlym? Don't. Please. Whatever you're thinking, please don't do this."

Helpless, she could only watch as Kahlym stood just out of arm's reach. Evainne pounded against the fragile-looking wall to no avail, tears burning hot paths down her cheeks. She groped for a crack, a seam—anything she could use to trigger an opening. Then she slammed her body into the flickering band of light again and again and again, her shoulder aching.

"Goddammit, Kahl! Let me out of here right fucking now!

Don't do this! Don't leave me here!" She screamed in rage, throat raw, while her heart broke in her silent cocoon.

The hairs on her arms stood on end as oxygen seeped out of her cage at a snail's pace and she focused her watery gaze on his sorrowful tourmaline orbs. Kahlym lifted his arm, fingertips resting a cat's whisker from her as she sucked down the remaining air in hungry gasps.

<You will be the only one who holds my heart, ziat'xahn.>

She pressed her palm against the pulsing ribbon of light as stars dotted her fading vision.

I love you.

His lips had whispered the words before everything around her disappeared.

<hr>

GONE.

Kahlym gasped as his world collapsed, and his legs turned to rubber, as if a physical blow had slammed into his chest. The air rushed out of the room, and he dropped to his knees.

This time, she was well and truly gone.

And his heart would never have reason to beat again.

Dear Ishtanti, what have I done?

The shattering of glass filtered through the blood thundering in his head, and he stared, watching from some point outside his body as R'uan swung a makeshift club into the transport control panel. The multicolored beam shimmered before winking out, leaving the room in a painful dim, and in the destructive silence, Evainne's heartbreaking pleas for mercy continued to ring in his ears.

How could he have been so stupid? He stared, frozen, as weak tears trailed down his face, unable to banish the haunting betrayal in her turbulent brown eyes. If he could bring her back, would she ever trust him again?

His friend shook him roughly, and Kahlym's gaze focused on

R'uan's determined lips as they formed silent words. His brain was locked in emptiness, his soul fighting to find a reason to remain alive.

A stinging slap jarred him back to the present. He blinked rapidly and shook his head, while R'uan gripped his shoulders and leveled his troubled gaze at him through narrowed eyes. Kahlym's cheek tingled, and he rubbed away the thought-clearing ache.

"She still lives, *kherdes-xahn*. I have the destination coordinates. But we have to go—now."

Windows rattled with another explosion. R'uan bobbed his head up and down, and Kahlym responded, dipping his chin slowly. No good would come if his moping caused his own death. Shoving back his grief, he steeled his spine and, with another sharp nod, he climbed to his feet. R'uan bolted toward the entryway, and he followed. With his body once again under his control, his legs chugged to keep pace with his gunner while he drew out his blaster and provided cover fire as the pair ran on.

She's safe, and she's alive.

The litany provided a powerful cadence, his footfalls beating out the rhythm of his driving thoughts. As long as she lived, he had a purpose.

Even if that purpose was to beg for her forgiveness for the rest of his days.

R'uan had assured him, as he prepared the transport link, of their ability to return her to them. But as they wove between the rubble, Kahlym took no comfort in this knowledge.

"All right, you guys," Brel's voice buzzed through the comm, barely discernible over the cacophony, *"if you're coming in, take the east route. We're gonna clear the road in two, but no telling how long it'll stay that way. Don't be late."*

Kahlym shifted his gaze to R'uan. The Ontaxian nodded in agreement, and in tandem, they rushed down the hall.

Kahlym rounded the corner just as the mounted ion cannon ripped an escape path through the approaching troops. He ducked back into the corridor, waited a heartbeat for the dust to settle, then made a mad dash for the gangplank of his vessel. Safety was within reach … when a resonating scream caught his attention. He grabbed on to the doorframe and jerked his head toward the far end of the docking bay.

"KAHLYM!" Anaxar bared his teeth. Kahlym felt the heat of his angered glare from across the vast distance. "What have you done, you wretched abomination?"

Kahlym stood tall, meeting his father's irate snarl. Then he stepped back and, resting one foot on the lowered ramp, shouted back, "I've protected what was never meant to be yours, asshole!"

Offering the man a final one-finger salute, Kahlym dove inside as the engines roared. Shots pinged off the hull as the platform sealed him in. He climbed back to his feet and brushed off his hands while the ship's rumbling drive blocked out the futile raging of his father.

As long as he knew of Evainne's whereabouts, Kahlym would continue to be of value to the man, and for that reason alone, he'd be spared. Hunted like a rabid beast, of course, but allowed to live.

He made his way to the pilot's chamber as the palace faded into the distance behind them. Ahead, battle freighter ships lumbered in their direction, but Dhaerin easily outmaneuvered the bulky vessels.

A nearby explosion rocked the ship, making it groan, and Kahlym was thrown off his feet.

"Come on. Hang in there, baby," he whispered, patting the wall at his cheek. He needed to survive this, if only to suffer for the rest of his days. *She's safe, and she's alive.* He replayed R'uan's words, though his heart refused to heed the soothing message. It simply beat out of habit, pumping blood through his body. Gone was the driving passion. He closed his eyes and Evainne's face appeared in the void, betrayal coloring her own brown eyes.

The ship jolted again, but this time it had slipped into the hyperlanes. With a relieved exhale, Kahlym headed toward the cockpit.

They needed a safe harbor and only one location came to mind, but a straight line of travel would be dangerous.

As he strode down the main corridor, he fought against the memories of his last trek along this exact path, and he banished the feel of her body in his arms, jaw clenched. He dashed the back of his hand across his rebellious, watering eyes as he took the two steps up to Dhaerin's grav chair.

"Get us to Ontaxa. Slow path."

Their code for "hit every waystation and change out the beacons ten times before final destination" was only used on extremely rare occasions.

He prayed his voice had carried his feigned strength, and he coughed, clearing away the emotions that thickened his throat. But from the pain reflected in the polished chrome bulkhead, he'd been less than successful. He'd deal with his heartache later. Right now, his crew needed a committed leader and his distant lover needed a worthy male.

I need to know that I'm your strength, not your weakness.

Her humble request resonated in his head, giving him the courage to face his friends. He tilted his chin up and squared his shoulders.

"You ready to see the best planet in the Seventh Quadrant, Evainne?" Dhaerin had tossed the question over his shoulder, eyes intent on their course.

The whirring pulse of the hyperdrive engines thrummed beneath the ensuing silence. Kahlym scanned the surrounding faces, each weary expression piercing his heart, their sympathetic pain driving the truth of his loss deeper into his aching soul. Brel stared at a distant spot, while R'uan and Falka helped the flustered cleric into an empty seat.

"She's gone."

The words' heavy weight dragged his gaze away from his crew to settle on an unremarkable seam in the hull. Kahlym remained in a fixed position, until Brel leaned into his field of vision, capturing his sullen stare.

Kahlym's heart broke even more than his sibling's; the crew united in their silent anguish. Words would only muddy the moment, and he dared not give voice to his own rampant fears. Instead, he waited until the grief in Brel's citrine eyes was gradually replaced by an understanding. Kahlym swallowed past the lump in his throat, pleading for some measure of forgiveness, and Brel obligated, dipping his chin.

"Gone?" Dhaerin quipped. "What the hell do you mean 'gone'? No way did those bastards get to her before us. I thought you said that was a last resort, not a first strike."

R'uan stepped in to defend his choice. "*Kherdes*, it was the only way to get her to safety."

"Bullshit!" Dhaerin raged, spinning his chair to face the ship's interior. "Did you even try, or were you so fucking stubborn to be right that you gave in without a fight?" Jumping to his feet, he squared off with Kahlym. "You managed to make it back just fine."

"Only because they were looking for her!" Kahlym roared, answering his friend's fury with his own frenzied pain. "The path to the ship was gone. There was no other solution." It didn't matter if he did agree with his pilot's reaction. Kahlym was still captain of this vessel and it was his duty to keep his crew—all of his crew— alive. "We need a safe place to rest," he said, "and Ontaxa is the best bet we have."

Looking at his crew, Kahlym paused, his stare catching every remaining pair of eyes until he turned to his pilot. A fierce tic had started on Dhaerin's tense jaw, and Kahlym held the striated brown-and-orange orbs, unwilling to show weakness. Sympathy with his mercurial pilot didn't alter their current reality. Dhaerin narrowed his eyes and slunk back into his seat, spinning away from the emotional scene.

"Yes, sir," he said, spitting out his venomous reply.

Kahlym drew upon the visceral anger from his long-time friend, using it to shore up his last sliver of decency. His jaw tightened, holding back his wanting to ask if Ontaxa had biolink facilities. If they didn't, he didn't want that news just yet; he'd face that question once they were planet-side. Until then, he'd do everything in his power to keep a promise he'd made to an angel.

I will not give in to despair, my love. For you are alive, and until the last breath leaves my body, I will never stop searching for you.

DIVINE RETRIBUTION

Hungry for more? Here is a tiny taste of the final leg of Evainne and Kahlym's journey: *Divine Retribution*.

"Bao! Open this door before I break it down!"

Evainne Wagner raged, her fists pounding against the smug barrier until her knuckles bled. She blatantly ignored the mutters at her back, hushed whispers about the "crazy round eye." Her Vietnamese might be a little rusty, but between their sneers and the space tech still implanted in her brain switching all the words in to English, she got the gist of their comments.

Granted, she was still dressed in a smoke stained green and ecru gossamer gown revealing more than concealing her assets and wearing ass-breaking sandals with a busted heel. She was certain she looked like an escapee from some toga party at Northeastern University, but her current goal was way more important than the perceived discomfort of passers-by.

She continued to beat the wood as the horror of her life replayed in her head.

Home.

She was back home.

Boston, Massachusetts. Earth. Milky Way.

And she was pissed.

Her eyes drifted shut and Kahlym's face jumped into the fore-ground, his tourmaline eyes glassing over with heart-breaking sadness before the chipped blue paint of her brownstone's door materialized before her. Tears pricked behind her shuttered lids and she bit her cheek.

No. She would not give into the loss or grief. Not yet. She still needed to use her anger to drive her to find the one person who could make this all disappear.

Growling, she mashed the doorbell, sending out a furious Morse code signal reading get the fuck down here. Intermixed as a strange downbeat, she added some kicking thumps to make her point even more clear. Time was of no importance; the sun was up. Good enough.

She paused, dragging down hot gulps of burning air. Preparing for another assault, she stopped her arm as she caught mumbles and footfalls on the other side of the door.

"Okay, okay. I'm—"

As soon as the door cracked open, she shoved past, nearly knocking Bao to the ground. Startled and sleepy, he stumbled back, rubbing a hand across his eyes as he tugged the white t-shirt completely on. He had gotten even bigger since the last time she saw him. Which said a lot, since he was a champion heavy weight Sumo wrestler to begin with. A couple frowning blinks later, his eyes snapped wide, surprise washing out his features.

"Evainne? Where the hell have you been? And what's with the get-up?"

She shook her head as she drove him backward, leading him through the hallway and into the kitchen. "Later. Where's Sifu?"

Bao fell into the first available chair, screwing up his face. "What? Why the—"

She glared, freezing the rest of his question. *Can this shit work here too?* Taking her own advice, she would think more on that later.

"Where. Is. Whetatoa."

Her heart raced as her mind spun in dangerous circles. How long had she been gone? Did time work the same in both universes? What if only seconds had passed, or if in the time it took her to run the half mile to get to Bao's front door, Kahlym had already lived and died?

The last query screamed in her mind and had propelled her legs to Olympic speeds. She fought that ugly beast even as she used the panic to give her actions more purpose.

Bao frowned, the deep crease across his forehead rippling and disappearing in his thick black hair. "He moved to a new space last week ago, which you would have known if you'd been around." His expression softened, concern relaxing his stern countenance. "Evainne, what happened to you?"

Another frantic shake of her head and she grabbed his arm, intent on yanking him out of the chair. "Take me there." She tugged and pointed her toes back to the entryway, only to be nearly pulled off her feet. The fierce glare returned to his eyes and he stayed glued to the low backed captain's chair. Maybe trying to single-handedly drag three hundred pounds of solid muscle around like a kid's toys was not the smartest thing she'd done all day. But she wasn't thinking with her head and time was not on her side.

She looked at him, swallowing past the growing lump of fear in her chest. "Bao, I promise. I'll explain everything once we find him. Please." She added her other hand and backpedaled, offering him the most pathetic smile she owned in her arsenal.

Precious seconds slipped by before Bao dropped his head and sighed loudly. Reluctant, he rose to his feet. "Fine. But you better have a good explanation for waking me up at the butt crack of dawn on a Saturday."

The urge to throw her arms around him and squeeze the stuffing out of him was great, but if she let down her guard, the tears would fall. Right now, she needed to contain the softer emotions, and keep the darker ones in the forefront. She nodded and continued to pull him toward the door.

Grumbling, Bao slipped on a pair of flip-flops by the front door and snatched a set of keys from bowl by the door. "It's just around the corner, and driving would be a-hang on!"

As soon as they crossed the threshold, she tapped into her Divine skills. There. About two blocks over and half way down the street, a pencil-thin column of deep lapis shot up like a rocket. Confident, she took off at a dead run, leaving Bao in the dust. He called out to her as he struggled to keep pace, but she was on a mission and refused to slow.

Now, why the fuck didn't you think of looking for him like THIS in the first place?

The red light on Boylston did force her to stop. If it wasn't such a busy thoroughfare, she would have dared the crossing. She paced and watched the cars zoom by, her predatory track short and dizzying. Huffing breath off to her side told her that Bao had managed to catch up. He placed a hand on her shoulder, though whether it was to keep his balance or to hold her in place, she could only guess.

"Shit, Evie. You think the devil was after you. What's the rush?"

Green flashed and Bao tightened his grip on her arm. With a stern glare, he escorted her across the street. "Hey, are you gonna tell me or what?"

She sped up as much as her physical leash allowed, her destination just a couple more storefronts away. "As soon as we get to Sifu's place, I will. I honestly don't think I could repeat it twice. You'd probably call the local looney police and have me locked in a little rubber room with one of those self-hugging shirts." Up ahead, a simple sign announced Jhuen Xaio Kung Fu.

She scoffed, shaking her head sadly as the truth revealed itself. Shrugging off Bao's hold, she stalked to the front door and gave the black security gate the same loving care as she had shown her friend's entry. A renewed purpose added powered to her knocks and her shouts.

"Geez, Evainne. Go easy."

Evainne snapped her gaze away from the groaning metal. "I don't have time to go easy."

Her knuckles bled as she continued to pound. Opting for another tactic, she closed her eyes and prayed the embedded unicomm translator chip worked at such a distance.

"Xandar, I need your help."

Kahlym's musical language fell heavy off her tongue and she rested her forehead against the frame, hoping to borrow strength from the building itself. Her heart stuttered, emptiness gradually taking over. The tears pressed hard against her closed lids, eager to make their escape and to bring her to her knees.

A click inches away pulled her back to the land of the hopeful. She hurriedly dashed the back of her hand against her face as the door swung open. Light created a halo around the shadowed figure hovering in the entryway.

Focusing her blurred vision, she marveled at the undeniable family resemblance. The strong jaw and wide, almond eyes were almost an exact match. His intriguing facial tattoos carried a new meaning beyond unique geometric patterns. She had attributed her instructor's unusually dark skin to either Middle Eastern or African descent. Yet now, all she could see was a taller version of Kahlym. But the eyes were wrong.

Never had she seen her sifu's eyes. All while she was studying, he wore thick black wraparound sunglasses. Also, he walked with a long staff. She assumed he was blind. Only now, she realized she was the one wandering in the dark. Pools of the most unnatural shade of blue stared at her, long black lashes brushing the tops of his cheeks as he blinked slowly.

"You learned my language easily, *learom-xahn.*"

Author's Notes

Thank you for allowing my stories into your life and I hope you stay along for the ride. Without readers like you, my characters would only live in my own imaginations.

Keep Believing in Magic!

About the Author

Tessa McFionn is a very native Californian and has called Southern California home for most of her life, growing up in San Diego and attending college in Northern California and Orange County, only to return to San Diego to work as a teacher. Insatiably curious and imaginative, she loves to learn and discover, making her wicked knowledge of trivial facts an unwelcomed guest at many Trivial Pursuit boards.

Her love of the fantastical began at a young age while her mother read to her and her brother such classics as *The Hobbit* and *Rikki Tikki Tavi*. She continued this love, devouring Terry Brooks, J.R.R. Tolkien, Ray Bradbury, and Isaac Asimov as well as comic books galore. Romance entered the field in the guise of Anne Rice's *An Interview with a Vampire*, and during college, she discovered the works of Sherrilyn Kenyon and Christine Feehan, and the rest is history.

Her first novel, *Spirit Fall*, came to her as she looked over the edge of a very dark place. Since then, she's added three more tales to the world of the Guardian Warriors and *Spirit Bound*, Book Two in the series, was awarded the 2016 Write Touch award for Paranormal Romance from WisRWA. But she never lost her love for science fiction and began a space opera, The Rise of the Stria, in March 2018 with the release of *To Discover a Divine*. After the original publishing house went under, she has now decided to continue the series on her own.

When not writing, she can be found at the movies or at Disneyland with her husband, as well as family, friends or anyone who wants to play at the Happiest Place on Earth. She also finds her artistic soul fed through her passions for theatre, dance and music. A proud parent of far too many high school seniors and two still living house plants, she also enjoys hockey, reading and playing Words with Friends to keep her vocabulary sharp. She has served as Treasurer, President-Elect, and President of the San Diego chapter of Romance Writers of America and loves spending time working with such amazingly intelligent and creative writers.